THE PUBLIC HATING

BOOKS BY STEVE ALLEN

BOP FABLES
FOURTEEN FOR TONIGHT
THE FUNNY MEN
WRY ON THE ROCKS
THE GIRLS ON THE TENTH FLOOR
THE QUESTION MAN
MARK IT AND STRIKE IT
NOT ALL OF YOUR LAUGHTER, NOT ALL OF YOUR TEARS
LETTER TO A CONSERVATIVE
THE GROUND IS OUR TABLE
BIGGER THAN A BREADBOX
A FLASH OF SWALLOWS
THE WAKE
PRINCESS SNIP-SNIP AND THE PUPPYKITTENS
CURSES!
WHAT TO SAY WHEN IT RAINS
SCHMOCK!-SCHMOCK!
MEETING OF MINDS
CHOPPED-UP CHINESE
RIPOFF: THE CORRUPTION THAT PLAGUES AMERICA
MEETING OF MINDS (Second Series)
EXPLAINING CHINA
FUNNY PEOPLE
THE TALK SHOW MURDERS
BELOVED SON: A STORY OF THE JESUS CULTS
MORE FUNNY PEOPLE
HOW TO MAKE A SPEECH
HOW TO BE FUNNY
MURDER ON THE GLITTER BOX
THE PASSIONATE NONSMOKER'S BILL OF RIGHTS
(With Bill Adler Jr.)
DUMBTH, AND 81 WAYS TO MAKE AMERICANS SMARTER
MEETING OF MINDS, SEASONS I-IV IN FOUR-VOLUME SET
THE PUBLIC HATING: A COLLECTION OF SHORT STORIES
MURDER IN MANHATTAN

THE PUBLIC
HATING

A Collection of Short Stories by
STEVE ALLEN

DEMBNER BOOKS
New York

Dembner Books
Published by Red Dembner Enterprises Corp.,
80 Eighth Avenue, New York, N.Y. 10011
Distributed by W. W. Norton & Company, Inc.,
500 Fifth Avenue, New York, N. Y. 10110

Library of Congress Cataloging-in-Publication Data

Allen, Steve, 1921–
   The public hating : a collection of short stories / Steve Allen.
      p.   cm.
   ISBN 0-942637-22-4
   I. Title.
PS3501.L5553P8   1990
813'.54—dc20
                                                    89-27702
                                                    CIP

Design by Antler & Baldwin, Inc.

CONTENTS

■ ■ ■

IRENE

■ ■ ■

After David Stanton lost his wife, he wept, of course, but at rather odd times. It did not happen when it might have been expected to, as in looking at old photographs, most of which he had purposely put away anyway, or at moments of recollection of past experiences, pleasant or unpleasant, but—to his surprise—it happened often when looking at strange women. It was not something that would occur when he encountered unknown women as such, of whom he might daily see hundreds, but only when he unexpectedly saw someone who shared one or more features with Irene.

Had any dozen or score of these women been gathered in one place, it would have been obvious that most of them bore little resemblance to one another, but in each, for Stanton, there was something that brought Irene to mind.

In one instance he had stared at a short, dark-haired woman who stood tapping an impatient foot, one hand on her left hip, as Irene often had. She was facing away, and some part of his brain, the part that recognizes objects from our past, at once perceived this now forever-lost feature.

The wiser level of his mind knew, of course, that he was not looking at Irene, but part of him responded as if he were. He felt an insane impulse to walk over to the young woman, to step around in front of her so that he could see her face and say, "Tapping that little foot again, eh?" He actually smiled at the mini-fantasy and then, a moment later, his eyes clouded.

A few days later he saw a woman getting into a cab in front of a hotel in Chicago, in which he was a resident for two days. In this case, it was only the sight of a thin wrist wearing a pair of small, inexpensive looking bracelets.

"Your wrists and hands," he had once told Irene, "are made of chicken bones. They look pathetic."

"Thanks a lot," she had said, speaking in a playfully sarcastic tone, pretending that he had insulted her but certainly understanding that his casual comment indicated a great, compassionate concern. Now, in Chicago, at least three years after the incident, he saw the same thin wrist on a stranger, and the same playful-looking, brightly colored fingernails, and it was as if he could step over to the cab before she entered and closed the door, take the thin-fingered hand in his own, and kiss it as if doing the same for a very young, beloved daughter.

In another instance he was watching a late-night television program, again in a hotel, this time in Denver. The Ted Koppel show had just ended and he had, almost without thinking, clicked the remote control to see what else was on. For a few minutes he watched a scene in a film, the name of which he had no way of knowing. A young woman with brown hair was lying asleep, her hair loosely flung across a white pillow, almost as if it had been blown into such a graceful pattern by a sea breeze.

"You have jungle-princess hair," he had said the first time he had seen Irene like that.

"I do?" she had asked coquettishly.

"Yes," he said. "I don't know if, in reality, there are any such people as jungle-princesses, nor, if there are, if they lie with their hair fanned out on white pillows, but that's what I think of when I see you like this."

"What else do you think of?" she had asked, continuing to smile impishly.

"You'd be surprised," he had replied with comically heavy implication, though at that moment, oddly enough, the possibility of making love had not entered his mind. She had just seemed so lovely, so feminine, that he had only wanted to kneel by the bed and somehow minister to her, as if tucking a child in at bedtime or gently waking someone who had been ill. So now again he stared, with a tremendous hunger, at the television screen and felt intense annoyance when the shot of the young woman disappeared and two other characters engaged in a whispered conversation in what turned out to be a hospital room.

"Let me see her again," he actually said aloud, though very softly, perfectly aware that no one could hear him. The universe, in any event, obliged, and again he saw the woman's lovely head on the pillow. This time, however, she turned more fully toward the camera, and since her face looked very little like Irene's, the spell of the moment vanished.

In yet another instance, in Beverly Hills, he had actually followed a strange woman on the street, for about a block and a half anyway, because of her remarkable resemblance, from the back, to Irene. What at first attracted his attention was the lavender skirt she was wearing. It was made of some sort of loose material, though not so loose across the hips, but it swayed slightly at the hemline as she walked so that it almost seemed she was dancing to unheard music.

His innermost reactions at that moment were surprisingly un-erotic, although powerfully romantic. Again, he well knew that the woman at whose back he was staring, not just at her hips but the waist, the shoulders, the curve of the neck, was not Irene, but because part of his brain automatically punched up her name on his invisible internal computer, he was powerless to resist the instruction to continue to stare at the woman. Had she stood motionless he would not have approached any closer. He was obliged to walk after her simply because she was moving away from him.

The young woman stopped, suddenly, to inspect some strikingly beautiful tailored suits in a shop window. He stopped too, keeping a respectful distance, feeling slightly idiotic. She could not possibly have noticed him, since her back had been turned to him, but at that moment she turned in his direction. He looked away, quickly embarrassed. When he looked back, she had disappeared.

He was at once seized with an aching sense of loss, tinged insanely with an element of panic. Reviewing the moment days later, it occurred to him that the strange woman's unexplained disappearance might have evoked a recollection from infancy in which, in some now forever-to-be-unknown public place, he had lost sight of his mother and felt utterly abandoned and almost invisible to the tall strangers who thronged about him.

A few weeks later, boarding a plane to New York, he had watched a young woman in the aisle putting a small bag in an overhead bin and there was something about her profile that was remarkably similar to Irene's. The smallish nose, the full lower lip, the lightly mascara'd lashes, the grey-blue of the eyes. He even heard the familiar tongue/teeth click of exasperation as the bag resisted her efforts to shove it into the open compartment. Again part of him plainly registered *Irene. Irene, my darling. Would you like to see the scar on my left elbow again?*

He had been injured, at the age of eight, by tripping on some chest-high weeds and falling on an adjacent sidewalk, splitting open the point of his elbow and drenching his lower arm with blood. The wound had never been stitched up, so there was an oddly shaped scar there for the rest of his life. He could not recall that anyone else had ever noticed it, since it was hidden in the loosely folded skin that is the normal part of human elbow covering, but Irene had. She had asked him, with true interest, what had happened to produce the wound. She clucked sympathetically and said, "Awwww," very softly, twice, even grimacing in sympathetic pain as he described the moment that he had tripped, running very fast, and the excruciating sensation of the bone coming into contact with the sidewalk. Ever after that, at odd and rare times, she would make little jokes about his elbow and the scar on it.

One of the reasons he had loved her, would always love her, though he would never see her again, would not, could not, was because of her sense of humor. There was no bitter wit to it, but they shared a sense of the inherent funniness of words and the relationship of one word to another. She too had a negative reaction to words like *trendy, yuppie,* phrases like *take a meeting, do lunch.*

So now he was staring at the sweet-faced young woman on the airplane who at that moment turned to seat herself. Full-face, she resembled Irene much less than he had thought, and the image of his forever-lost evaporated in that instant.

Two hours later, while walking back up the aisle after going to the john, he stared intently at the young stranger's face for a moment, trying to turn her into Irene, but the realities of her facial construction resisted his fantasy. She was just a stranger, who, though good-looking enough, was of no particular interest to him.

In one instance his reaction was decidedly erotic rather than achingly romantic. A young woman with Irene's legs, even the same kind of high-heeled shoes and a tight-fitting skirt, was riding in an open hansom cab on 59th Street. He stared at the legs hungrily, and in the moment he was excited. It was not just that he "wanted sex," whatever that meant. There were, no doubt, women he knew, or strangers he might easily meet, with whom he could have made some sort of arrangement. All of that was beside the point. He had a strong desire for Irene, and, at that moment, Irene was the lovely, firm, curved legs he was staring at. He actually groaned slightly, the typical sounds of New York traffic covering the soft volume of his voice, and said, "Oh, my baby, my baby, I want you," making sure that his lips moved as little as possible. The hansom driver, a young woman with a mannish look, flicked her whip lightly and the ancient horse that pulled her carriage trotted off. In an instant he could no longer see Irene's legs, with their honey-color. He stood for a moment staring at the sidewalk but not seeing it. What registered on his internal monitor was, again, the honey-colored legs, the creamy few inches of skin above the top of the stocking line, the lavender silk panties she often wore because she knew the color appealed to him. Then he shook his head, as if to clear his mind, muttered, "I'm in a bad way," chuckled aloud at the old-fashionedness of the phrase, and continued on his way.

Since there was no possibility of ever seeing her again, the rational part of his mind would have been content to forget her— though such words sound cruel—and to begin to rebuild the part of his life that could be reconstructed, but the moments of there-she-is recognition were never willed, they simply occurred, in the way that breezes or sweet scents from our childhood casually occur. He would sometimes call her *puppy* in his mind in such moments. It had been one of his ways of addressing her.

Part of the problem with the other women he had known since he had lost Irene was that it simply did not seem natural to discuss ideas with them. He, as a semanticist, and she, as a professor of English, had, from the first, used words to talk about words. When he was away from her but thinking of her he rarely used her name but frequently thought or even whisperingly spoke the word *baby*, but whether he was using it in her absence or presence, it was not employed in the vulgar slang sense as in, "Hey, baby, what's happening?" or the way most men used it to apply to almost any object. "This baby can go from zero to 60 miles an hour in 8 seconds flat." He used the word, oddly enough, as if he were talking to, or about, an actual baby, a sweet, smiling infant. She had not been so helpless nor, for that matter, had she always smiled. There was something in him that at certain times wanted to address that aspect of her so that when he applied the word it was used in the same way as *kitten* or *puppy*, to mean something tremendously appealing and playful. She had shared his amusement at all cliches, and he had been fascinated and entertained by her sense of the comic aspect of assorted human weaknesses and peculiarities. It is possible, after all, to have generally satisfactory sexual encounters or relationships with a theoretically infinite list of others, but the special laughter, and the philosophical sensibility that gave rise to the laughter, the sense of speaking the same language, these could not so easily be found again.

His sensitivity to her, on several levels, had been exquisite. "I swear," he had said once, while holding her hand and kissing her forearm as if it were an object he had never seen before, "that I could recognize your skin-temperature, in the way that we recognize or remember things by their sight, smell, or sound. They could conduct a scientific test—blindfold me and let me hold just the left arm of a hundred different women. I swear I could identify you by the temperature and the texture of your skin."

"You probably couldn't," she said laughing, "but I love hearing about it."

One day several weeks later he was speaking in Boston on the subject of love as it had been addressed by major poets over the centuries, including the unknown authors of the Bible's Song of Solomon. As he looked up from the first paragraph on the third page of his text, he suddenly saw Irene seated in the front row, smiling at him in her unique Mona Lisa way. He knew that she could not be there, yet his mind registered that she was. When he looked back down at the page his vision was strangely blurred. Fortunately he knew the subject matter well enough that he was able to continue rather than stand there, like an idiot, saying nothing. To cover the mingled embarrassment and panic he was feeling he paused, poured himself half a glass of water from a small pitcher inside the lectern, took a sip, and then looked back at his text. But he had lost both his place and his general concentration.

The room was very quiet. He did not know how many seconds had passed since the moment of shock, though he knew he had been speaking. "Of all the human emotions," he suddenly heard himself saying, "love remains the most mysterious. Psychological science knows quite a lot, now, about joy, fear, anger, sadness. Unfortunately the emotions can never be studied in total isolation, as in other fields of science we can study specific material objects. The emotions intermingle. They affect each other."

Feeling partially insane, he was no longer doing what experienced speakers always do, which is to look to different parts of the room, the front, the back, the sides, the center, or pick out specific faces to whom to communicate certain points along the way. He was speaking now to Irene only.

"One fascinating aspect of the emotions," he said, "is that they act quite independently of the will. We do not decide to become afraid. We do not make a conscious decision that anger would be an inappropriate response in the face of a particular threat. No one has ever reasoned his way into a state of depression. The same is true of love. It always, always comes as a surprise. If we are very fortunate, it will be a sweet surprise. In other cases, if there is no room for the accommodation of a new relationship in our lives, or if the object of our interest is unworthy, then the surprise will be of a more tragic sort. But it is reason that knows that. The response of love itself is totally unmindful of such surrounding factors."

Suddenly, glancing down, he discovered that he could again see and read the print, which included a reference to Shakespeare. But somehow he found himself still speaking extemporaneously, though having literally no idea toward what end.

"Shakespeare," he said, "perhaps the most gifted poet to write of love, dealt with it, as you know, in the form of his sonnets and also certain of his plays. Three of his best known characters, Romeo, Othello, and Hamlet, far from being enriched by love, were undone by it. And all of us, alas, have had a sense of that in our own lives. This is not to say that if we could have foreseen our futures, we would have sacrificed the possibility of loving and being loved, but merely that life will never let us be totally content with it.

"Another reason," he continued, still looking straight at the beautiful face of Irene, smiling more broadly now from the first row, her lower face framed by a lavender and blue scarf, "a factor that further deepens the mystery, is the connection between love and lust. At its peak, in its best, most vibrant forms of expression, love and a sense of erotic romanticism, acted out in purely physical, even animalistic terms, have a way of reigning supreme in us, whether its seeds have fallen on fertile or rocky soil. Yet another element of the great mystery is that there is invariably something unique about love relationships. No two of us—literally no two people on earth, no two who have ever lived—perceive love in precisely the same way. If we all did respond to love's appeal in some narrowly defined manner, then, I suppose, any one of us might be made happy by any other of us. But that is not what we find, in reality. You can show the average man a hundred women who are quite beautiful, intelligent, civilized and charming, and yet there will be something about just two or three of them—perhaps even one—that will speak to his heart in a way that none of the others can."

David Stanton did not, later, remember the rest of what he said, but he gradually became aware that the gentleman who had introduced him, now sitting at the end of the first row, was raising his left arm, pointing to his wristwatch and making purposely unobtrusive hand signals.

Stanton shook his head, to clear it, and turned to the last two pages of his speech. "I'm sorry" he said, "I seem to have wandered rather far afield here and I'm afraid we've gotten a bit behind schedule."

When he finished, there was the usual warm applause, which he scarcely noticed. Walking down the four stairs at stage right, he moved toward the audience, which was now standing, not in the act of an ovation but merely intent on moving out of the auditorium. Irene, who had so inflamed and distracted him, was now turned away and walking toward the center aisle. Seeing the woman from the back, he thought, "My God, it's not her."

Hurrying forward he stood beside the woman and said, "Pardon me, but I—"

"Oh, Mr. Stanton," she said, indeed not Irene at all, "I was fascinated by what you had to say."

"Were you?" he said, at a loss for words, his mind racing. "We haven't met before, have we?"

She laughed. "I'm quite sure we haven't," she said. "I would have remembered that. I've admired your work for quite some time."

"That's very kind of you," he said.

"Is something wrong?" she asked, speaking more softly.

"No," he said, "I just thought—you look so strikingly like someone I knew—once."

"Once?" she said, not sure how to take the word.

"It doesn't matter," he said, "but I—I feel I should thank you for the expression on your face as I was speaking. It was very encouraging."

It was while he was saying the word *encouraging* that his voice broke.

She reached forward in an automatically warm way, and took his hand in hers. "Is there anything I can do?" she said.

He stepped backward, hideously embarrassed and strangely stricken.

"Thank you," he said, then hurried away toward a door near the side of the stage, blindly signing two autographs along the way, muttering, "Thank you, thank you. You're very kind."

A few minutes later up in his room, surveying the broad panoramic expanse of that portion of the city visible from the 37th floor, he suddenly said aloud, though softly, "That's idiotic," responding to another part of his mind that had, a moment earlier, suggested opening a window, very quickly, and jumping out. Then he laughed, seeing that the windows were unopenable anyway.

Since he could not kill himself and thought, in fact, that he would not have done so anyway, despite his misery, he undressed, went into the bathroom, and masturbated, with tears in his eyes, first speaking to Irene very quietly and tenderly and then finally wildly shouting her name, visualizing her breasts, her mouth, hearing, quite clearly, her responses to his love-making.

THE CATS

■ ■ ■

When she heard the first rumble of thunder Blanche touched the tip of her tongue to the back of her upper front teeth, making the traditional sound of annoyance. Then she left the kitchen and walked to the living room and closed the windows.

A thin, spattered film of water lay on each sill. She wiped all of it away with the end of her apron and stood for a moment looking absently out at the traffic on Seventy-eighth Street. A taxi had double-parked and two middle-aged women had gotten out and were standing in the drizzling rain, taking too much time to pay the driver. Several cars were lined up and there was much honking of horns.

"Come on, 'ere," somebody called from down the street.

Blanche turned away from the window, walked to the television set, and turned it on. After a moment a voice said "—twice the work in half the time. And remember, it cleans as it scours as it shines." Before the picture even came up Blanche turned the station-selector knob. As she did so, a woman's face came fuzzily into view on the glass plate.

"—certainly be a conversation piece," the woman was saying. It was Jinx. Blanche took a package of cigarettes out of her apron pocket, lighted one, and sat down on a hassock.

Jinx put aside the delicate glass bowl she was holding and smiled broadly, away from the camera. The picture widened to include another woman. Blanche giggled. It was Mrs. Hollis.

"—delighted you could take the time out to visit us this afternoon," Jinx was saying.

"Thanks," Mrs. Hollis said, a little breathlessly, "but I'm so sorry

11

I was late. Honestly, I just *couldn't* get a cab, and then you know crosstown traffic."

Both women laughed and so did Blanche.

"If I didn't call you, you *still* be asleep," said Blanche to the television set. She sat listening to Jinx and Mrs. Hollis talk about Mrs. Hollis' new novel, about her newspaper column, and about her French poodle. At the mention of the dog's name Blanche wrinkled her nose in displeasure.

"—a successful career woman, a housewife, and a mother," Jinx said. "It's truly remarkable how you do it all."

"Psshh," Blanche said softly.

At that moment Mr. Hollis walked through the living room. Blanche sat upright, then stood, frightened, and tried to hide the cigarette. Mr. Hollis pretended not to notice.

"I won't be home for dinner, Blanche," he said.

"Yes, sir," Blanche said. "You want me to tell Mrs. Hollis anything?" As she said it she pointed to the screen.

Mr. Hollis did not become interested.

"Just tell her I won't be home for dinner," he repeated.

Blanche knew precisely what Mrs. Hollis did when she left the comfortable brownstone on Seventy-eighth Street, East, but she had never arrived at a really clear understanding as to what Mr. Hollis did or where he went or even, exactly, what he was.

"I don't know," she had said to her sister, coming down on the Fifth Avenue bus out of Harlem early in the morning. "He read a lot and he drink a lot and he talk to a lot of important people, but I'll be go-ta-hell if I know just what he do."

"Maybe," her sister had ventured with a knowing chuckle, "he just sit home and count the money Mrs. Hollis make."

"No," Blanche had said. "He got money in his own name. He ain't one of them gigolo husbands. I know he ain't that, but I jes' don't know what he *is*."

"What he and Mis' Hollis talk about him doin'?"

"Well, when they ain't fightin' they talk about plays and TV shows and like that. He got somethin' to do with show business, I guess, but he's pretty close-mouthed."

Now, standing before her, pulling on his gloves, Mr. Hollis said, "Brucie get off all right this morning?"

"Yes, sir," Blanche said. "He ate good and they picked him up right on time."

"Good," Mr. Hollis said and then, with no other word, walked out of the house.

When she heard the downstairs door click Blanche sat on the hassock again and looked at the television set. Jinx and Mrs. Hollis were talking about earrings.

Blanche sat motionless for several minutes, watching them, and then the back doorbell rang in a shave-and-a-haircut pattern, twice.

"Keep your shirt on," Blanche said as she crossed the spacious kitchen. It had to be Carter.

It was.

"You all wet, man," she said when she saw him.

"I'll live," Carter said, smiling broadly. "Mr. Hollis up yet?"

"You missed him. He jes' went out."

Carter stepped in, wiping moisture from the back of his brown neck.

"Whee-hoo," he said. "It's really whalin' out there."

"Don't look too bad out to me," Blanche said.

"No," said Carter, "that's 'cause you lookin' at it from inside."

"You remember the eggplant?" Blanche said as Carter placed the two shopping bags on the kitchen table.

"Yep," he said, pointing to one of the bags, "and it's the craziest, if you dig eggplant."

They worked in silence for a few minutes, putting things away, and then Carter said, "Hey, how about puttin' down some coffee?"

"All right," Blanche said.

"Ooop-shoop," said Carter, getting out two cups and saucers.

"You goin' call the cleaners?" Blanche said.

"Salt peanuts, salt peanuts," Carter sang softly. "I already did. They goofed."

"What?"

"Stuff won't be ready till tomorrow."

When the coffee was ready Carter drank it eagerly. It burned his throat a little.

"Cool," Carter said. "You order ice yet?"

"Not yet," Blanche said.

"How many people be here tonight?"

"I don't know. Maybe fifty."

"Ouch," said Carter. "They'll be whalin' all night." Then he said, "You know, Blanche, if you wasn't so fat I'd like to—"

"Aw, you shut up," Blanche said, laughing heartily with embarrassment.

Carter carefully washed and dried his cup and saucer. "I'm goin' up and play a little," he said.

"Don't you fool around up there too long."

"Mokay," said Carter.

He walked up the thickly carpeted, winding staircase to the living room, pausing at the first landing to listen to Blanche splashing water in the kitchen. Then he stepped up to the liquor cabinet opposite the false fireplace and poured himself a good drink of straight rye whisky. Downing it quickly in four short gulps, he carefully replaced the bottle, put the glass in the pocket of his suède jacket, and sat down at the piano.

With his left hand, low on the keyboard, he played an E-flat octave. Against it in the treble he played a straight A chord. At the fine, stark, dramatic quality of the combination he smiled broadly.

"Blanche," he called at the top of his voice.

"What?" faintly.

"Man, that thing you showed me sounds *fine!*"

Cursing the stiffness of his fingers, he began to play again, trying first the blues, with the modern changes. Instead of playing the straight B-flat chord all the way through the first three measures, he changed the chord on each beat, playing slow, lush tenths, going from B-flat to C minor to D minor and then back again. With the right hand he played a traditional blues phrase, humming softly and tapping gently with his foot on the sustaining pedal; not enough to sustain the chords and run one into the other, but just enough to get a pounding, echo-y beat from the hollow parts of the piano.

Blanche listened to him for ten minutes, then, after she had put the clothes in the automatic washer, she went upstairs and sat next to him on the piano bench.

"Show me those chords to 'Lover Man,'" Carter said, sliding off the seat.

Blanche positioned herself and straightened her skirt.

"You use like a D minor to start here," she said, "and you play the left hand like this." She hit a D and G simultaneously in the lower register. Carter shivered in delight at the rich, pleasant dissonance.

"Crazy," he said.

Blanche closed her eyes and began to sing quietly in a throaty voice. When she got to the bridge of the song Carter slid back on the bench and began to play fill-in notes with his right hand.

"Yeah," he said appreciatively as she altered the melody in the last eight bars, ad-libbing a new line, but in perfect agreement with the composer's harmonies.

"Hi," Bruce said.

They whirled and then looked at each other like trapped conspirators. Blanche paused and then said, "Yes, you're right, Carter. This piano *does* need tuning. Brucie, how come you ain't in school?"

"I didn't want to go," said Bruce, twirling his leather pilot's hat.

He was sitting at the head of the stairs, looking at them pleasantly. "Don't stop playing."

"We weren't playing," Carter said. "We just were testing the piano. How come you ain't in school? You got picked up and everything."

"Oh, I *went*," said Bruce, "but I just walked in one door and out the other. I didn't want to go to class today."

"How come?" Blanche said.

"I don't know," Bruce said. "I didn't have my homework done, and I just didn't feel like it. Is my father home?"

"No," Carter said, "and it's a good thing for you he ain't."

"No, it isn't," Bruce said. "Go on, play some more."

"I got work to do," Blanche said.

"Then how come you were playing?"

"We was testing the piano."

"You don't have to *sing* to test the piano, do you?"

"No," Carter admitted. "You don't *have* to exactly, but it helps."

"Test it some more then," Bruce said, taking off his rubbers. "I want to hear you."

"But we got more important things to do, boy," Blanche said.

"Then why weren't you doing them?"

"What you gonna do when your mother finds out you ditchin' school?" said Carter, trying to change the subject.

"She won't find out for a long time," Bruce said.

"What makes you think she won't?" Carter said.

"*You're* not going to tell her, are you?" said Bruce, looking directly at Carter and then at the piano.

"Why, no," Carter said. "I guess I'm not, but she'll find out some time."

"Maybe she won't," said Bruce. Then in a businesslike voice he added, "If you don't tell her either, Blanche, I won't tell her that you and Carter were playing the piano and singing."

Blanche laughed.

"Listen to him," she said. "Brucie, you're makin' a Federal case out of this thing."

"Sing something else," Bruce said. "Please."

"Maybe," suggested Carter, "you better do it, Blanche."

Blanche looked from the man to the boy, then sat down.

"What would you like to hear?" she said.

"Anything you want," Bruce said. "I like to listen to you. I'd lots rather listen to you right now than be in school."

"All right," Blanche said, sighing.

She hit a G seventh chord and looked at the ceiling for inspiration.

"My funny valentine," she sang slowly, her voice low, "sweet, comic valentine. You make me smile with my heart."

Bruce put his chin on his knees and wrapped his arms around his calves.

"Your looks are laughable," she sang, smiling warmly at Bruce in the mirror, "unphotographable, but you're my favorite work of art."

"Crazy," whispered Carter, tapping his foot on the carpet very slowly.

It began to rain again and the shy, sad whisper of the rain on the windows gave to the piano a sort of warm-fireplace, golden quality. The three were figures huddling for warmth.

"Is your figure less than Greek?" Blanche sang. "Is your mouth a little weak? When you open it to speak . . . are you smart?"

The braces on Brucie's teeth glinted dully in the light from the one lamp at the far end of the room. He leaned forward eagerly; Blanche was singing softly, almost inaudibly. Her fingers paused over a plaintive chord and Carter sweetly hummed a low note of harmony.

Outside taxis swished lazily past the house. The sound of their wet tires seemed part of the music. From a million miles away the city added dreamily to the orchestra, with ships in the river lowing like the ghosts of blind beasts, the muffled clatter of the Third Avenue El filling in a contrapuntal feathery staccato, and now and then the faint English trumpet of an auto horn seeming, by its very remoteness, to make the piano and voice in the room intensely close and personal.

Blanche's eyes were closed now and her head was thrown slightly back. She was still keeping a slow, steady beat with her fingers, but the voice lagged behind tantalizingly, like the pouring of rich honey, seeming now to be almost out of synchronization with the music, now to be catching up in a way that pulled Bruce forward, chewing the piece of gum that was in his mouth in the rhythm of the song, his head lifting regularly, his chin still braced on his knees.

"Don't change a hair for me," Blanche sang and Bruce loved her, feeling loved in his inadequacies.

"Not if you care for me," she whispered, and he felt fierce and loyal.

"Stay, little valentine, stay!"

Tenderly, Blanche fingered, as if on a harp, a rippling trio of chords. Carter hummed, a faint wisp of a smile in his eyes, which were fastened on the carpet. Bruce blew his nose.

"Each day is Valentine's day." A clock ticked somewhere cozily.

When the last chord had died away they all sat motionless for perhaps five seconds and then Bruce said, "That was beautiful, Blanche. I like that song."

"Thank you," Blanche said.

"Yep," said Carter, chuckling. "This is *all right!*" He looked at their reflections in the wall mirror behind the piano. "Here we are: three cats really swingin'!"

THE SIDEWALK

■ ■ ■

When I came around the corner at Fifty-fourth Street I saw Seventy on his hands and knees. His face was screwed up in concentration and his nose was close to the sidewalk.

"Hi," I said.

"Hi," he said. "Careful. Don't walk here where it's wet."

"Why not?" I said. He dipped a small brush into a glass of soapy water and brushed vigorously at the pavement. Half of one square of concrete was brushed clean.

"I'm trying to get the sidewalk clean," he answered.

"What for?"

"Oh, it's a long story," he said, "but I gotta get it all clean. I figure this soap'll do the trick, then I can hose it down to wash the soap off."

"What's the idea?" I said.

"It's a long story."

I reached into the pocket of my jacket and took out a small, dark red rubber ball. While he brushed the sidewalk I stood there throwing the ball against the small space between two windows of the apartment house that stretched from the alley to the corner.

"Careful," Seventy said, "don't walk here where it's wet."

"Who's walking?" I said.

"I didn't say you were," Seventy said. "I just said be careful."

"All right," I said, "but what the hell's the big idea? You gonna clean up the whole city?"

"No, he said. "Just this one square here." The square of cement bounded east and west by two cracks and north and south by the curb and a sparse lawn was now almost wholly moistened, cleaned by Seventy's brush.

19

"Al ain't home yet," Seventy said. "Go in the alley and find a tin can or a milk bottle."

"What for?"

"If Al ain't home I can't borrow his hose, so I'll need a tin can or something for the water."

"What water?"

"Judas, you're a dumb bastard. The water to wash all the soap off, what water do you think?"

"Oh," I said, frowning. I walked down the street a few steps and turned into the alley. Halfway down its length I found a milk bottle. When I brought it to him he walked across the grass and filled the bottle from the pipe that jutted back from the brick wall. Then he shook it to clean the inside of the bottle, emptied the water on the grass, and refilled the bottle.

"This should do it," he said, splashing the water down hard on the pavement. The fluid scooped up tiny soap bubbles and cleaned little patches where soap had dried to a powdery film. Six times he filled the milk bottle and emptied its contents on the sidewalk. At last, satisfied with its cleanliness, he sat down on the curb in his faded brown corduroys and unbuttoned his collar.

"Now what?" I said.

"Now we're all set," he said.

"All set for what?" I asked. He looked at me the way people look at a dog that just isn't learning the simplest of tricks.

"Judas, you're a dumb bastard," he said, "but I guess I'll have to lay it all out for you. I just cleaned me off a little stretch of sidewalk here."

"Thanks a lot," I said, with all the sarcasm I could muster. "I thought maybe you were playing baseball or something." This struck me as a crushingly clever retort.

"Tell you what," Seventy said. "Maybe you can help me out. You got a quarter?"

"Yeah. I've got thirty-five cents. Why?"

"Why do you think," Seventy said. "Because I want to borrow it, that's why." I gave him the quarter and he said, "If this little deal comes off I'll give you back fifty cents for your quarter. Okay?"

"Okay," I said. "What do we do now?"

"Head for the Bluebird Diner," he said, standing up and dusting off his pants. At the Bluebird he carefully examined the menu as I drained both glasses of water the counter man had set before us.

"What'll it be?" the counter man asked tiredly.

"The chicken à la king should do it," Seventy told him.

"You want it on the dinner?" the man said.

"No," Seventy said. "To go. And just the chicken à la king in a carton or something. Nothing else."

The man looked at me. "You want anything?" he said.

"No," I said. "I'm with him." Walking back to Fifty-fourth I lovingly fingered the warm paper bag and the carton inside it. I could feel the heat from the creamy chicken warming my cold fingers.

"The sidewalk should be dried off by now," Seventy said.

"I guess you're right," I said, as we rounded the corner. I could see that the film of water had disappeared and the square of pavement Seventy had so diligently cleaned gave no immediate evidence of having been so recently scoured.

"Well," he said, squinting his eyes and pursing his lips, "I guess we're just about all set." I started to say "For what?" but checked myself. Seventy hated to be prodded and I refused to lower myself by any further demonstrations of insatiable curiosity.

"One thing, though," he added. "We'll have to figure out some way to keep people from walking on it."

"Walking on what?" I said, without thinking, then bit my lip.

"Tell you what," he said, not pressing his advantage, "let's pull that horse over here." He referred to a yellow wooden sawhorse flanked by two oil lanterns that the city had left in the street to warn motorists of the presence of an unusually deep depression in the asphalt.

"Isn't that liable to cause trouble?" I asked.

"No," he said. "The two red lanterns will guard the bump and besides we can put the thing back later."

When we had carried the guard horse to the curb and slanted it diagonally across the washed square of pavement Seventy picked up the bag of chicken à la king, deftly opened the carton, and without a word splattered its contents down on the sidewalk.

"You crazy?" I asked.

"When are you gonna stop asking stupid questions?" he said. "What time is it?"

"I don't know. It was about half-past five when we left the Bluebird."

"Okay, then it's about time Nick should be gettin' home from work. Let's go down to Woodlawn 'cause I gotta get the bread before he gets off the bus."

By this time I was so angry I wouldn't have asked another question if my life had depended on it. When we got to Woodlawn Avenue we went down the street to the A.&P. and bought a loaf of bread, sliced. Seventy made sure it was sliced. Without talking we hurried out of the A.&P. and walked up to Fifty-third Street.

"Let's not stand right here on the corner," Seventy said. "Let's wait down here by the shoe store, so's it'll look like we were just passing by."

I didn't say anything. We waited near the shoe store and in about five minutes the bus stopped near the corner. Seventy hurried toward it and then slowed down and sauntered past the drugstore just as Nick was getting off the bus.

"Let on you don't see him," Seventy whispered. We turned the corner and walked on ahead of Nick, listening to his cleated heels clicking on the pavement behind us. Nick always wore cleats on the heels of his shiny, pointed shoes. Nick was a pretty sharp operator.

His full name was Nick Depopolous and around the neighbor-hood he liked to be referred to as Nick, the Greek, which he was. I think he had read something in a magazine once about the well-known gambler, Nick the Greek, and had selected the man as a personal idol. Nick needn't have patterned himself after anybody. He was tall, well-built, good-looking in a sort of George Raftish way, a natty dresser, and popular with the girls. He worked downtown as a shipping clerk, but he spent a lot of time around the Green Mill Poolroom on Fifty-fifth Street and he liked to gamble. Nick would take a bet on anything, and though he rarely wagered more than ten or fifteen dollars at a time, this made him a big gambler in the eyes of most of the kids in the neighborhood.

"Hi, Seventy." Nick had come abreast of us. Seventy's face lit up. He could not have acted more surprised if the King of England had come up behind us.

"Why, Nick," he said, "I haven't seen you in a week or so. Where've you been keeping yourself?"

"Oh, here and there," Nick said. "What's new with you guys?"

"Nothing much" I said.

We walked on for a few feet in silence, then Seventy said, "How the ponies treating you, Nick?"

"Fair enough," Nick answered. "Almost had a daily double this afternoon." Nick was only eighteen but to me he seemed a man of the world.

"This guy'll kill you," Seventy said to me. "Bets on anything. Nick, tell him about the time you bet Al Dietz he didn't know what color socks he was wearing."

"Sucker bet," Nick said modestly. "Nothing to it."

Seventy laughed in vast admiration. "Get him," he said. "Nothing to it. How about the time you bet old man Walters ten bucks his cigarette lighter wouldn't light the first time he tried it?"

"Sucker bet," Nick said, thrusting his lower lip out with slight pride.

Seventy laughed again. "I'm tellin' ya, there's nothing this guy won't bet on. Funny part of it is, he usually wins."

"No kidding?" I said.

"That's right," Seventy said as we turned the corner.

"Why, I saw him one time when he bet Bob Petrolli that he could swallow a live goldfish. Did it, too. Didn't ya, Nick?"

"Yep," Nick admitted. "If the price is right, I guess a guy'll do just about anything."

"Yessirree," Seventy said. "That's the way I feel about it, too. A guy might think he couldn't eat a goldfish, but you put a sawbuck on the line and there's a lot of guys would try it. Right, Nick?"

"Right you are," Nick said. "Of course, the price has to be right."

"And the guy has to have guts, too," Seventy said.

"Oh, of course," Nick agreed. "If you ain't got guts, you got no right to make a bet in the first place."

"I got just as much guts as you have, Nick, only I don't seem to have the money to back it up," Seventy said, with sudden abandon. A flicker of surprise at his tone crossed Nick's face. We had almost walked up to the cleaned square of pavement, the spilled chicken à la king that lay splashed on the pavement, and the sawhorse that partially blocked the path.

"So you got guts," Nick said.

"You're darned right," Seventy said. "Eating live goldfish!" He sneered. "Why, if somebody was to make me the right kind of a bet I'd even *eat that*." He pointed with a rigid finger at the cold, creamy mess that he had thrown on the sidewalk.

I was looking at Nick. When he saw what Seventy was pointing at, his face screwed up with displeasure and he turned his eyes away, stepping gingerly across the splattered area. I held my breath. Nick walked on a few feet, then halted and turned around. He looked at Seventy.

"What did you say?" he asked.

"I said that if somebody made me the right kind of a bet, I'd even eat that!" He pointed again, but Nick's eyes refused to lower. They were momentarily expressionless, then a methodical glint came into them. Nick slanted his head to one side and regarded Seventy with a superior smile.

"You talk big," he said. "I got twenty-five dollars I'll put up against your five that says you can't do no such thing. That is," he smiled with even more contempt, "if you can raise five bucks."

"Don't you worry about me," Seventy said. There was a pause.

"Well, big boy," Nick said. "How about it? We got a bet or have you chickened out already?" Seventy hesitated. I couldn't help admiring his timing.

"That's what I thought," Nick said. "You punks around here talk pretty big, but when it comes to putting up you ain't got what it takes."

"That does it," Seventy said. "You got a bet!"

"Okay," Nick said. "So I got a bet. But it don't look to me as if I'm gonna lose it. As a matter of fact," he said, "I'll do you a favor. You can welsh out right now and we'll call the whole thing off."

Seventy didn't answer. Instead he opened the wax paper wrapped on the bread he was carrying and took out one slice. Tearing it in half, he solemnly got down on his knees and carefully sopped up a large gob of chicken à la king from the spotless pavement. Nick's eyes almost popped out of his head.

"Holy God!" he said.

Expressionlessly Seventy lifted the slice of bread to his mouth, bit off a large piece, and wiped more chicken from the sidewalk with the rest of the slice, then put it into his mouth, closed his eyes tight as if suffering great pain, and wolfed the bread and chicken down.

Nick was pale now. Through tight lips he gasped,

"That's enough. Cut it out!" With trembling fingers he withdrew his wallet from a back pocket, produced two tens and a five, and handed them to Seventy, then without a word he turned and hurried away, groaning slightly.

Seventy and I went back to the A.&P., got five ones for the five, and Seventy handed me one of the bills.

He came by that nickname because even though he was only fifteen he had the wisdom of an old man. I haven't seen him in years now, but I guess he's doing all right.

JOE SHULMAN
IS DEAD

■ ■ ■

Joe Shulman is dead. We were sitting here in Nick's front room, in the Village, drinking, when Bill stepped out to take a phone call and then after a minute he came back in, waited till we stopped laughing at something, and said, "I don't mean to be a drag but Joe Shulman just died."

There was a flurry of soft "Oh, no's" and we all began frowning and looking at our drinks and the floor and the iced celery and carrots on the low, round white coffee table and at anything except each other's eyes.

I didn't actually know Joe intimately. He wasn't really what you would call a close friend, and yet he was the kind of man I would have liked to have for a good friend. It was only the business, the damned busy business, with its endless hustle and travel and meet and talk and decide and flip and then at last, as in Joe's case, die, before you had a chance to spend leisure time with the few people you met who seemed to be worth knowing better.

Joe was a bass player. String bass. He was my favorite. I wouldn't say he was the very best in the business, but for some reason I enjoyed playing with him the most. I play only moderately good jazz, but with Joe standing next to the piano, swinging back and forth with his eyes closing from time to time like a sleepy baby's, and his mouth framing a perpetual slight smile, I always played my best. Perhaps it was because I knew that he approved of what I was playing. Some bass players play for themselves, for their own enjoyment. Others are perfectionists who in a subtle way let you know that you're not

25

quite on their level. But with Joe you always were supported by a combination of swinging, relaxed beat and a personal contact that let it be understood that besides being a musical experience your playing together was a type of warm social contact. There was a poetic sort of conversation that took place between his beat-up old bass and your piano. Mostly he played with his wife Barbara Carroll, but when you went to hear Barbara, if you were a pianist, she always asked you to sit in.

She is a fine jazz pianist herself, and she seemed to play her best after Joe joined her trio. I remember the general time; it was around 1953 and Jayne and I were still studying each other. Jayne's mother and father were missionaries. She was born in China and didn't see America till she was seven, so she was not like any other woman you might meet in New York. She didn't know the names of old movie stars, she didn't know the words of old songs, and she didn't understand jazz. All I knew about her at first was that she was beautiful and intelligent and the kind of woman I wanted to invite into my world to become—well, to take over, actually. But I used to take her to the jazz spots around town and explain the music to her. She was a good student. One of the places I took her to was The Embers on East 54th Street. We used to sit close together at a table against the wall and I would put my hand on her knee under the tablecloth and softly tap out the rhythm of the music. I introduced her to Barbara and Joe, and Joe seemed to take a particular interest in our romance. He would step over to the bar and discuss with the bartender a very particular sort of oversized martini and then he would bring two of them back to our table and we would drink them and fall more in love with each other and with the whole world. Alcohol may be an evil thing if that's the way you feel about it, but it is not entirely evil in that it can release in a man a certain capacity for universal love that otherwise frequently remains locked deep within him and in some individuals never gets a chance to get to the surface at all.

So Joe would keep bringing these martinis to us and he would laugh at my jokes and tell Jayne how beautiful she was and I guess you might say that he was sort of our Cupid. We would have eventually gotten married without him, no doubt, but he surrounded the early days of our courtship with an amber Embers haze of good feeling and logs in the fireplace and hands across the table and laughter and the deeply felt happy rhythm of good music.

I remember one time I was having dinner at the apartment when

Joe called me up and said that Barbara was sick and he had a question to ask me and he figured I'd say no but he was going to ask anyway, just for the heck of it. He asked me if I'd go to fill in for Barbara at the Embers for two nights and, man, it was ridiculous. I mean, here I was thinking it was the best invitation I'd ever had and he thought I'd say no. Anyway, I played there for two nights and Barbara thought I was doing her a big favor. Those two nights were a ball, and with Joe booming out the big fat beat hour after hour I felt that I was in good hands and it gave me the greatest possible confidence.

After Jayne and I got married we saw Joe rarely, but each time we ran across the Barbara Carroll trio it was a happy time. Usually it was by surprise. We'd be invited to a party at somebody's house and we'd be there talking and suddenly Barbara and Joe would come in and that meant that eventually somebody would open up the piano and Joe's bass would appear from some closet where he'd quietly slipped it when he'd entered and there would be music; and if I played I'd play far beyond my customary creative ability. Joe would lay down his rock-steady and yet unobstrusive beat and he'd keep smiling and whispering to me, like a father encouraging a child. He was young, about my own age, but as a musician he was much my senior, and he always made me feel that I was well taken care of when I was with him. Joe was an enthusiast: I guess that's the best thing anybody can say about him, and it's higher praise than it might seem at first thought. The world needs more enthusiasts. Most people are critics, putter-downers. Joe made you feel better than you were and as a result you *became* better. I'm sure he had experimented with drugs and ignored rather than consciously broken the Commandments, but by some sort of deep, elementary standard he was a good man. There was nothing vicious in him and yet he was the sort of person who I'm sure would be criticized by people who consider themselves worthy but who are every ready to bare their fangs.

Joe had a funny habit of closing his eyes when he played and doing a little stationary sort of dance, rocking back and forth within about a ten-inch arc, tipping his head first from one side then to the other.

I'm writing this now on a borrowed typewriter in a cubicle at Nick's house, while out in the front room the party rolls on. I'm enjoying the party, but I just had to step in here and put these few meager ideas on paper while they were on my mind. It was just a few minutes ago that Bill said, "Joe Shulman just died. Heart attack," and I don't fully understand the motivation that drove me in here to this little sweatbox and the Italian portable. I have my shirt and my undershirt off and just to my left on the table a cockamamie modernistic lamp is slanting its light through a low glass of scarlet wine. Maybe it's just a means of saying good-by to Joe, but damn it, there's no way of knowing that he's getting the message, and so I have the crazy idea that I ought to rush into the other room now and say to all of the gang in there:

"Listen, you're all going to die someday—soon or late—and it'll probably happen to some of you unexpectedly and to others when you've been scattered to a far corner, so don't think I'm too weird but I thought maybe I would say good-by to you now and tell you that I've really enjoyed knowing you and that I admire you. So now when you die you'll at least have had the glad hand from me. The way it happened to Joe and the way it happens to a lot of them, it's as if they were suddenly cut off while making a phone call. Joe was in his thirties and—oh, hell."

Naturally I won't say anything when I walk back in there.

It's sort of sad about the last time I saw Joe. I had to go to Chicago to meet with one of my sponsors a few months ago and after I checked into the Sherman I spent two days running back and forth to meetings and conferences and interviews. The second day, while leaving the old Medina Temple Building on North Michigan, I heard a voice that I thought had called my name. At that moment I was leaning forward to enter a taxi and a few seconds later, while the driver was making a U-turn, I glanced out the right-hand window and there were Barbara and Joe, smiling and waving. The driver slowed down a bit and I stuck my head out and yelled, "Where are you working?"

"The London House," Joe shouted. "Call us."

I said I would and then they were disappearing in the distance and I was rushing back to the Sherman house and the treadmill.

I never got to see Joe after that. Goddamn it. I don't know now that what I feel so maudlin about is him or what. Is it the realization that the world is just too much? Oh, God, why don't we walk around every single minute with our eyes wide open, drinking it all in, because it's being taken away from us little by little every day. I know now why some people believe in reincarnation: it has to be an idea born out of the same sense of incompleteness that I'm feeling right now as I sit here sweating and wishing I had more talent so I could tell you what I mean because, believe me, these words are doing nothing more than expressing the very vaguest outlines of my conception. Time runs out on all of us.

So what if I had lost a couple of hours' sleep on that last Chicago trip and gone over to the London House and listened to Barbara and Joe? I might have sat in and it would have been a ball, but it wouldn't have made the feeling of loss now any smaller. In fact, the better that now ever-lost evening would have been, the worse would be the present feeling.

Joe was young and he had blue eyes and light sandy hair and he was hip and relaxed and I swear that musicians at their best are a very fine type of people. I've never known a vicious musician unless he was a very bad musician. There's something about the business of playing that keeps a man young, younger than he would be if he were driving a bus or auditing in a bank. And that's why Joe died younger than even his years indicate.

To tell you what kind of fellow he was, let me say first that the thing I do the very worst is play the clarinet. I took a few lessons once in connection with making a picture, and although every now and then I kid myself that I'll practice diligently for a couple of years and maybe eventually make it with the instrument, I actually realize that it takes eight or ten years to become good at it and that what with being busy and all, I'm never going to make it. But one night at a party at Bill's house I had a few drinks and the next thing I know I'm opening up the clarinet case and putting the plumbing together and somehow in my condition I have the idea that when I put the instrument in my mouth I'm going to play something worth while. It doesn't happen, of course. My tone isn't too bad for a beginner, but when you're handicapped by inadequate technical mastery of an instrument like the clarinet you're just handicapped, that's all.

But all of a sudden I'm playing, with Barbara at the piano and Joe at the bass, and I'm damned if they didn't make me play over my head. Nothing you'd care to hear again or talk about, of course, but still it's remarkable that I never played the clarinet that well before or since.

So that's about it. That's about all I know about Joe. I don't know where he came from or where he went to school or what his religion was or how he spent his time when he wasn't playing. All the moments we spent together probably wouldn't have added up to twenty-four hours. But let's work out the arithmetic that way. Let's put all the joking and the martini talk and the sitting-in and the swinging and the smiling and the understanding together and add it up to one twenty-four-hour period. And let's say it was one of the happiest days of my life. I owe it to Joe Shulman.

THE GIRLS ON
THE TENTH FLOOR

■ ■ ■

The Village is a pretty wild place. Something's always happening here, I mean. Like you take the place I stop in sometimes after I knock off work: Gus' Elbow Room. You probably know Gus. He tends his own bar. Yeah, the heavy-set fellow with the bags under his eyes. Fifteen years ago when I was punk reporter for the *Trib* Gus was working as a doorman for Slats Ryan over on Eighth. Now he's got his own joint. Does all right too. Oh, nothing big like some of the uptown spots, but he's his own boss, you know what I mean?

You wouldn't think Gus would be a very rough customer to look at him. He isn't much more than five seven or eight and he looks fat. But that isn't fat. It's muscle. In the Village you never know when you're going to need muscle.

I remember one time I was sitting at the bar, it must have been about ten-thirty one night, and a couple of strangers walked in. Everybody in the village is a stranger in one way or another. In fact, a stranger bunch of people you will never meet in your life; but these particular strangers were even strange to the Village, if you know what I mean.

They looked like a couple of king-size trouble-makers. One of them was tall, raw-boned with big fists, and he rapped on the bar for a beer the way the fella tells you to do on television. The other was shorter, but he had a wild glint in his eye, like he was looking to pick a fight or something. They came in talking kind of loud and foul-mouthed and we all gave them the once-over when they sat down.

Gus is used to odd-balls, though, and they didn't faze him.

31

Besides, the three guys at the far end of the bar were cops. Not that they could have been of much help to Gus, though, because they were all on the narcotics undercover squad, and when I call them plain-clothes men I want you to understand that they are wearing the plainest clothes in town: khaki pants and torn sweaters and long-shoremen's jackets. The Village makes you as a cop in two minutes if you go in dressed in a business suit. You either got to dress in shantung pants and fancy shirts like a fairy or else you have to dress like a slob. So only Gus and I knew these fellows were on the force, and if any trouble came up it would have made a bit of a problem for them if they took part in the fracas inasmuch as it might have forced them to reveal their hand.

Anyway, the two newcomers sit down at the bar and right away they're shooting off their mouths and acting like a couple of cowboys in off the range or sailors back from overseas or something. Turns out they're just a couple of studs from Jersey City and there's no mystery as to what they're doing in town.

"Hey, Mac," one of them yelled at Gus, "come here."

Gus walked over politely.

"Where can we get some broads?" the shorter fellow said.

"I don't know," Gus said. Right away I knew he didn't like the boys. Actually Gus can tell you where and how to get anything in the Village. He's been around a long time and he has good friends on both sides of the law.

"Ah, come on," said the taller man. "You know what we're talkin' about?"

"Yes," said Gus, "I know what you're talkin' about."

"So?"

"So what?"

The tall man's face screwed up into an express of complete disgust.

"Look, Mac," he said, "we didn't come in here to make trouble, so why don't you be a nice fella? You didn't open for business yesterday. This ain't no goddamned tearoom you're runnin' here. I ask you again, where can my buddy and me get a couple of broads for the night?"

I got the idea Gus didn't like the way the fellow was leaning forward over the bar, making a face like he was going to spit.

"I don't know," Gus said. "Why don't you put an ad in the paper?" And he walked back to the other end of the bar.

I thought maybe there was going to be trouble right then and there, but something about the blankness on Gus' face and the quiet way he said what he said must have puzzled the two jokers from Jersey. They just looked at each other for a minute, then hunched down on their stools and stared into their beer. Somebody dropped a dime in the juke box and Frank Sinatra began to sing. Gus and the three coppers started talking baseball.

Maybe it's unfortunate that this particular night Gus *wasn't* running a tearoom. Because after they got a few beers into them the two strangers came back to life. They sat muttering to each other for a few minutes, and then the big one jerked a thumb at Gus again.

"Hey you," he said. "Come here."

Gus walked over to them.

"I'm askin' you for the last time, Fatso. Where can me and my buddy get fixed up tonight?"

"Where you fellas from?" Gus said.

"None of your goddamn business," the shorter man said. "You heard what my friend asked you. Why don't you answer him?"

"'Cause he asked me too loud," Gus said. The coppers turned around on their stools, ready for action.

"Oh, a wise guy, eh?" the tall man said.

"No," said Gus. "Look, why don't you fellas just pick up your change and go home? It'll be simpler that way."

"Get him," said the short man, smiling with his mouth but not his eyes. "What are you, *tough* guy?"

"No," said Gus. "I'm a bartender. Not a pimp."

"What did you say?" the big guy demanded belligerently. I knew he was pretty drunk then. He was acting as if Gus had called *him* a pimp. The word was like a match dropped into a box of sawdust.

The big man got up off his stool and leaned over the bar. "What did you say?" he repeated.

"I said I'm a bartender, not a pimp."

"Over in Jersey we knew how to take care of guys like you."

"This ain't Jersey," Gus said, not retreating an inch. "Why don't you get lost?"

The shorter man got up off his stool and in so doing knocked it down. The clatter of falling furniture charged the room with electricity. I got a grip on the neck of an empty beer bottle.

When the man had picked up the stool Gus suddenly said, "Wait a minute. I got an idea."

"What is it?" the tall man growled.

"You fellas are that hard up," said Gus, "I may be able to take care of you."

"Now you're talkin', Fatso," said the shorter man.

"Yea," said Gus. Then he turned to me. "Charlie," he said, "what's the address of that big hotel for girls over on Tenth Street?"

My eyes bugged out a little. There's no hotel for girls on Tenth Street, but there *is* a place called the Women's House of Detention. It's the city lock-up for young females.

"It's the corner of Tenth and Greenwich Avenue," I said.

"Thanks," Gus said, writing the address on a card. He handed it to the tall man.

"It's a big joint," he said, "but don't let that throw you. You're in the big city now."

The tall man threw a bill on the bar and began to move toward the door.

"Thanks, Buster," he said. "You wised up just in time."

"Incidentally," Gus said, "this place has great protection. They even got a cop guarding the front door, but don't mind him."

"Whadda you mean?" said the shorter man.

"He's on salary," said Gus. "He's just there to keep the peace. Don't take any back talk from him. If he gets smart just belt him one."

"You betcha," said the taller man. "We'll take care of him."

"Oh, and one more thing," Gus said. "The best dames are on the tenth floor. Don't let the madam give you any *old* stuff. Insist on the tenth floor. All young blondes, ya know what I mean?"

"Gotcha," said the shorter man and the two disappeared.

When the door was closed we all busted out laughing. Then I thought of something.

"Hey, Gus," I said, "that was a pretty good way to get rid of 'em for now, but what happens when they get wise?"

"Oh, I don't know," said Gus. "They come back and I bust their skulls with this." He held up a child's baseball bat that he kept behind the bar.

"All the same," said one of the policemen, "I wouldn't like to be you when they find out what's what."

"Well," said Gus. "We'll see."

I later found out from Stelmazek, the night guard at the Detention Home, what happened when the boys from Jersey got there. There's no sign out front, by the way, so Gus' trap was a neat one. The place *looks* like a hotel. When Stelmazek heard the night bell ring he walked over and opened the door.

The two men tried to walk past him. He shoved them back.

"Visiting hours in the afternoon," he said.

"We ain't visiting nobody, Pop," one of the men said. "Where are the broads?"

"What the hell are you talkin' about?" Stelmazek said.

"Here," said the tall man, reaching in his pocket, "here's a five-spot for yourself. Now lead up to the broads!"

"Get outta here," Stelmazek said and closed the door.

There was a moment of silence then several moments of vigorous pounding. Stelmazek opened the door.

"Look, Pop," one of the men said, "don't get smart. They warned us about you. Now don't get nasty again or I'll belt you one."

"Yeah," said the other man. "Stop the crap and let us in. And listen, don't try to give us any of the old stuff, you understand? We want the broads on the tenth floor. Cream of the crop!"

"Get outta here right now," Stelmazek said, "or I'll kick you down the stairs."

Another officer came along the hall toward the door, drawn by the commotion.

"You and what army?" cried the shorter man.

At that Stelmazek threw the door open wide and punched the shorter man in the mouth. He fell over backward and rolled down two or three steps. Stelmazek and the other officer leaped at the tall man and the three fell into the vestibule, fighting. The first man must have suddenly figured out the double-cross because he took to his feet and disappeared down the street, leaving his friend to do battle. To make a long story short I think the tall guy eventually did three days for disturbing the peace. I don't know if they ever caught up with the other fellow.

That isn't the end of the tale, of course, because when we all heard what happened we figured it would be only a matter of time before the two guys came back to the Elbow Room to even the score with Gus. But weeks passed and nothing happened. We began to think the two had been smart enough to learn their lesson and stay on their own side of the river.

We found out we were wrong. One night about three months after their first visit the two men came back. I was sitting at the bar, as chance would have it, although I don't want you to get the idea that

I spend all my time at Gus' place. I usually drop in two, maybe three nights a week, but for Gus' sake I was glad I was on hand this night.

That is, I was glad for a couple of seconds when the two Jersey boys walked in, but then I noticed they're not alone. Behind them I see two other customers and they look even rougher than the first two. For a second I thought maybe they weren't all together, but I had guessed wrong. They all walked over to the bar very buddy-buddy and sat down at the far end, talking loud and acting for all the world like a bunch of guys who had come in to bust up the joint.

The three coppers weren't on hand this time either. There was only me and one woman at the bar, the cook in the kitchen, and two young fairies having dinner in one of the booths. It looked bad.

I know Gus had his baseball bat but we were outnumbered. He walked over to them as if they were all perfect strangers.

"What'll it be?" he said.

"Four beers," one of them said. "And make it snappy."

Gus didn't answer. He drew four beers and set them carefully on the bar. Then he walked down to the other end of the room and pretended to watch television.

After about five minutes I see the big guy jerk his thumb at Gus. I figured the time had come to do something, so I nonchalantly stepped over to the telephone booth by the men's room and put in a call to precinct police. Unfortunately it was Saturday night. It took half a minute for them to answer the phone and when they did they said they couldn't come right over.

"Look," I said, "nothing's happened yet but I'm pretty sure there's going to be trouble."

"We got a lot of trouble tonight," the cop on the line said. "But relax. I'll have somebody look in. May take twenty minutes or so."

I hung up. A lot can happen in twenty minutes. It takes two seconds to throw a glass through a bar mirror or give a bartender a clout on the head. I looked at Gus. He's dead game, that's for sure, but this time he looked worried. I looked at myself in the mirror. I looked worried too. Reflected in the mirror I could also see the baseball bat he kept under the bar. But I didn't know whether he'd try to use it against four men. There was too good a chance they'd take it away from him and use it themselves. Something like that is a good weapon only if you're fighting one or two men. Nothing short of a gun is any good against four and I knew Gus didn't keep a revolver on the premises.

Ten minutes ticked by. On television George Gobel was making everybody laugh, but he wasn't doing so good at the Elbow Room. It was pretty quiet, like waiting for a bomb to go off. The four strangers drank another round and their talk became rougher, louder.

Then it happened. The tall man of the original two stood up and walked down to our end of the bar. He leaned in toward Gus, who pretended not to notice.

"Hey, you," he said softly.

"Yeah?" said Gus.

"You're the wise guy pulled that smart trick on my friend and me a few weeks ago, ain't you?"

"Why," said Gus," I guess maybe I am. Why?" He kept his eye on the stranger's hands, which were spread out on the bar, palms down.

"You think that was a very nice thing to do?" said the man.

"I don't know," said Gus. "It just came to me at the time. Maybe you guys were askin' for it. What's the matter, can't you take a joke?"

"Yeah, sure," the man said. "I can take a joke. Don't you worry about that. In fact, that's what I want to talk to you about. Come here," he gestured. "I wanna whisper something to you."

I turned partly sideways so that when he made his move I could get a good shot at him. I figured if we could get one of them out of the way fast we might stand a chance against the other three.

Gus leaned forward, warily. His right hand was out of sight behind the bar.

"What do you want?" he said.

"Well, I'll tell you," said the stranger. "At first me and my buddy were pretty sore, but you see them two guys we brought in with us? We want you to do us a favor."

"What?" said Gus, his jaw dropping.

"I'm gonna call you down to the other end of the bar in a minute and ask you about some broads for our two friends. I want you to hook them just the way you hooked us. Okay?"

"Okay," said Gus, bringing his right hand back up into sight.

Before the four guys left, Gus set up a round on the house. I had a shot myself.

THE AWARD
■ ■ ■

Clare walked up to my desk with a long face.

"What's the good word?" I said, trying to be cheerful.

"Read it and weep," she said, handing me a letter. It was from Marty Davis.

"Dear Harry," the letter said. "Thank you for your letter of February 14 and for the kind invitation you extended to Bob and myself. He is extremely flattered, naturally, that your organization should choose to name him Mr. Entertainment for the year, but unfortunately he will be making a film in Japan this spring and we will all be leaving for Tokyo early in April, which means he couldn't attend your banquet in New York on April 27."

I didn't bother to read any further.

"Well," I said. "Two down. Where do we go from here?"

"I don't know," Clare said. "I thought sure Gleason would be able to do it or I would have gotten the letter off to Hope a long time ago."

"What's that got to do with it?" I said.

"Nothing," she said, "except Jackie giving us the bad news so late made us lose three valuable weeks."

"I am hip," I said, "but don't worry. We've done it before and we can do it again."

"I don't know," she said. "It gets harder every year . . . comedians moving to the Coast and all. Why the hell do they go through this rigmarole anyway? Why don't people just send in their money, period?"

"Hush," I said. "You start talking like that and we'll be out of work."

You see, Clare and I are partners in a very fascinating business:

39

fund-raising. The average organization doesn't know beans about raising money, so they call in specialists. That's us. We're set up to handle the entire operation: organize lunches, dances, benefits, banquets, telephone appeals, direct-mail campaigns—you know, the whole business. We work on a very modest percentage, although some of our colleagues work on flat salary. But either way I'm sure you'll agree there's nothing unethical about it. The money goes to charity and everybody's happy.

Except that six years ago, wanting to make a good impression when we signed on this particular account, Clare and I decided to kick up some dust and get a little newspaper and newsreel attention by holding a lush banquet at the Waldorf and passing out Citations of Merit to some big show-business names.

It's a good dodge and I must admit we didn't invent it. The actors are a push-over, of course. Just tell them they've won an award and they jump at the bait. Then we charge fifty or a hundred bucks a plate and the cash customers pour in, as much to gawk at the celebrities as to help the organization. As I said before, it's all for sweet charity, and for a long time it's been running like clockwork.

Lately, though, it's been getting tough to line up top-drawer names. About three years ago we put ourselves out on a limb by naming Groucho Marx as Mr. Entertainment, and he was a smash. Got a million laughs at the dinner, was quoted in everybody's column, and attracted a lot of attention to the organization, which of course is what Clare and I are most interested in. The next year, naturally, we had to get somebody more or less as big as Groucho so we invited Arthur Godfrey. But he wasn't having any. He sent us a nice check, and frankly I've never been so disgusted by a large contribution. Money we can get pretty easily these days. It was a big drawing card for our banquet that we really needed, and when Arthur turned us down I began to worry a little. Next we tried Sid Caesar, but when Sid found out he would have to make a speech of acceptance he, too, begged off because he only does bits and sketches and doesn't like to talk in public "as himself," as they say in the trade.

We finally got somebody, of course, and everything worked out fine. But each year it's been getting tougher. Last year we had to go through Berle, Gobel, Skelton, and Garry Moore before we pinned somebody down. And to tell you the truth, I think some of these guys have a lot of nerve saying no to us. After all, they're being honored by a great organization with thousands of contributing members and some mighty imposing names on the letterhead. It's true that there's no voting or anything—Clare and I, we just pick the names ourselves—but, even so, it's a big thing. We send them a wire first:

> I AM PLEASED TO INFORM YOU THAT OUR ORGANIZATION HAS JUST NAMED YOU MR. ENTERTAINMENT OF 1956 FOR THE GENERAL EXCELLENCE OF YOUR TELEVISION PERFORMANCES DURING THE PAST YEAR.

It has to be television, by the way. Movies or radio or records don't mean a thing in connection with a deal like this. The guy has to be working in television.

> PLEASE ACCEPT MY PERSONAL CONGRATULATIONS. DETAILS CONCERNING FORMAL PRESENTATION OF YOUR AWARD SUPPLIED IN LETTER TO FOLLOW.

We send the wire out over the signature of our honorary president, you understand, who is always somebody mighty important. We've had General MacArthur, Oscar Hammerstein, and Governor Dewey, just to give you an idea. Naturally, being busy men, they don't have the time to handle any of the details of their office, so what they're actually doing is just allowing us to use their names. Like if you were to get a wire from me, Harry Slater, you'd probably throw it away, but getting a wire signed General Sarnoff or Herbert Hoover, you sit up and take notice.

We send out three copies of this wire. One to the guy himself, one to his agent or manager, and one to his publicity man. Usually it does the trick, or anyway it did up until recently when some of the boys began playing hard to get. If we get a turn-down we make a few quick phone calls, tell 'em to keep our correspondence confidential, and then start all over again with some other target. But, as I say, I think some of these guys have a lot of nerve saying no to us. A lot of them say they can't fly in from the Coast, that they're busy doing their shows every week, and so on, but if a guy really wants to make a trip he'll do it. Groucho had flown in from the Coast, although it's true his show is on film and he has more free time than the guys who work live. Also he had to come here anyway to do a show for Max Liebman, and our timing just happened to be lucky.

So anyway, here we were, Clare and I, with rejection slips from Hope and Gleason, and banquet time rushing in on us like the Notre Dame forward wall.

"Comedians are getting tough," I said. "What about singers. How does Perry Como strike you?"

"It would be a pleasure," Clare said.

"Cut the comedy," I said. "Do you think he'd go for it?"

"I don't know," she said. "What about the speech bit?"

"He's not a cretin," I said. "He can talk."

"But he strikes me as the kind who doesn't like to," she said.

Clare's a better judge of human nature than I am so I didn't argue with her. She takes care of the subtler problems we run up against, and handles a lot of the detail work. I like to tell myself that I do the big thinking for the two of us.

"He could sing," I said.

"All right. Shall we send a wire?"

I reached for the phone. "We might lose a couple of days that way," I said. "What's Sol Green's number?"

Sol's a publicity man who's well liked at NBC and specializes in handling Perry. When I gave him the pitch he said, "Sounds wonderful, Harry. Can I call you back?"

"I'll be here," I said.

He called back in twenty minutes. "Jeez," he said, "I forgot. That very night Perry is getting an award at the Astor. Red Cross or Community Chest or something."

I took Clare to lunch at "21." Figured it would give our morale a little boost. When we got back to the office there was a message to call Ed Sullivan's secretary. I think I had promised Ed an exclusive on our award story. You really have to break a thing like this open for everybody, but it doesn't do any harm now and then to let one of the boys get a lick at it a few hours early.

I told Ed's girl I had no news.

I was looking out the window at some pigeons that were trying to keep out of the rain when Clare said, "What about Jimmy Thomas?"

For a long time I looked at the pigeons, going over names in my mind. Groucho, Caesar, Berle, Gleason, Hope, Skelton, Silvers, Como. They were all off the list for one reason or another. Buttons, Cox, and a few other weren't working at the moment.

"Sugar plum," I said, "I think you have hit it. At least we'll give it a try."

Thomas was a new boy. Not as big yet as the old hands, but getting good ratings and a great press, which was important. To me, I mean. Personally, I didn't entirely dig his talent but I knew a lot of people who did. To me he seemed cast in Godfrey's mold, although he had a youthful, fresh appeal; but I knew a few people who thought he was the funniest thing since Charlie Chaplin.

"Where does Thomas hail from?" I said. "Cincinnati?"

"Chicago," Clare said.

"Good. We'll get good breaks there."

"You're chicken-counting," Clare said, and she was right. I didn't have Thomas' name on the dotted line yet.

I thought about him while I reached for the phone. Jimmy had started out down South as a disc jockey and had landed in Chicago after the war. His easygoing, country-boy charm and his way of handing out a line of gab between records had made him, within three years, the toast of the town, so CBS finally brought him to New York. But somebody goofed and they had him doing quiz shows for a couple of years, which made him a big favorite with the afternoon crowd but didn't make much of an impression at Lindy's. Finally, though, he had gotten a summer-replacement spot on a kind of last-minute fluke, and that did it. He was off to the races.

Funny thing about television. In the old days you worked for years to become a star. In TV one good show could do it. And, Jimmy did a good show; I'll have to admit that. He worked mostly ad-lib, although he had writers, and his peculiar combination of boy-next-door style and sharp wit made him the critics' darling. Not since Buttons and Gobel has anybody made it that fast. Within six weeks his name was as well known around the country as anybody in the business. It remained to be seen, of course, whether or not he could last, but for the time being he was certainly riding high.

I got his press agent on the line. "Andy," I said, playing it carefully, "I've just heard news that I thought you might be interested in."

"What's that?" he said.

"Been talking to the gang over here and they're very hot to give Jimmy the big one this year. You know, the Mr. Entertainment award. It's between him and Gleason, as it stands at the moment."

"Jeez," Andy said. "It would be a great thing for Jim. When are they voting? When will you know?"

Andy hasn't been in the business long. He used to write or something.

"Oh," I said, "maybe this afternoon, maybe not for a couple of days. Reason I'm calling you now is just to get a line on a few things. Like would Jimmy be available to accept the award on the twenty-seventh of April? In case he wins, I mean."

"Don't see why not," Andy said. "He never gets away and he has nothing booked in the way of benefits or anything, after—let me see—the middle of March."

"Well," I said, "I'll tell them that over here and we'll see what happens."

"Swell," Andy said. "Very nice of you to call, Harry."

I played it cool and killed a couple of hours to bring Andy and Thomas to a boil. Got some dictation done, went and got a haircut, and then came back and began doing a little thinking as to the dais line-up for the banquet. I figured it would be the usual: somebody from the mayor's office; somebody speaking for the governor, a couple of columnists, whatever glamour dolls were scheduled to be in town to plug pictures; a couple of other comics or emcees from CBS, Thomas' network; three or four officers of the organization, and a toastmaster. Jessel had done it for us two years before, so we probably couldn't get him.

While I was jotting down some names Andy called back. It was twenty minutes past four.

"I've talked to Jim," he said, "and he's very pleased to be in the running. He would definitely be available on the twenty-seventh."

"Funny thing you should call at just this minute," I said. "I had the phone in my hand trying to call *you*. Good news."

"Really?"

"Yep. It was never even close. They love Gleason but Jimmy is hot this year."

"Gee, that's wonderful."

"You bet it is," I said, "but then Jim deserves it. I love his show myself."

"Thanks," Andy said. "I'll tell him."

"You should get the wire from the old man any minute," I said, signaling Clare to get it out on the other phone. "Then in a couple of days we'll fill you in with the minor details."

"Wonderful," Andy said. "I'll let you guys make the first announcement, then I'll follow it up. You let me know how you want to handle it."

"Oh, by the way," I said, "maybe Jim could work a couple of plugs for the organization into the show some time this week."

"No problem," Andy said. "Shoot it over and we'll put it on."

Frankly, I pride myself on never overlooking anything. Thomas does one of those chatty shows where you can get plugs in easy. It's tougher if you're working with somebody like Hope or Berle.

Within a week we had the dais line-up all nailed down. We were able to get Phil Silvers. Phil couldn't be on hand for the whole thing but he committed himself to come in for ten minutes and say a few words. Carmine De Sapio signed on because he likes our organization and because I suggested he could make a brief pitch about his candidate. I like Carmine. He's the kind of a guy who'll usually come through for you. Then we got Rhonda Fleming because her picture was opening the say day as the banquet; Earl Wilson because he prided himself on being the guy who had "discovered" Thomas when he was working in Chicago; Jaye P. Morgan because she had been named the Queen of our Winter Fund-Raising Drive and thought she owed us something; Mike Wallace because he was still kind of new to the banquet circuit, and was impressed at being invited and wanted to be a nice guy about it; Herbert Bayard Swope because he was on our Board of Trustees; and two CBS vice-presidents because it was part of their day's work. The other four chairs, as I say, were taken by officers of the organization. They were all *part-time* officers, of course, as they had their own business to attend to in addition to their charitable activities, but they were all ready, willing, and able to attend because they got a kick out of hobnobbing with the celebrities.

If I do say so myself everything went off smooth as glass.

The Grand Ballroom of the Waldorf was darned near filled up the night of the banquet and we had pretty lights and a small band playing dinner music.

We hadn't had any luck getting a topnotch emcee, so we finally had to settle for Peter O'Brien from the Mayor's office, who is pretty good. He's kind of a minor-league Grover Whalen as far as I'm concerned, but he tells a fair story, the ladies like him, and he handles a banquet with all the ease of a man who has practically lived on chicken, peas, and ice cream.

The feed was pretty good, and about nine-forty-five I gave O'Brien the high sign and sent the man over to adjust the microphone. I felt fine. The pictures had already been taken, the money was all in, I had had a couple of drinks and, all in all, life was rosy.

While I was watching the guy adjust the mike I noticed that Andy Sloan, Thomas' man, was approaching my table. He hunched down next to me.

"Say," he said, "Jim was just wondering—who did the voting that got him this award?"

I've always thought it was pretty corny in stories where people say their blood ran cold, but, believe me, that's the way I felt right then. I personally always had figured Thomas as kind of a smart-aleck type and I was afraid that his question meant trouble.

"Why, what do you mean, Andy?" I stalled.

"You know, who decided that he's this year's Mr. Entertainment? Was there some kind of vote? Jim just wants to know in connection with his speech."

I started to say, "That's what I was afraid of," but I held my tongue.

"Well," I said, "you know how these things work. There's no actual vote. It was just the committee. Same way we do it every year. Like for Groucho and the rest of them."

"Who's on the committee?"

"Well, uh—I mean it's not a *formal* committee or anything. We just discuss it up at the office and we do a lot of thinking as to who's the most deserving guy and like that."

"I see," Andy said. "Okay, thanks. I'll tell Jim."

I figured there was no sense running after him.

"What were you two whispering about?" Clare said.

"Listen," I said. "Wasn't it Thomas who made that speech about fluoridation on his show a few weeks ago?"

"Yes," she said. "Why do you ask?"

"I don't see the Thomas show too often. Does he think he's some sort of a–like a—you know, an Edward R. Murrow?"

"Yes, maybe a little. But what's up?"

"The jig. Sloan just came nosing around to find out how we actually do the deciding about the award."

"So?"

"So I told him."

"Why didn't you lie?"

"I don't know. What good would that have done? They could check later."

"Are you afraid Thomas is going to mention something about it in his speech?"

"Two minds," I said, "with but a single thought. The papers would eat it up. We'd be out of work in the morning."

Clare put her hand to her head and just stared at the tablecloth.

I looked across the room. Sloan and Thomas had their heads together, with Sloan doing the talking and Thomas frowning. After a moment he lifted his head and looked at me. I pretended not to notice and gawked at the giant chandelier for a couple of seconds. When I looked back, Thomas was still staring at me, with what the fiction boys would probably describe as a sardonic smile on his face.

At that moment O'Brien rapped for order, cleared his throat, and said, "Good evening, ladies and gentlemen. Can you hear me?"

A man at a nearby table shouted "Yes!"

"Not you, Charley." O'Brien laughed. "I said ladies and *gentlemen.*"

You had to hand it to Pete. He was fast on his feet.

After he handled a few formal introductions and announcements, Pete introduced Mr. Salzberger, our chairman, who lumbered to the microphone, spilled a glass of water, discussed finances briefly, and sat down.

Pete then told a few stories and got the crowd in a good mood. Me, I didn't laugh.

After that it was Carmine, whose remarks had something to do with the opportunities in our great nation for young men with something fresh and worth-while to say, although he had a little trouble working in praise for both Jimmy Thomas and his candidate. Then came Rhonda Fleming, who said she couldn't really think of very much to say because she wasn't a practiced public speaker but that to prove just how much she loved Jim, she was going to give him a big kiss right then and there, and she did, and the crowd ate it up. Thomas wasn't exactly displeased either. I mean, after all.

She closed with a few words about the organization and only said "worthy cause" twice, which is less than par for the course.

Then Earl said a few words, and I do mean a few words because he isn't much of a talker, which is true of a lot of writers, but he spoke sincerely anyway and did an okay job. Then O'Brien put Phil on because he had to get out early and he was great, of course, as always. We should have given him the award. He's not the type that asks questions.

"It's very wonderful to be here at the—" he said and then he looked at a small card in his hand and said, "the Waldorf." It broke everybody up because he was pretending not to know where he was, you know.

"I think it's a fine thing that you're giving this well-deserved citation to Jimmy Thomas," he said, "although frankly I think there is one other man to whom the award could have gone—myself."

Phil actually is a very shy, modest guy, you understand, but sometimes he does these jokes where he seems to be bold and brazen and the people eat it up. Anyway, he went on like that for about eight minutes and he even had Thomas laughing, which is pretty good because being the guest of honor at one of these affairs is a little unnerving and you are apt to be kind of distracted during the speeches and what-have-you. I was hoping Thomas would choke.

At long last we were heading for the home stretch and O'Brien picked up the large, shiny plaque we had had made up.

"As you all know," Peter said, "the Mr. Entertainment Award that this organization presents every year is one of the most respected in the annals of show business. Extreme care is given to the selection of candidates for this great honor, and when a man is privileged to have his name engraved on one of these plaques, it is a tremendously significant thing, both to the man involved, to the organization, and to . . . uh . . . those of us who support this worthy effort."

I looked at Clare and smiled to hide the fact that I felt sick.

"We all know," he was saying, "the tireless devotion and unflagging zeal with which show people contribute their time and talents to one charitable cause or another. It has been said that an actor is the only man in the world who will time and time again give away the only thing he has to sell: his God-given ability."

I didn't quite see what that had to do with Jimmy's getting the award, but the crowd seemed to be lapping it up and, besides, I suppose Thomas had done his share of benefits, although I must say he had never done anything in particular for our organization before. But be that as it may, O'Brien was warming to his task, as they say.

"This young man," he said, "who came out of the great city of Chicago just a few years ago, has done what very few men in our history have been able to do. He has won the heart of New York, the respect of its people, and the admiration of its leaders. New York is proud to consider Jimmy Thomas an adopted son."

At this there was a great wave of applause.

"And how has he accomplished all this?" O'Brien asked. "By consistently telecasting good, clean entertainment" (more applause), "by bringing a smile to many a troubled countenance, by giving unselfishly of his time and . . . uh . . . talent . . . and . . . uh . . . by showing the world what is meant by good, clean American entertainment."

The audience applauded again. Clare and I exchanged glances.

"Jimmy Thomas," O'Brien said, plunging into a brief biography, "was the only child of Alfred and Agnes Thomas of Baltimore, Maryland. As a boy he attended school in Baltimore, became interested in dramatics, and finally started his radio career on a Baltimore station. His professional progress was interrupted by a three-year stretch in the United States Navy" (more applause) "after which he migrated to Chicago and began the phenomenal success story that has reached its climax, so to speak, here in this room tonight. But I am certain that, in another sense, this is not the climax of the career of Jimmy Thomas. For he is yet a young man. He has horizons before him. Uncharted seas to sail. Battles to win. And great honors to . . . uh . . . attain. No, it will be many a year before Jimmy Thomas reaches the climax, the apex, of his climb to fame and the full love of . . . uh . . . his fellow Americans. And we know he will . . . uh . . . do all that we . . . uh . . . so confidently predict for him here tonight. At this time, it gives me extreme pleasure, Jim, to present to you this plaque." Thomas rose to his feet and stood, somewhat sheepishly, next to O'Brien. "It gives me extreme pleasure to present to you this citation for meritorious entertainment service to the people of America during the past twelve months and to officially proclaim you, acting as I am on behalf of this great organization, Mr. Entertainment of 1956!"

The whole audience leaped to its feet and gave Thomas a lengthy ovation.

When it subsided he bowed, looked directly at me, and then spoke slowly. "Thank you, Mr. O'Brien, ladies and gentlemen, and distinguished guests. I know this has been a long evening for you and I'm not going to take very much of your time now with a speech or anything remotely resembling a speech. I just want to say a few words about this award . . . and about what it means."

I couldn't look at Clare.

"You know, those of us in the entertainment field receive quite a few awards. Our offices are full to overflowing with plaques and citations and gold cups and silver cups and what-have-you. Not all of these awards, frankly, are of earth-shattering importance. Some are presented not so much for the honor of the recipient as for the publicizing of the donor."

I looked at the Old Man, wondering if he had sized up the situation, but his face was a mask as he sat turned slightly sideways, staring at Thomas.

"But I want to make it clear," our award winner went on, "that I am truly grateful . . . to all of you . . . for the kind words said here tonight . . . and for this very handsome plaque. I know what your organization stands for . . . and what its ideals are. And I like thinking that those ideals are somehow embodied in, or connected with, this particular award."

I looked at Clare. She looked kind of funny. Like she almost had tears in her eyes or something.

"Those of us in television," Jimmy said, "sometimes are apt to get so interested in the very *doing* of our programs that we almost forget the audience, strange as that may sound. It isn't that we're unaware of the audience; it's just that the simple mechanics of our work sometimes induces in us a peculiar kind of . . . well, you might call it . . . selfishness. And that's why it's particularly heart-warming to receive some demonstration such as this of the fact that you don't hold that selfishness against us, that you do have some measure of charitable feeling toward us, and that you look to us to bring some pleasure into your lives.

"Despite what you may hear, we *are* interested in you, of course. Sometimes I wish I could go into your homes physically and do my program. At times I feel that the camera stands in the way of our getting to know each other, and it is, as I say, an evening like this and an event like this, that does bring me face to face with you and that enables me to thank you very sincerely and very humbly for your response and your affection. I"—he paused and scratched his head with that peculiar country-boy gesture that made him seem so folksy—"I guess I just finished my speech, folks, so . . . so I think I'll just sit down. Thank you again, from the bottom of my heart."

The crowd gave Thomas a swell hand and I was a little surprised when I noticed who was applauding the loudest. It was me. To this day I still haven't made up my mind how much of a smart aleck Thomas is, but I have to admit he had the good sense to realize that the last thing the people want is a cold, hard fact shoved down their throats.

That's about all there is to this little saga. When you started reading it you probably figured me for a cynical bastard who just wanted to give you the low-down on the citation business, but that isn't my angle. I mean, as we all left the Waldorf that night Jimmy Thomas was happy, the audience was happy, the treasury was bulging, and Clare and I were set for another year. Don't give me any of that ends-and-means malarky. I like my work very much. Wouldn't change it for anything.

Oh, and one more thing. This year when you're taking care of the Community Chest and the Red Cross and the March of Dimes and the rest, remember the organization, too, will you?

THE SECRET
■ ■ ■

I didn't know I was dead until I walked into the bathroom and looked in the mirror.

In fact I didn't even know it at that exact moment. The only thing I knew for sure then was that I couldn't see anything in the mirror except the wallpaper behind me and the small table with the hairbrushes on it low against the wall.

I think I just stood there for perhaps ten seconds. Then I reached out and tried to touch the mirror, because I thought I was still asleep on the couch in the den and I figured that if I moved around a bit, so to speak, in my dream I could sort of jar myself awake. I know it isn't a very logical way to think, but in moments of stress we all do unusual things.

The first moment I really knew I was dead was when I couldn't feel the mirror. I couldn't even see the hand I had stretched out to touch it. That's when I knew there was nothing physical about me. I had identity, I was conscious, but I was invisible. I knew then I had to be either dead or a raving maniac.

Just to be sure, I stepped back into the den. I felt better when I saw my body lying on the couch. I guess that sounds like a peculiar thing to say too, but what I mean is, I'd rather be dead than insane. Maybe *you* wouldn't but that's what makes horse races.

My next sensation (that's the only word I can think of to convey my meaning to you) was that there was something pressing on my mind, some nagging matter I had almost forgotten. It was very much like the feeling you sometimes have when you walk over to a bookshelf or a clothes closet, let's say, and then suddenly just stand

51

there and say to yourself, "Now why did I come over here?" I felt a bit as if I had an imminent appointment.

I went over to the couch and looked down at myself. The magazine was open on the floor where it had slipped from my hand, and my right foot had fallen down as if I might have been making an effort to get up when I died.

It must have been the round of golf that did it. Larkin had warned me about exertion as long as three years ago, but after a fearful six months I had gotten steadily more overconfident. I was physically big, robust, muscular. I had played football at college. Inactivity annoyed the hell out of me. I remembered the headache that had plagued me over the last three holes, the feeling of utter weariness in the locker room after the game. But the cold shower had refreshed me a bit and a drink had relaxed me. I felt pretty good when I got home, except for an inner weariness and a lingering trace of the headache.

It had come while I was asleep, that's why I didn't recognize it. I mean if it comes in the form of a death-bed scene, with people standing around you shaking their heads, or if it comes in the form of a bullet from an angry gun, or in the form of drowning, well, it certainly comes as no surprise. But it came to me while I was lying there asleep in the den after reading a magazine. What with the sun and the exercise and the drink, I was a little groggy anyway and my dreams were sort of wild and confused. Naturally when I found myself standing in front of the mirror I thought it was all just another part of a dream.

It wasn't, of course. You know that. You do if you read the papers, anyway, because they played it up pretty big on page one. "Westchester Man 'Dead' for 16 Minutes." That was the headline in the *Herald Tribune*. In the Chicago *Daily News* the headline on the story was "New Yorker 'Dead,' Revived by Doctors." Notice those quotation marks around the word *dead*. That's always the way the papers handle it. I say always because it happens all the time. Last year alone there were nine of us around the country. Ask any of us about it and we'll just laugh good-naturedly and tell you that the papers were right, we weren't dead. Of course we'll tell you that. What else could we tell you?

So there I was, beside the couch, staring down at myself. I remember looking around the room, but I was alone. They hadn't come yet. I felt a flicker of some kind that would be hard to describe—an urgency, an anxiety, a realization that I had left a few things undone. Then I tried a ridiculous thing. I tried to get back into myself. But it wouldn't work. I couldn't do it alone.

Jo would have to help, although we had just had a bitter argument. She had been in the kitchen when I had gone in to take a nap. I hurried to the kitchen. She was still there. Shelling peas, I think, and talking to the cook. "Jo," I said, but of course she couldn't hear me. I moved close to her and tried to tell her. I felt like a dog trying to interest a distracted master.

"Agnes," she said, "would you please close the window."

That's all she said. Then she stood up, wiped her hands, and walked out of the kitchen and down the hall to the den. I don't know how I did it; but in a vague way she had gotten the message.

She let out a tiny scream when she saw the color of my face. Then she shook me twice and then she said, "Oh, my God," and started to cry, quietly. She did not go to pieces. Thank God she didn't go to pieces or I wouldn't be able to tell the tale today.

Still crying, she ran to the hall phone and called Larkin. He ordered an ambulance and met it at the house inside of ten minutes. In all, only twelve minutes had elapsed since I had tried to look at myself in the mirror.

I remember Larkin came in on the run without talking. He ran past me as I stood at the door of the den and knelt down beside my body on the couch.

"When did you find him?" he said.

"Ten minutes ago," Jo said.

He took something out of his bag and injected the body with adrenalin, and then they bundled "me" off to the hospital. I followed. It was five minutes away.

I never would have believed a crew could work so fast. Oxygen. More adrenalin. And then one of the doctors pushed a button and the table my body was on began to lift slowly, first at one end and then at the other, like a slow teeter-totter.

"Watch for blood pressure," Larkin whispered to an assistant, who squeezed a rubber bulb.

I was so fascinated watching them I did not at first realize I had visitors.

"Interesting," a voice said.

"Yes," I answered, without consciously directing my attention away from the body on the tilting table. Then I felt at one and the same time a pang of fear and the release of the nagging anxiety that had troubled me earlier.

I must have been expecting them. There was one on each side of me.

The second one looked at the body, then at Larkin and the others. "Do you think they'll succeed?" he said.

"I don't know," I said. "I hope so."

The answer seemed significant. The two looked at each other.

"We must be very certain," he said. "Would it matter so much to you either way?"

"Why, yes," I said. "I suppose it would. I mean, there's work I've left unfinished."

"Work isn't important *now*, is it?" asked the first one.

"No," I agreed. "It isn't. But there are other things. Things I have to do for Jo. For the children."

Again the two seemed to confer, silently.

"What sort of things?"

"Oh," I said, "there are some business details I've left up in the air. There'll be legal trouble, I'm sure, about the distribution of the assets of my firm."

"Is that all?" the first one said, coming close to me. Larkin began to shake his head slowly. He looked as if he were losing hope.

Then I thought of something else. "You'll laugh," I said, "but something silly just came into my mind."

"What is it?" asked the second one.

"I would like to apologize to Jo," I said, "because we had an argument this afternoon. I'd forgotten I'd promised to take her and the children out to dinner and a movie. We had an argument about it. I suppose it sounds ridiculous at a time like this to talk about something that may seem so trivial, but that's what I'd like to do. I'd like to apologize to her for the things I said, and I'd like to keep that date. I'd like to take the children to see that movie, even if it is some cowboys-and-Indians thing that'll bore the hell out of me."

That's when it all began to happen. I can't say that suddenly the two were gone. To say *I* was gone would be more to the point. They didn't leave me. I left them. I was still unconscious, but now I was on the table. I was back inside my head. I was dreaming and I was dizzy. I didn't know what was happening in the room then, of course. I didn't know anything till later that night when I woke up. I felt weak and shaky and for a few minutes I wasn't aware that Larkin and some other doctors and Jo were standing around my bed. There was some kind of an oxygen tent over my chest and head, and my mouth felt dry and stiff. My tongue was like a piece of wood but I was alive. And I could see Jo. She looked tired and wan but she looked mighty beautiful to me.

The next day the men from the papers came around and interviewed me. They wrote that I was in good spirits and was sitting up in bed swapping jokes with the nurses, which was something of an exaggeration.

It was almost a month before I could keep that date with Jo and the kids, and by that time the picture wasn't even playing in our neighborhood. We had to drive all the way over to Claremont to see it, but we stopped at a nice tearoom on the way and had a wonderful dinner.

People still ask me what I felt while I was "dead." They always say it just that way, getting quotation marks into their voices, treating it as something a little bit amusing, the way the newspapers did. And I go along with it, of course. You can't say to them, "Why, yes, I was dead." They'd lock you up.

Funny thing about it all was that I'd always been more or less afraid of the idea of death. But after dying, I wasn't. I always knew I'd eventually go again, but it never worried me. I did my best to make a go of my relationships with other people and that was about the size of it. One other thing I did was write this little story and give it to a friend of mine, to be published only after my death.

If you're reading it, that means I've gone again. But this time I won't be back.

ONE REASON TELEVISION
IS SO TERRIBLE

■ ■ ■

This is a true story.

I know that's a dumb way to begin, but I've never written a short story before.

I've never written anything, in fact, with the exception of thousands of memos and a few hundred personal letters.

I wouldn't even be writing this now if it weren't for the fact that I'm finally free to do so. For the last nine years, the narrative itself—the real-life facts of it, that is—have been gnawing at me inside, like an ulcer. It didn't matter how high I rose in the program department at CBS or NBC, the two television networks I've worked for, I still couldn't forget what happened.

When I tell you the story, you'll see why. You may, at first, think less of me for not having gone public with the information long before now. You may even think that the main reason for my reticence was cowardice.

You'd be absolutely right, at least so far as my first motivation was concerned. Eventually, when I got to the point where I suppose I could have spoken out, what stayed my hand was more a matter of good old corporate loyalty. These last few years I could have stood the heat personally, but the network itself was on such shaky ground, the parent company had suffered such severe losses, that I figured—what the hell, why rock the boat?

I *know* I've just mixed metaphors. That must happen a lot when you're new at the writing game.

The funny thing about my not being able to write too well is that for the past fourteen years I've been passing judgment on a thousand-and-one men and women who, for the most part, wrote very well indeed. But then I guess that's par-for-the-course in all sorts of businesses. Executives who couldn't fix a flat tire or put a nut and bolt together without hurting themselves, give orders to engineers and designers who can actually create automobiles. Executives who couldn't act, write, operate a camera, or direct a picture, give orders to creative people who can. We even elect men to the presidency of the United States who are not economists, are usually the rankest amateurs at the delicate art of foreign policy, never ran a business (*never met a payroll* is the cliche), and sometimes, in fact, never truly distinguished themselves at anything much except the business of getting elected.

I spell this out so that you won't think that non-writers' making life-and-death decisions that affect writers is the root cause of the low quality of so many television programs.

You see, there are exceptions to every rule and there certainly are to this one. Some executives are former writers. Their decisions, so far as I can see, are no better than those of guys like me, who bring nothing to the job except intelligence, dedication, a true zestful interest in our work, and—initially, at least—a perhaps naive, romantic hope that we personally can do something to elevate the quality of the programs our networks carry.

We're not on the job very long, it's true, before we are disabused of that lovely notion, but my point here is that, in general, our hearts are in the right place.

I've just gone back to the top of this story and re-read what I've written, and I'll tell you the truth—if a writer had turned it in to me, as part of a script, I wouldn't accept it.

"Where's that early action?" I'd be asking him.

Where's the zinger? Where's the fresh angle that will make the viewer sit up and take notice right away?

But to defend my all-too-weak narrative powers against my analytical, critical self, I'll just say that if I had jumped into the story itself right at the top, you probably wouldn't have believed it. O.K., now let's get down to details.

If you know nothing about television other than what you see on your screens, you may think that network programming executives get creative ideas and then hire people to convert them into broadcastable reality. That does happen, but rarely. The regular method involves professionally creative people's thinking of fresh ideas and then coming into our offices, sitting down, and pitching them to us.

If you're reading this in Leavenworth, Kansas, or Providence, Rhode Island, I wouldn't want you to get on the next plane and camp out in the reception area at any of the three network headquarters, since that's not how the thing is done either. We do business with pros, for the most part, and—obviously—by appointment only. I suppose this means that somewhere out there a few ideas are floating around that will never become realities simply because the people who conceive them are living in other parts of the country and working as school teachers, dentists, truck drivers, or Methodist ministers, but I honestly don't know what to do about that part of the problem. In any event, it does not, for better or for worse, affect the quality of television, since at any given moment simple supply-and-demand factors mean that only a tiny percentage of ideas presented to networks can ever get on the air. Moreover, this would be the case even if every single idea were absolutely brilliant. Most of the professionals with whom we do business are represented by agents or—more correctly—agencies. Actually, agents are salesmen. But instead of selling automobiles, toothpaste, office supplies, or hardware, they sell human beings, which is to say that they find employment for actors, actresses, writers, directors, composers, and the other talented men and women who create motion pictures, television and radio programs, plays, books, etc.

The system creaks a bit, as all systems do, in practice, and it has its share of incompetents, schmucks and crooks; but, by and large, it works.

The funny thing is that the system would work just as well and maybe even better if it were discovered—say, next Wednesday after everybody had woken up—that all agencies and agents had mysteriously disappeared in the night. In other words, television and radio would continue to function, and so would Broadway and Hollywood. A writer's secretary could set up an appointment for him just as easily as his agent could, and at considerably less cost. But that's all fantasy. Let's get back to the reality.

The one part of my job I've never enjoyed is having to say no. And, of course, I have to say no 57 times for every once I can smile at a writer or producer and say, "Hey, this is terrific. We'd like to do it." But people like me are hired because we presumably have reasonable judgment about the programming proposals presented to us and, just like doctors and dentists, we eventually become accustomed to inducing moments of pain in those we do business with since there's no way to avoid it.

I want to stress that part of the story so you'll understand that in saying No-thanks to so many writers, producers, and studios, I—and my dozens of counterparts at the three networks—are also saying No-thanks to the various agencies representing the creative people we've talked to. I have nothing against agents, as a class. In fact, they have my sympathy: first, their job is tougher than my own, or I should say, what has been my own for the past 14 years; and second, since there is only a relatively small number of important agencies in town, they receive a far greater number of rejections than acceptances.

In the case of some of the more important, old-line offices, the top executives rarely bestir themselves to personally pitch a show to a network. Such house-calls are usually left to captains and lieutenants. But this story—the interesting part of it, anyway—starts with a phone call I got one day from one of the generals, Matt Klein, of the Walter Mansfield Agency.

"Dick," he said, all cheerful and up-beat, "how are ya?"

"Just fine, Matt," I said. "How's yourself?"

"Couldn't be better. Listen, I was talking to Eddie Martin this morning, and he tells me you guys turned down the Hey, Doctor idea."

"Yes, that's right," I said.

"You didn't think it was funny enough?"

"No," I said, "that wasn't it. It was, if anything, too funny. But the underlying structure of it just didn't seem strong enough. I've seen worse shows on television. Hell, I've probably been responsible for a few. But the business has changed in the last few years, as you know, and this idea just seems a little old-fashioned to me."

"I see," he said. "Well, listen, I have a memo that was just put on my desk this morning, and the fellows tell me that your decision looks like part of a pattern."

"I'm sorry," I said. "For a moment here I don't know what we're talking about."

"What I'm talking about," he said, "is that Hey, Doctor is the fifth straight show of ours you've turned down."

"Is that right?" I said. "To tell you the truth, I don't keep track of such factors, but I'll take your word for it."

"You don't have anything against us over here, do you?"

"God, no," I said. "Why would I?"

"I can't think of a reason in the world," Klein said, "but I just wanted to be very sure about that."

"Matt," I said, "I—and the rest of the fellows here, too—give very careful study to every single proposal that's presented to us. We'd be pretty dumb if we didn't. Think how embarrassed we'd be if we turned down an idea and one of the other networks picked it up and it became a hit."

"It's happened," said Klein, chuckling.

"I'm hip," I said. "But seriously, I've always been very conscientious about that. In fact, I'm so eager to find great show ideas that I don't care who the hell brings them in. A uniformed Nazi or any other kind of schmuck could come in here, and if he had a sensational idea, I'd find some way of doing business with him."

"Well, that's all very fine," Klein said, "but the fact remains that you've turned down the last five shows we've pitched to you, and all of us over here were very high on Hey, Doctor."

"Matt," I said, beginning to be a little irritated at the conversation, "what do you want me to do? Go against my own best judgment?"

"I'll tell you what I want you to do," he said. "I want you to have lunch with Harry Lerner. He'll fly out from New York."

Lerner was top brass. He'd been with the Mansfield office for 40 years.

"Why? So he can try to talk me into Hey, Doctor?"

"No," Klein said, "not necessarily. But I think that talking to him can do you some good."

"Listen, Matt," I said, "I'll be happy to have lunch with Harry Lerner any time, any place. But if the only reason for our getting together is for him to try to get me to reverse my decision on this, then I think Harry would be wasting his valuable time."

"Dick," Matt said, his voice suddenly sounding considerably less friendly, "can I level with you? I don't think we ought to do any more reasoning about this. I strongly recommend that you have lunch with Harry, and as soon as possible."

The pressure was almost oozing out of my telephone. For a moment I stared out the window of my office building, frowning, feeling increasingly annoyed.

"How about Thursday?" Klein said.

"I'm hung up for lunch for the rest of the week, Matt," I said.

Klein's voice turned colder. "O.K.," he said, "I'll get back to you."

The following morning, at about ten after 6:00, I was awakened out of a sound sleep by the jangling of the bedside phone.

"Mr. Randolph?" said a cheerful feminine voice, in response to my half-asleep mumble.

"Yes."

"Sorry to call so early, sir, but Mr. Adams has to leave for a meeting."

"What?" I said, not too intelligently. Why the hell would the Chairman of the Board of my network's parent company be calling me, from New York, so early?

"Hello, Dick?" It was Adams all right.

"Yes? Hello, Bob."

"Hope I didn't wake you old man, but I just have a minute, and I wanted to take up something important with you."

"Yea, sure," I said, swinging around to place my feet on the floor.

"It's about this meeting I'd like you to have with Harry Lerner."

"*You'd* like me to have?" I said.

"Right as rain," Adams said briskly, in his usual friendly but no-nonsense tone.

"Do you know what it is that Lerner wants to talk to me about?"

"I do and I don't," Adams said. "But, just to save time here, do get together with him, O.K.?"

"Certainly," I said. "But, Bob, I just wanted to be sure that you personally knew the background of this. It concerns a terrible idea called Hey, Doctor, that the Mansfield office has pitched to us. It's old-fashioned, it's not what we're doing these days at all, and everybody in the department agreed with me that it's not for us."

"I see," Adams said. "Well look, Dick, I've got to run, but do have lunch with Lerner. And if I were you, I wouldn't close my mind completely to the Hey, Doctor idea."

There was no chance of getting back to sleep after the call. I went to the kitchen, squeezed some fresh orange juice, and popped two slices of whole-grain bread into the toaster. But nothing, not the juice, not the warm toast with coffee, not a hot shower, not what would have been an otherwise pleasant drive to the office with the top down on my convertible, through a beautiful California Spring morning, could elevate my mood. The Big-Boss-in-the-Sky himself wanted me to compromise the integrity of his own network because of some God-damned power play. Jesus, how high do you have to rank, on how firm ground do you have to stand, before you can at last say to the wheeler-dealers and connivers of the world, "No, by God.

I had to take this shit when I was low-man-on-the-totem-pole, but I don't have to take it now." Here was the high-man-on-the-totem pole, the God-damned pole himself, and he was still kissing ass.

Pardon the bluntness of my language, Dear Reader—as writers used to say a century ago—but I'm writing out of anger now, out of an outraged sense of justice. Please understand, I'm no longer a naive kid. I know the ropes. I know the degree of corruption that runs through every part of our system, from the Mom-and-Pop grocery store down the street right up to the White House, but I'll tell you, I hate it. I'll always hate it.

But if the call from Adams upset me this much, I didn't know how lucky I was. The worst was yet to come.

The lunch with Lerner at La Sere was a million laughs. For the first ten minutes or so, the guy was all pleasantries. He simply would not get down to business. He was even solicitous about my lunch order. "I had the veal with anchovies here the other day," he said. "Absolutely delicious."

"Thanks," I said, forcing a smile. "I believe I'll try it." We talked about the races, about how the Dodgers were doing, about the problems with the Marines in Central America. Lerner even told me a new dirty joke, and it was funny. A hell of a lot funnier than Hey, Doctor.

He waited until after the first sip of wine to get to the point.

"Dick," he said, "how old are you?"

"Thirty-five."

"And how long have you been at NBC now?"

"Seven years. How long have you been with the Martin office?" I asked, being deliberately impertinent, but keeping a smile on my face. He paused for a moment, to let me know that he didn't like the volley, but never once during our conversation did he permit himself to be less than charming.

"And before you joined NBC, you were with CBS, I understand, for four years."

"That's right," I said, surprised that he knew.

"Well," he said, "you're one of the brightest guys at the network, and I've heard some terrific things about you."

"Thank you," I said.

"I think you're gonna do great," he said. "There's so much good talk about you around town that, as I'm sure you know, you could step out and go to one of the studios, or into private production any time and you'd have no problems."

"I suppose so."

"You'd have no problems," he said, "unless you'd made enemies. Then you could have problems."

"You're absolutely right," I said, "but so far as I'm aware, at least, I haven't made any enemies yet. Not on purpose anyway."

"Ah," he said, "that's just it. Most of us, I suppose, don't deliberately make enemies. Maybe it always happens by accident. You know, a guy means well, gives it his best shot, but maybe he doesn't realize that somebody else gets hit by that shot."

"Harry," I said, "put yourself in my place. Do you mind if I speak very frankly about Hey, Doctor? I told Matt Klein that it was funny, but old-fashioned. Since you and I are speaking frankly to each other, I must tell you that, in my carefully considered opinion, Hey, Doctor stinks. I can say that openly to you since you didn't create it, so there's no way that your personal feelings could be hurt here. I wouldn't speak that bluntly to Jimmy St. Leger, who dreamed it up, or Jack Kiley, who wants to produce it. But it really is awful."

Lerner sighed deeply and looked at the lattice-work on the ceiling.

"Dick," he said, "I didn't invite you to lunch today to talk about Hey, Doctor."

"You didn't?"

"No. I came here to talk about you."

"So? What about me?"

"You're very bright," he said, "and personable and—like I said before—I think you're going to do very well in this business. Some of you guys start with the networks just to get your feet wet, to get some training and experience, get a track record, then jump else-where. Some of you decide to stay right where you are and move up the corporate ladder. I have the impression that that's what you're interested in. O.K. I'm in a position to make it happen."

"*You* are in the position to make that happen?" For the first time in the conversation I was actually caught off-guard.

"You heard me," he said.

For the moment, I honestly couldn't think of an answer.

"Oh, I don't mean that I can personally push a button and get you a particular job on a particular day at a particular salary. That's not how the system works. But if—and, mind you, I'm just saying *if*—if the Mansfield Office, for whatever reasons, did not like you, you would never get that job."

For a moment, I didn't say anything. In some small, dark corner of my mind, a fantasy flickered. I saw myself like a young Jimmy Stewart in *Mr. Smith Goes To Washington,* suddenly standing up, tipping over the God-damned table, and once and for all telling Harry Lerner, and all his kind in our business—and every God-damned business in the world—what they look like from the moral point of view.

I entertained that fantasy for, I would suppose, about four seconds.

"O.K., Harry," I said, "you've made your point, very clearly. Couldn't have made it clearer, in fact."

"You know," he said, suddenly very fatherly, all smiles, "there's really no reason for you to be angry about this."

"There isn't?"

"Not at all," he said. "I didn't make up the rules of our business. But I know them, real well, and I play by them. You ought to, too."

"Is that right?" I said.

"It's the rightest God-damned thing you'll ever hear," he said, but still speaking in a fatherly, genial tone. The son-of-a-bitch, if you can believe it, actually patted my hand as he said it.

If this were an imaginary story, if it were a plot line of a made-for-TV movie that the studio had just bought, then as regards casting for the role of Harry Lerner, I suppose I would have recommended a sort of overbearing, slightly sinister actor like the late Lee J. Cobb or maybe Rod Steiger; but Lerner, in reality, looked not at all threatening. With his neatly-clipped white hair, his rimless glasses, his genial smile, he looked like a friendly old dentist.

The rest of our conversation was small-talk.

On the way back to the office, I pulled my car over to the side of the road, got out, and threw up. Then I drove to a phone booth and called the office. "Irene," I said, "I'm not going to be able to get back to the office today. Cancel that 4:00 o'clock appointment, will you? I'll see you in the morning."

I drove down to the beach, parked the car, and walked along the sand for about two hours. I thought of quitting, but I felt that it would have accomplished nothing.

There were more surprises in store for me.

When I got to the office shortly after 10:00 the following morning, my secretary said, "Mr. O'Rourke would like to see you, right away."

Bill O'Rourke was the head of programming. Still is.

"Dick," he said, as soon as I walked in, "I know how you felt about the Hey, Doctor thing. That's why I wanted to let you know, first thing this morning, that we've decided to pick it up."

"Really?"

"Yeah."

There would have been no point in reminding O'Rourke that the show, the outline, the sample script—all were third-rate. He'd already told me that himself, three weeks earlier.

If you watch much television, you'll already know that the series got on the air, got lousy ratings, and was dropped after six weeks. Not even the Walter Mansfield office has the power to keep on the air a show that represents a bleeding wound in a network's schedule. But now you know how much power the agency does have. The saddest fact of all is that this is not an isolated story. I know of three similar incidents; and there must be dozens—maybe scores—that have never come to my attention. I wouldn't be free to tell the story even now if it weren't for the fact that I'm independently wealthy and that, because of my law degree and background in the industry, our new President has just named me to a seat on the Federal Communications Commission.

Maybe shining a bright light, however temporarily, into this ugly, dark corner, will slightly discourage such practices.

But I doubt it.

THE
ITALIAN VOICES

■ ■ ■

The countryside north of Rome was hot although it was quite late in the summer. From time to time, when the road stretched flat before him, Stan could see the quick shimmering silver of a mirage in the distance, reflecting a slice of light from the cloudless sky.

For the most part, however, the highway ran curved, up and around and down, twisting almost randomly through the vineyards and wheatfields. The Chevrolet took the hills and turns confidently, the kilometric speedometer giving the impression that it was even going a great deal faster than it actually was. On the radio the Armed Forces channel was broadcasting jazz records, and as Stan's left hand gripped the wheel his right tapped out a bongo-beat tatoo on the center-knob of the steering shaft. Just outside of Perugia the radio began to play one of his own records and he laughed softly at the surprise of hearing the familiar intro, the muted trumpets.

It was one of his older sides, the big band version of Neal Hefti's classic *"Why Not?"* His head nodded in approval of the beat as the brass stated the theme, and then he narrowed his eyes, listening carefully, following his trumpet solo on the second chorus. It was good. The record was nine years old but sounded as if it might have been made yesterday.

Nine years. Stan, trying to picture the band as it had been then, was surprised that he could not recall all the faces. Then he remembered that two of the men were dead. Ziggy Trace, the wild hot-shot clarinet player, irresponsible, always in trouble, who unaccountably one day had been taken with a fit of common sense, suddenly reached

67

a plateau of maturity, gone west to a job with the Warner Brothers' studio orchestra, married, settled down, gotten into the real-estate business as a sideline, and then died one bright afternoon in his swimming pool. And there had been Buddy Arthur, drummer, with reflexes like a ferret's, nerves that had demanded more than the normal degree of stimulation. He had died from an overdose of heroin in a lonely hotel room in Chicago. Stan listened to Buddy's powerful but properly subtle beat now, moving his head slowly from side to side in rhythm, speeding through the Italian afternoon.

Soon, he reflected—and no matter how many years it took it would still be soon—soon *all* the men on this record would be dead. He would be a ghost leader, leading a ghost band, a band that perhaps, if musical tastes should change drastically, would clutter up the future. Already there were the extreme modernists, one of whom had described the Basie band as playing "dreary rock-and-roll." Would the day come when even Charlie Parker's or Bud Powell's records would be laughed at as hopelessly out-of-date? Unless history reversed itself, Stan thought, that day was inevitable.

And yet certain forms of art survived. The past week in Rome had brought that truth to his attention. Change took place here but respect for antiquity remained. The tawny and green hills through which he was driving had seen much change.

In a few minutes he was within the Perugia city limits, circuitously climbing the great hill upon which the ancient community sprawled. He became confused by a street sign and pulled over to the curb to ask directions of a man who was peering into the insides of a stalled Lambretta.

"Dove albergo Bufani?" Stan said, employing his meagre Berlitz-handbook Italian. He was unable to understand much of the answer but the word *sinistro* and a gesture gave him the information he needed.

With no further difficulty he found the Bufani hotel, checked in, and was shown to his room. When the bellboy had left, frowning glumly at his tip, Stan walked out onto the room's tiny balcony and looked down into the venerable valley of the upper Tiber river. Before him lay a sleepy panorama of furry olive-green, checkered with red tile roof-tops in the foreground, endless terraced vineyards and quiet grain-fields in the distance. The tranquil appearance of the long view contrasted strangely with the angry droning of motor-scooters and squawking of auto-horns in the hairpin curve of the street below.

Tired of standing, Stan stepped back into the room and brought a small chair out into the slanting amber sunshine. Just to his right the top of a tall tower thrust itself up from the side of the hill below. He was surprised to see in the hollowed-out bell-chamber not a bell but an assortment of clothes drying on a line, flapping gently in the warm breeze that floated up from the valley floor.

Idly he reached in his pocket for the Berlitz book, to look up the word for *clothes*. It was odd; he was full-blooded Italian and yet spoke scarcely a word of the language of his ancestors. It was as Stan Manucci that he had first made his reputation among his fellow musicians, starting in 1939 with Teddy Powell, moving into the Goodman trumpet section, and then on to the Les Brown band. The change of name had come about because a booker had said, "Stan, you're going to make it on your own, but not with a name like Manucci." He had been right, of course. At the time Stan had not given the matter much thought. He had just picked up the first name that came into his head: Jackson, in honor of a Negro trumpet-man he had known as a boy on Chicago's South Side. But now, in retrospect, sitting in the afternoon sun in a country where names like Jackson seemed peculiar, it occurred to him that no matter how small a minority the American English Protestants were, theirs would always be the dominant social influence in the United States, so that in most cases, before a Jew, an Italian, a Greek, or a Pole could presume to present himself as an idol in the theater or popular-music world he had to change his name.

The Negroes didn't have to change *their* names, he started to say to himself, and then laughed, recalling that their names had all been changed for them by the owners of the plantations on which their grandparents had worked as slaves. He considered for a moment how it would sound to his ears if the Negro musicians he knew had names like Uganda and Umgawa and when he admitted to himself that these would seem absurd he realized that, without ever having reasoned it out, he was part of the unthinking majority, a small unresisting cell in the tissue of his society.

Later, after a quiet dinner in the hotel dining-room, he decided to go out for a walk. The round of European jazz-concerts had come to an end a week before and now he was realizing an ambition of long standing, to see Europe not in the fleeting, scuffling way that one-night concert stands necessitated, but in a leisurely manner, driving a rented car himself, alone.

The square in front of the hotel was packed with people, out for a breath of evening air, staying away, Stan supposed, as long as possible from their hot, squalid apartments. They walked and talked in groups, the very young and the very old, here in this square at the top of the mountain. Turning left Stan walked, without plan, until he came to a huge plaza, from the center of which a large and graceful fountain broadcast the cooling sound of splashing water. On one side of the plaza loomed an ancient cathedral; from its interior there came the muffled tones of a medieval chant, combining the lament of many voices with that of a throbbing pipe-organ.

He walked to the fountain to inspect it more closely and then turned at random and moved down a side street. People sitting in sidewalk cafes surveyed him blankly as he strolled past. And then in the next moment he was standing before a small movie theatre, staring intently at a poster showing his ex-wife in the arms of Humphrey Bogart. He found himself wanting companionship, not because he was lonesome, but simply because he wanted an ear into which he could say, "Isn't this the damndest thing? Here I am a million miles from nowhere, or 85 miles north of Rome, or some-place, and what do I run into but one of Marion's old pictures!"

Since he was alone he said these words to himself, and then walked into the theatre and bought a ticket and went in and sat down in the darkness. He felt slightly stunned and yet excited at the pro-spect of seeing Marion again, even if only on the screen. The picture had already started and he had not been able to translate the title of it printed on the poster, but he realized it was one of her films that he had never seen, because he could not recall having ever seen her playing opposite Humphrey Bogart.

It must have been a picture that she had made even before he had met her. He reflected that when she came on the screen he would be seeing, in a sense, a woman unknown to him, a woman he had not yet met. By the look of the car that Bogart was driving, Stan estimated the picture had been made in about 1944 or '45.

That would be about two years before Marion's fate had joined his own. Then he saw her, wearing a golden camel's hair polo-coat, frowning as she ran across a rainswept highway and into a telephone booth. As soon as she began to speak he laughed, and then in embarrassment smothered the laugh with a cough. Marion was speaking in Italian.

But of course. The entire soundtrack would have Italian voices dubbed in and, because he was in Perugia, no English sub-titles. He sat, alone down front in the half-empty theatre, because his glasses were not quite strong enough, and listened to his ex-wife speak

Italian. He could not, naturally, understand her. It occurred to him that he had never been able to understand her and at the wry joke he pursed his lips, staring eagerly at the screen, drinking her face in.

The face had never changed. It had looked like this the moment thousands of nights back when, standing on the stage of the Palladium Ballroom on Sunset Boulevard during a disc-jockey charity benefit show, he had looked into the wings and seen her waiting to go on. She had stood quietly, swaying almost imperceptibly to the rhythm of *Sentimental Journey*, the hem of her tight gold lamé dress swinging back and forth. They had exchanged smiles and then the next minute Peter Potter, the disc-jockey, had stepped to the microphone and introduced her, and she had come out and made a brief speech and then walked off backstage, and disappeared.

He had not been able to forget the face then any more than he could now. He could still remember Ziggy Trace's joke when, two weeks later, he had said "I'm going to marry Marion Wilson."

"Who do you think you are: Harry James?" Ziggy had said.

What was the cliche? They said it couldn't last. They had been right. This beautiful woman, speaking at the present moment the strange musical language of his grandmother, had, he thought, not existed in reality. She had existed chiefly in the world of make-believe and had not been happy when away from it. This voice he was hearing now was not her own, as so much of her in the old days had not been her own. The movie-screen sophistication, the devil-may-care-sex, the puckish sense of humor had all, it seems, been the creations of writers and directors. But he had still been in love with the real Marion, the woman consisting of a true face, a beautiful face, a full rounded body, and a sad, little-girl soul. He had fallen in love, he supposed, with the illusion and then been attracted even more desperately by the reality. But there was no living with the reality. There could be romance, there could be sex, but there could be no living, at least not for long, not permanently.

It was so partly because Marion had stopped developing as a human being too early, her physical beauty having destined her, conceivably against her will, to function as a public face, a public body, a thing of beauty that the world must own, and to which it must pay homage. So all that they had been able to do was love each other very much, within the limits of their capabilities, and be unhappy. Then, too, the simple mechanics of the business had made things difficult. She worked by day, he by night. She was frequently on location, he often had to play out-of-town engagements. So they

saw her movies and they listened to his records and their bodies held
them together for a time but eventually their minds became distracted and then the years had rushed past, which was something
known to them only when they looked back over their shoulders
along the direction in which time had disappeared, and now he was
sitting in the darkness in this small Italian town feeling maudlin to
the point where he noted, with a sudden twinge of helpless anger,
that his eyes were wet.

At that moment something that Bogart said amused the audience
and the theatre rang with a brief burst of laughter. Then there was a
great close-up of Marion and a heart-wrenching cry from a score of
violins. Stan looked first at one great luminous eye and then at the
other. Then he followed the girlish curve of the nose down to the
open, moist-lipped mouth. It was strange, he thought; he had known
that he loved her, or at least that he would have to say yes if anyone
said *do you still love her*? And yet he had not known for a long time
that he loved her just this much.

Then the scene faded out and opened on a long shot of the beach
at Santa Monica, the very beach where they had gone swimming by
night, by moonlight, so many times in the old days, and he decided
that he had had enough and got up and left the theatre.

He was ·surprised to discover that it was now almost dark
outside. He stopped for a drink at a sidewalk cafe and then went back
to the hotel, showered, took a mild sleeping pill, and turned in.

In the morning, driving again through the hills, headed for
Venice, he decided that in the next reasonably large town he would
send a cable to Helen and the children, to tell them that he was fine
and that he would be home soon. Southern California was much like
Italy scenically, he reflected. It would be good to lie in the hammock
in the back yard again with the children, to swim in the pool with
Helen on the hot San Fernando Valley nights, to sit by the side of the
pool, sipping ice cold orange-juice and gin. He would tell them all
about the trip, all about the jazz concerts in Stockholm and London
and Brussels, and all about seeing the land of his people and learning
to appreciate its ancient glories, but he very probably would never
mention to them the night in Perugia when he had accidentally
stumbled on the ghost of his long-dead first wife.

HOUSTON INCIDENT

■ ■ ■

"It's a long road that has no turning."

The man was middle-aged, over fifty, Mac guessed, and he had come up from the rear walking slowly, just fast enough to bring himself abreast of the boy. His face had a heavy stubble of beard and his wrinkled coat did not match his pants. Slightly drunk, he had the easy but ignominious grace of the professional panhandler. Mac expected him to ask for money.

"What did you say?"

"I say it's a long road that has no turning," the man repeated.

"Yep, I guess it is."

They walked along in silence for a few moments, Mac's stomach aching and gnawing on itself in the grip of hunger. He kept his eye on the curb. Once in a great while you could find a coin in the gutter, and a coin meant a loaf of bread or a candy bar or a carton of milk and the stopping of the pain in the stomach.

"You on the road?" the man said.

"Yes."

"Headed West?"

"That's right."

"The coast?"

"Yep."

More silence as they walked along in the pale Southern autumn sunlight, through the streets of Houston.

"Where you from?"

"Chicago."

The pavement pressed up hard against the soles of Mac's feet. He was tired of walking and his back ached.

"Hungry?"

"What?" His head spun at the thought of food. He suddenly developed the craft, the tight controlled excitement of the animal.

"I'm goin' in here for a cuppa coffee." The man indicated an open-air bar. "Want to join me?"

"Why, yes, I guess that wouldn't be a bad idea at that." He struggled to act casual.

They strolled in off the hot pavement, into the dim, musty half-saloon half-chili joint. Mac stared eagerly at the giant coffee-maker that gleamed and hissed against the wall, tasted with his eyes the rows of steaming frankfurters that lay in open trays behind the bar.

"Just a coffee," said his host.

"I'll have a coffee, too and . . . uh . . . I believe, a hot dog."

Wolfing it down, he closed his eyes and leaned back against the bar, feeling the wooden railing firm against his back. The coffee sloshed down his esophagus and curled out warmly along the lining of his stomach. The frankfurter meat was of poor quality, but he had never enjoyed turkey or filet mignon more. He forced himself to take smaller bites as he neared the end of the sandwich.

"Care for another?"

"Why, yes, I think I might."

Twenty minutes later he was finishing his fifth hot dog and third cup of coffee.

"You look like you could use a bath, Slim."

In a fatherly way the man slipped his arm around Mac's shoulder and looked into his face.

"Yes, sir. I figured soon as I saw you, I said, here's a boy, I said, who could use a good bath. Not that he's the kind who wouldn't take one if he could, I said, but here's the kind of a boy who just hasn't had a chance lately."

The man's whiskyish breath caused Mac to draw back a bit and as he did so a gnarled, brown-spotted hand patted him affectionately on the thigh. Mac took his foot off the bar rail and inched away. There was something weird about this operator, but a bath . . . a bath would be the most welcome thing in the world now that he had filled his stomach. A bath and a good shave would put him back on top of the world. Even if he had to put his filthy clothes back on, at least his body would be clean underneath them.

"My hotel's just around the corner," the man said as they left the bar. He put his arm up over Mac's worn suède jacket-back. A wave of revulsion swept him and he started to say, "Ixnay," but then he realized he might hurt the man's feelings. Without seeming to notice the man's arm he quickened his step so that he slipped away and the offending arm dropped of its own weight.

Going up in the elevator, he noticed that the attendant's uniform was greasy and torn. The building smelled ancient, dirty. The room was on the eighth floor and as soon as the man unlocked the door he walked in and poured himself a drink from a half-empty bottle on the dresser.

"Care for a snifter?" he said.

"No, thanks."

"You don't like me." Mac felt a quick chill, as of fear, go through him. He was in no mood for an emotional scene, least of all for one the full significance of which he did not, because of his tender years, understand.

"You don't like me, do you?" the man repeated, with a twisted smile.

"Why, certainly," Mac said, hedging. "What makes you think I've got anything against you? I'm very grateful to you, as a matter of fact, for the hot dogs and the coffee and everything."

"All right," the man said. "I just thought maybe you didn't like me." He slumped on the bed and waved a welcoming hand around the room. "Go ahead," he said. "Make yourself at home. Take your bath."

"Where's the john?" Mac said.

"At the end of the hall."

"How do I get down there?"

"Oh, it's all right. You can just put a towel around yourself. There's never anybody in the hall in the afternoon."

Self-consciously Mac sat on a chair across the room and took off his shoes and socks. Then, standing, he removed his jacket, sweater, shirt, and pants.

"I'll wear my underwear down the hall," he said. "Do you have a towel and soap?"

"Sure," the man said, "but first why don't you have a little drink?"

"No, thanks, really. If it's all the same to you, I'd just as soon take the bath first." He didn't know why he had said *first*. It implied that he would be willing to have a drink later and he had no taste for liquor. He wanted to take a bath and then leave the hotel. He wanted to get away from the man, but strangely he could feel no anger in his heart, no actual ill will against the half-drunk unfortunate who leered at him blankly from across the room. He felt, rather, pity. He wanted to avoid offending the man. He wanted to avoid an argument.

In the shower he forgot the stranger and laughed aloud in the sheer exultation of the moment. The hot water streamed through his hair, hit his face, splashed down over his body as he lathered and turned and luxuriated in its blood-cheering warmth.

He thought of a line from Rupert Brooke . . . *the benison of hot water.* He laughed again, mouth turned up to catch the hot spray, eyes blinking, staring up into the needle holes in the spout, lathering his itching stomach, his loins, sudsing his hair, rinsing it, sudsing it again and again, feeling clean and strong, blinking, grasping, singing, standing like a savage in a monsoon, letting the water clean him out down to his soul, watching triumphantly as dirty suds washed down his legs, filtered off into the outlet on the floor. He sudsed his hair again, lathering his whole body, lifting his arms and his face to the warm, delicious torrent, poking his slippery fingers into his ears and washing his face again and again till his eyes stung from the soap.

He stood with bowed head under the water for at least another ten minutes, reluctant to give up the sensation. He was standing thus, almost asleep, when the shower curtain was jerked violently to one side.

"Howdy, big fella," the man said, stepping partly into the shower. He put his hand out and touched Mac's hip. Water dotted his sleeve.

"Hey, wait a minute! That's enough, I mean, this is no place to get smart."

"What's the matter?" The man seemed drunker, more desperate.

"Why, nothing's the matter. I just want to finish up taking this shower, that's all. Now just relax and go on back to your room. I'll be back there in a couple of minutes."

Pouting slightly, the man retreated.

"I didn't mean no harm," he said.

His heart pounding, Mac turned off the water and dried himself. In his underwear he slipped back down the hall. It would be difficult now. The stranger had made his move.

"Feel better?"

"Yes, thanks," reaching for the trousers, slipping into them. "That bath really hit the spot."

"What's your hurry? Wouldn't you like to catch a little shut-eye?"

"Well, to tell you the truth, I really would, but I'll tell you . . . I . . . I have to go mail a letter."

The excuse was so lamely offered they avoided looking at each other for a moment. Then the man started to sob.

"You don't like me," he said, sniffling. "I told you before you didn't. I knew it."

"Aw, don't cry. I like you all right. It's just that I have to get out of here and mail these letters."

"But you won't come back." He had the pathetic expression of an about-to-be-abandoned dog.

"Sure I will." Anything to get away.

"No, you won't. I bought you all those hot dogs and the coffee and fixed you up here so you could take a shower and everything and now you're sore and you won't come back." The man rubbed the back of his hand across his nose and belched. Then he rose and poured himself another drink, whimpering.

"Don't cry," Mac said. "See, here are the letters I'm talking about." He pulled two letters out of the pocket of his jacket. "I'm not kidding. I really have to mail them." He sat down on the chair and put on his stockings and shoes as quickly as he could, his fingers trembling.

"I don't know, what the hell," the man said sobbing and looking at the floor.

His hand on the doorknob Mac turned and tried to smile reassuringly. A heartfelt sorrow for the man was mingled with his disgust.

"Thanks," he said. "Thanks for everything. You take it easy here and I'll go mail these letters and if I get a chance I'll drop back a little later. I really will if it's possible."

Without waiting for an answer, he closed the door and walked swiftly down the hall to the elevator, listening to see if the man would follow. In a moment he was out in the street. The sun was lower in the sky. He turned toward it, walking very briskly, and stepped out into the street, walking parallel to the curb, lifting his thumb to passing cars.

EVERYBODY HATES
DAVID STARBUCK

■ ■ ■

The police are not surprised when, in connection with a highly publicized murder that has gone unsolved, a number of people come forth to confess to the crime.

It is, on the other hand, unusual if not unknown for a man to confess to having committed a murder when beyond the shadow of a doubt a suicide rather than a killing was involved. That is why nobody paid any attention to Walt Swanson when he said he had murdered David Starbuck. Starbuck killed himself in the bathroom of his palatial Palm Springs home on the night of September 14th. There were at least 30 people who knew that Swanson had spent the night at the bar of the Villa Loma, a spaghetti-and-rendezvous joint on the Sunset Strip.

The door of Starbuck's toilet was locked from the inside. He had slashed his wrists, stretched out on the pink tile floor with a folded rug-mat under his head, and died almost peacefully. As one wag said when Swanson first confessed that *he* had cut Starbuck's wrists, although it was clearly established that he had been in Beverly Hills on the night in question, "Must have had a mighty long razor."

The police spent a little time checking Swanson's story, marked him as a psycho, and told him to get lost. I guess I'm the only one who knows that he was telling the truth after all, because I listened to the *whole* story.

To say that Starbuck was not widely admired is to win the understatement championship of any year. The movie business is never short of phonies but Dave was the champ. He came out here in the late Thirties with a reputation as a hot-shot salesman and there was always the vague idea that he had *had* to come West, that something he had been involved in in the East had not been strictly kosher. The idea was founded on bedrock. Dave had gotten into the habit of selling things he didn't own. In Hollywood he soon found that this trick could be valuable. First he palmed himself off as a writer, sold a book he hadn't written, stole half the profits from the poor bum who did write it, wangled a share of the production arrangement and found himself with a smash on his hands. From there on in there was no stopping him.

By 1945 he was second in command at World-American, living in Bel Air with his fourth wife, and climbing fast by reason of his shrewd and ruthless ability to manipulate men with big talent and small guts.

But I am getting ahead of myself, as they say. Let's go back a wife or two. We never knew just who Dave was married to back East. She never made the trip. He stole his second woman from Walt Swanson. Nobody but the old-timers remember much about Walt now, but in his time he was the greatest cameraman of them all. Some of the old stars wouldn't make a picture without him. Eventually he started directing and he would have made a fine director except that he began belting the bottle. Charming as he was sober, he was a mean drunk. They put up with his bats for a couple of years but eventually the word got around that hiring him for a picture meant added costs in lost shooting time. He never had a prayer after that. Well, no, he did have one chance. Dave Starbuck hired him for a picture and made a rather peculiar deal with him.

"Walt," Dave said, "here's the arrangement. Nobody else in town will hire you because you're a stewbum, right? Here's my offer. I'll give you your regular price for this picture and you get it the day we're through shooting, in one lump. Unless you start drinking. The first day you're drunk on the set the money drops to 50 percent. If you pull it a second time you get 25 percent. Take it or leave it."

Walt took it. You have to eat.

The third week of shooting Starbuck hired an out-of-work writer to take Walt to lunch and get him loaded. Then he came around to the set after lunch, walked up to Swanson, smiled broadly, smelled Walt's breath and said. "Cheer up, baby. At 50 percent you're still being overpaid." Walt's ego being what it was, he went on a week's bender. Starbuck threatened to throw him off the picture. Eventually he paid him peanuts and kicked him out. In desperation Walt sent his wife around to plead for a break.

"Listen, sweetie," Dave said, "what do you want from me? We made a deal."

"But Dave," Swanson's wife said, "Walt's having a rough time. He did a good job for you, didn't he?"

Dave looked at Swanson's wife. She had good legs and was years younger than Walt.

"Listen, Myrna," he said, "doesn't it make you feel sorta cheap to have to go around town begging for handouts for a has-been like Walt? You deserve better than that. You're a looker. I happen to know you have talent. You should be acting again. Whadda ya say we forget about the deal Walt and I made? It's all over. He made his bed. Let him lie in it. But let's say you have a small part in my next picture, at pretty good money. Now how's that?"

Well, when you're a former callgirl, when you'd love to do a little picture work, when you're married to a man 20 years your senior, and when you married him in the first place just because you were tired and he offered someplace to rest, a pitch like Starbuck's is pretty hard to resist. To spare the painful details, within six months Myrna had left Walt and moved in with Dave.

That did it for the poor bastard. He was no good after that. Never directed another picture. It must have been about that time that he first thought of killing Starbuck. He wasn't the first, of course, nor the only one, but he must have been head of the club.

The philosophers tell us that when you lust after a woman in your heart, or long to commit a murder, you're already on record, even if you never get to realize your ambition. On that basis I guess quite a few of us around town are guilty of the murder of David Starbuck. But here's how Walt Swanson did it.

By 1955 he was all washed up as a director, although Alcoholics Anonymous had put him back in one physical piece for the time being. To pay for the booze he had sold everything he had and now to keep eating he had to take any odd job he could get. An old friend eventually landed him a spot with Consolidated Film Service, a subsidiary of the Consolidated Studio, that did film exchange work. For example, when a wealthy producer wanted to go to the movies, well, it didn't work out that way. The movies went to him. His secretary just called the film exchange, ordered a certain picture, or maybe a double feature, and the films were shipped to the producer's home, to be shown in his private projection room, for his private pleasure. Walt Swanson thought it was a pretty grim joke the first time he got an order to ship a can of film to Starbuck's Bel Air pleasure-dome.

Then one day he learned that Starbuck had an ulcer. A snatch of conversation overheard at a restaurant and Walt's own stomach tingled in a momentary frenzy of vengeful glee. So the bastard could be hurt after all, if only by his conscience, his own fears. At the time that Walt noted this fact he did not file it away in any sort of conscious realization that eventually he would be able to call it out, to employ it. It was just something he heard about and was glad about and that was that.

The catalyst was dropped into the seething caldron of his mind a year later when he read a story in the *Hollywood Reporter* about subliminal advertising. A theatre in New Jersey had cut into a motion picture film commercial announcements that flashed on the screen too quickly to be seen consciously but, according to the theory, not too quickly to transmit to the eye and the subconscious mind an impression which subsequently would suggest action to the individual. In the test case the action suggested was the purchase of a particular soft drink. Sales of the drink increased markedly on the night of the test.

It was after reading that story that Walt Swanson began to get even with David Starbuck. At first the idea of murder was not actually in his mind. He only wanted to hurt, to lash out, to avenge himself. The first thing he did was to print up two small cards, using white ink on black paper. On card said "Dave Starbuck, you stink." The other one said "Everybody hates David Starbuck." Then he borrowed a handoperated movie camera from a friend, shot stills of the two cards, clipped out the film frames, put them into his wallet and waited.

Within a week Starbuck's secretary called to order a picture. When Walt received the shipping slip he got the film out of the vault, set it up on spools, scissored a line and inserted one of the still frames he had shot at home. Twenty minutes farther along on the reel he slipped in the second insert.

The picture was a comedy but that night after running it Dave Starbuck didn't feel amused. A certain insensitivity had always been part of his make-up, but faced even if subconsciously with the knowledge that he was actively disliked, and being at the same time unable to erect any of his customary defenses, he became vaguely depressed.

Swanson at first, and for a long time afterward, had no sure way of knowing how effective his attack was, but eventually he began to pick up stray bits of information that convinced him that he was striking telling blows. Column items about suddenly planned vacations, rumors about physical checkups, stories about angry blowups in conference rooms. And only Swanson knew the reason. Once a week for a whole year he sent his invisible arrows into Starbuck's hide. "Starbuck, you're no good." "Dave, you're a heel." "Starbuck, you're sick."

And every Monday when the film would come back to the exchange, Walt would scissor out his inserts and patch up the reel, leaving no evidence.

"Starbuck, your wife despises you!"

"David Starbuck is a jerk!"

"Starbuck you are the lowest of the low."

Starbuck's irritation increased to the point where he became careless about his attitude toward his superiors, and in Hollywood no matter how high up you are you have to answer to somebody: chairmen of the board, stockholders' groups. One night at a party he told the head of his studio's New York office to go to hell. From that moment he started to slide downhill, although at first his speed was so slow nobody was quite sure he was moving.

It was about that time that Swanson aimed his *coup de grace*. The next time Starbuck had a picture run off he received this message: "Dave, why don't you kill yourself?"

The following week it was "Kill yourself, Dave. It's the only way out."

Starbuck put up with eight weeks of it. He began to fall apart. Having no friends to sympathize with him, he went from bad to worse fast. Then one day he went to Palm Springs, spent all afternoon lying in the sun by his swimming pool, got drunk, went into the bathroom, locked the door, lay down on the pink tile floor, folded the fluffy lamb's wool bath mat under his head, slashed his wrists with a single-edge razor and bled to death, slowly, lying still.

After it happened Walt began drinking again. I wouldn't be telling the story now except that, as some of you may know, poor Walt got careless with a cigarette one night in the lab and burned himself up along with a hell of a lot of film. A few weeks before the end he told me the story one night at the Villa Loma bar.

Good thing Walt didn't work in a TV film lab.

THE SOUTHERN ACCENT

■ ■ ■

My father died when I was a boy and from then on I was raised by women, but there was one man I remember being around the house pretty often. Uncle Jack. Oh, I had a stepfather for a while, but he faded out of the picture before I was six years old and I don't remember him very clearly. And there was Uncle Bill, but he usually worked in some other city like Allentown, Pennsylvania, or Los Angeles. He only came home to Chicago to visit and then, at the end, to die.

But Jack was around quite a lot. He would go away for five or six months at a time, usually to a soldiers' home. Sometimes he would go to the one in Danville, Illinois, and sometimes to one in Wisconsin; I think it was at West Allis. Sometimes, too, he would just go away, period, and neither my mother nor any of her sisters would have the slightest idea where he had gone.

"I'm worried sick," my mother would say. "We haven't heard from Jack in eight weeks."

"Oh, don't worry, Bella," her sister Kate would say; "he'll turn up. If anything had happened to him you'd have heard about it."

Kate was just as worried as Mother, but they'd take turns cheering each other up. Both of them were confirmed pessimists but never at the same time. Whichever one picked up the pessimism first sort of had a claim on it. The other would automatically assume the role of the optimist, although always with a certain lack of conviction.

Sure enough, Jack would turn up eventually or else they'd get a brief letter from him. It was always just one page long and it always began "Dear Sister." It was neither an overly friendly letter nor a cold

85

one, but the fact that he had cared enough to write made the letter a
gladsome thing to the women. The handwriting was always neat and
all the words were spelled correctly, although the punctuation and
the grammar left something to be desired. No one in my mother's
family had ever got beyond a fifth-grade education.

The letters usually went something like this:

> *Just thought I would drop you a line to tell you that I have
> been here at Danville for the past couple of months. I have gained
> twelve pounds and am eating like an army mule. The weather here
> is good and I am off the drink and feeling fine. I hope you are all
> well. Take care of yourselves.*
>
> *Your loving brother.*

I never did know why Jack kept going away and coming back,
although his departures usually followed a siege of heavy drinking
and a big fight. He would be on the straight and narrow for several
weeks, and then all of a sudden one day he wouldn't show up at all for
maybe two days. When he would come home he'd be drunk and ugly
and mean and he'd insult my mother and all her sisters and swear
and throw up in the bathroom. And his clothes would be dirty, as if
he had slept on the sidewalk or in some alley.

He'd rant and rave around the house for maybe twenty-four
hours and he'd smash drinking glasses and threaten to kill Kate and
my mother, but he never laid a hand on them and through it all he
was never angry or cross with me. That part was funny. Uncle Bill
was actually a better human being than Jack, I suppose; he was
intelligent, usually had a good job, was a neat dresser, and had a lot
of friends. But he was always very strict with me. So for that one
crazy reason I preferred Jack.

When he was sober and in good spirits Uncle Jack would take me
to Lincoln Park Zoo or to the circus or just for long walks in the park.
At every street we crossed he'd lecture me about looking both ways
for traffic; and as we walked along in the morning air he'd tell me to
take deep breaths and to keep my back straight like a soldier. I had
been sickly as a young child and, having spent such a lot of time in
bed being pampered and fussed over, I suppose I had gotten a little
delicate in personality as well as in body. I think this worried Jack
because he was always telling me about people like Teddy Roosevelt
and Jack Dempsey, and he was always telling me to throw back my

shoulders and to breathe deeply and to drink lots of milk and to get lots of exercise.

Like a lot of the Irish who grew up back of the Yards, he had never had an opportunity to be trained in any particular trade. That's not a real excuse for not making anything of yourself, of course, but it has something to do with it. Jack's own father was a strict, violent-tempered immigrant who married a docile, saintly girl and had sixteen children by her. Most of them died either at birth or shortly after, but those who grew up were rebellious and wild, all of them. Frankly, there wasn't one person in my mother's family who had what you and I would call good sense. They had a lot of other abilities: they were bright, amusing, popular, charitable, honest to an uncommon degree, religious in their own particular way, and, except for Jack, hard-working. But they were all wild and unpredictable and terrible-tempered like their father. The father was so hard and the mother so soft that the children's personalities got twisted out of shape. They never learned tolerance or logic or intellectual curiosity or a love for the arts. They lived at either the father's or the mother's emotional extreme. They were either loving each other furiously or hating each other with an equal fury. The hatred never lasted, of course, but it was in the saddle just long enough to break up home after home. I can remember living in at least a dozen different places when I was a child, and in each case the reason for moving was that there had been a fight and somebody had said, "I can't stand this. I've got to get out of this neighborhood and find some peace."

So Jack had the least sense of all, but I liked him. He used to feel the muscle of my scrawny upper arm and pretend to marvel at its firmness. And no matter how drunk he got, no matter how angry his hidden resentments made him at the rest of the world, he could always, even in the midst of his violent rages, be gentle with me. And he had reason, sometimes, to be angry with me too. I remember one time when we lived on Cottage Grove Avenue our apartment had a long, narrow, dark hallway that ran from the living room, past a bedroom and a bathroom, back to the dining room. I used to be afraid of the dark, I think, and I never liked to walk through this hallway. One day when I was hurrying along its dismal length, Uncle Jack made a sudden noise behind a drapery and said, "Boo!" Although he meant to frighten me he was just playing, but I didn't understand that at the time. I was in the instant overcome by fear and shock and in my sudden rage I kicked at him as hard as I could. I was only about seven, but I had on new shoes and in my anger I must have put great force into the kick. I remember the point of the new shoe caught his leg squarely on the shinbone and he exhaled slightly as he felt the pain. But he didn't get angry at me. He just held me at arm's length for a moment till I calmed down and then he laughed a little and apologized. He carried the scar on his shin for many months.

That must have been one of the times when he would go off and sit by himself somewhere in the house and read and whistle. When his mind was on something else he either whistled or softly sang an old song called "Sunbonnet Sue."

"Sunbonnet Sue . . . Sunbonnet Sue," he would whisper softly, "sunshine and roses run second to you. I kissed you twice . . . it was so nice . . . under your bonnet of blue."

So far as I was ever able to learn, the singing of this lyric was Uncle Jack's one concession to the fact that love and/or sex existed in the world. He never married and he never spoke of women except, as I say, when he sang. "It was only kind of a kid-kiss, but it tasted much nicer than pie. What else could I do? I was dead stuck on you . . . when you were a kid so high." I don't even know if those were the right words, but that's the way he used to sing it.

Jack was what you would call a confirmed bachelor, but not of the usual type, if there is a usual type. By that I mean he was not an artistic homosexual, nor was he the Caspar Milquetoast mama's boy. Physically he was big, manly. He looked like a stevedore or a truck driver. He always wore second-hand dark blue suits and a rough-looking gray cap. Except on rare occasions he would not wear a tie, and his shirts were the sort worn by railroad men. He drank hard and got into fist fights at the drop of a hat. When he was young I presume he fought because he was almost certain to win; but as he got older he used to come home obviously the loser of these saloon altercations, his shirt sometimes encrusted with blood and his face and lips cut and swollen. He didn't have enough sense to stop picking fights with other, younger men.

No, Jack was a bachelor of a type that I think might possibly be peculiar to the Irish. I seem to recall reading an article a couple of years ago in some magazine that said that the birth rate in Ireland is falling at an alarming rate and that there are far too many bachelors and old maids over there. Nobody has as yet pinned down the precise reasons, but there are a lot of theories. Some blame the Church, but there are many Catholic countries and only Ireland has this peculiar problem. Some blame the climate, others the poverty of the farmers, others the puritanical traditions of the country. Whatever the reason, it produces a certain number of men like Jack: virile, fearless, completely masculine, but shy with women to an unnatural degree, unsophisticated, narrow-minded, old-fashioned, out of contact with their time, almost monastically sexless.

If there was any explanation of Jack's inability to hold a job, it might be the one sometimes put forth by my mother: that as the baby of the family he was the most protected by his mother. But these days it is the fashion to say that it is the oldest child in the family who usually has the roughest road and that the baby, because he gets more love and attention, has more confidence in himself and his world.

I'm no psychiatrist and I can't figure it out any more than the rest of the family could. You can point to social environment and you've got a pretty fair argument, because the South Side of Chicago in the early years of the century was a rough, brawling place to grow up in, with plenty of saloons and pool halls but no playgrounds or libraries or young people's dances. But then again, millions of other people grew up in that same environment and they didn't all turn out to be hard-drinking saloon fighters.

When I got a little older I sometimes used to envy men like Jack their lack of interest in sex. And I suppose men like Jack envy me my lack of interest in liquor. I've been lucky, of course, in that you can channel your sexual appetite correctly, but there's no earthly good can come of a lusty appetite for alcohol.

But maybe I'm getting off the track. Another reason I liked Jack was that he had a great sense of humor. He never told jokes or stories and he wasn't the life of the party type by a long shot; but in ordinary conversation he could perceive and isolate the humorous element. Too, he had a few little meaningless phrases he used to say to me that always amused me although I never really understood them.

"Do you know Tap Max?" he used to say to me when he was just slightly drunk.

"Who's that?" I would demand, in mock seriousness because I knew he was playing with me.

"He's a friend of Calingo Red's," Jack would say.

"Who's Calingo Red?"

"He works with Tap Max."

Once in a while Jack would say something about Tap Max or Calingo Red being in the Rocky Mountains working on some railroad or other, but I never found out who they were. Jack used to talk a lot about railroads. He worked for different lines, and of course when he

traveled it was always on freights. I think he always fancied himself
a railroad man, although he had probably not worked long at any
particular railroad jobs either. He used to dress like railroad men and
roll his own cigarettes with Bull Durham tobacco (I used to save the
little cloth bags to keep marbles in), and in his back pocket he always
carried a large dark blue handkerchief with white dots.

I liked him, too, because he was a solid masculine influence in
the sometimes cloyingly feminine world in which I lived as a child.
My aunt used to praise him sometimes when he was away. "He was
a handsome man when he was younger," she would say. "He looked
like Gary Cooper." I never thought Jack looked like Gary Cooper but
he had the same tall, lean open-airness about him. He used to talk not
only of railroads but of the Far West and of farms and mountains and
army life and the oil fields. He had traveled a lot. The one place I do
not believe he ever visited was the South. And that was peculiar
because when he got drunk he would speak with a Southern accent.

Not when he was angry, of course; just when he was trying to be
amusing.

I remember one night when we lived on 60th Street just off
Halsted and he came home drunk and wild. He broke some dishes in
the kitchen and chased Kate to bed and told my mother to go to hell,
so the three of us went to bed and left him roaming around the house,
cursing and mumbling to himself and bumping into things.

I slept with my aunt in the front bedroom. There was a very
small porch just off this bedroom which could be entered from the
living room. After I lay in the darkness whispering to my aunt for
perhaps half an hour a storm began to come up. I remember
watching the lights of cars making patterns on the ceiling and walls
of the room as they drove past in the rain.

It was then we heard the door to the porch open.

"He's going out there in the rain," my aunt hissed.

Sure enough, Jack walked out on the small porch, muttering to
himself; I saw him clearly as a flash of lightning washed the scene
white. And then I laughed because he had come home with a peculiar
haircut, with the hair much too short and looking almost like a
convict's, and he was standing out on the porch in his long underwear.

There was an old-fashioned deck chair on the porch and I knew
if he tried to sit in it he would have trouble; I was not surprised when
suddenly I heard the sound of the chair being knocked and pulled
about and Jack swearing.

"Is he going to sleep out there in the rain?" I asked my aunt, giggling at the prospect.

"Shut up," she whispered. "If he hears you laughing he'll keep that foolishness up all night, if it doesn't make him mad."

The wind was stronger now and I heard Jack say in a loud voice, "Blow, you son-of-a-bitch, blow!" The wind obliged and he must have been drenched to the skin. I seem to recall that he had been having trouble with his false teeth and that he was not wearing them that night. He must have presented a fearsome appearance. "My God," my aunt said, "if anybody sees him out there like that we'll all be arrested."

At this moment the wind died down a bit, and as the rain was not falling heavily I was able to hear the click-click of a man's heels coming down the sidewalk that ran right below the porch. When my aunt heard the footsteps she said, "Jesus, Mary, and Joseph."

Then in the momentary stillness, over the soft sighing of the wind, as the heel sounds passed just below our window I heard Jack say, "Say, brothah . . ."

From below there came a startled, "What!"

"Pahdon me, podnuh," said Jack, speaking with the mellow accents of the South, "but ah was wonderin' if pe'haps you maught have a cigarette."

I remember getting a fit of the giggles and laughing so hard my aunt had to press her hand over my mouth. I don't remember what happened after that. I must have fallen asleep happy.

THE HOUSE
IN BEL AIR

■ ■ ■

When they got out of the limousine at the airport, a uniformed TWA man stepped up and said, "Miss Lane?" Harry Sonnenberg said, "Yes," as he helped Cora out of the car.

"As soon as you check in," the man said, "you can go right aboard."

"Thank you," Cora said, adjusting her sun glasses. She walked into the waiting room and paused momentarily at the ticket counter.

"You go ahead with the fella," Harry said. "I'll take care of all this. See ya in a minute."

When she had disappeared into a private lounge behind the counter, a photographer approached Harry. "Would Miss Lane mind posing for a quick shot waving bye-bye?" he said. "TWA."

"No, it's all right," Harry said. "No cheesecake this time."

"Fine," the man said, looking disappointed.

Cora posed for the picture, smiling blankly, then turned to climb the steps into the plane. Somebody whistled as the night wind whipping across the field pressed her mink coat tightly against the roundness of her hips, and she turned and smiled again in an impersonal, practiced way.

When Harry had put her overnight bag in her berth, he handed her the Los Angeles papers.

"You all set?" he said.

"Fine, thanks," she said. Harry was painless, colorless, odorless, tasteless: the perfect man for his job, which was putting actresses on airplanes, meeting them when they got off, pacifying columnists, handling the million-and-one minor details of publicity for the studio.

Before the plane had reached the Nevada-California border, Cora was ready for bed. She took a sleeping pill, accepted a glass of champagne from the stewardness who served nightcaps, allowed herself to be talked to flirtingly by a producer from another studio who happened to be on the flight, and turned in. Lying in her berth with her knees up, she read the funny papers and the gossip columns till her eyelids became heavy.

She slept soundly.

In New York she suffered through a three-day whirlwind of pictures, interviews, night clubs, theaters, appointments at the hairdresser's, appointments at the beauty parlor, and one appointment with a doctor, to see if she was pregnant. She was not.

The next morning a man from the studio home office took her in the conventional Cadillac limousine to the airport and put her on the United Flight for Chicago.

"Well," he said when he had made her comfortable, "I'll bet you'll be glad to relax for a few days and see your family, eh?"

"Yes," she said.

"Somebody will meet you at the airport in Chicago," he said.

The man who met her three hours later was new at the job and seemed embarrassed, but he handled the baggage and saw her to a suite at the Ambassador East for which the studio had made the arrangements.

After he had left she called the house. Her mother's voice sounded harsh.

"It's me, Mom," Cora said.

"Oh, hello, angel," her mother said. "Where are ya?"

"I'm in town, at a hotel."

"Oh, my God, we woulda met ya. I thought you were coming tomorra."

"Didn't you get the last wire? Oh, never mind. Anyway, I'm here."

"Wonderful. Listen, I'll have Tom drive downtown after he gets off at the yards and pick you—"

"No, Mom, don't bother," Cora said. "I'll have somebody bring me out. Don't worry about that."

"It's no bother," her mother said. "Tom would love to do it."

Cora felt a knot in her stomach.

"Mom," she said, "will you listen? I don't *want* Uncle Tom to pick me up. I'll come out as soon as I can. Myself."

"All right," her mother said, "but I think you're crazy. Tom would just love to drive down there and get ya. You must be dead, traveling and all, and it wouldn't take him more than twenty minutes on the outer drive to—"

"Listen," Cora said. "How is everybody? I mean how are you all?"

"Oh, we're fine, Marge," her mother said. Hearing her real name was always a shock to Cora, although a very slight one. She had been Cora Lane for six years. She liked being Cora Lane. She had never particularly liked being Margaret Monihan. Margaret Monihan had had brown hair and had been heavy, though sensuous. Cora Lane was brilliantly blond, slimmer, perfumed, expensively stockinged and shod, dramatically dressed.

When she had finished talking to her mother she took her shoes off and lay down on the bed to read the papers. First she read Parson's column and was pleased to find a reference to herself. "Cora Lane's dates with handsome Bill Keith," Louella had written, "are lifting a few eyebrows, but the smart money in the Lane sweepstakes is still on Mike Gordon. One report has it that they'll marry in April."

She had not been in the house for more than ten minutes when her mother mentioned the item.

"You still going with that Jewish fella?" was the way she put it.

"Mother," Cora said, exasperated.

"What's the matter?" her mother said, blank-faced.

"His name is Mike Gordon."

"Did I say anything wrong?"

"Oh, never mind."

"Oh, you mean my calling him a Jew? Well, he is, ain't he? I mean is there any crime in mentioning that fact?"

"Not at all," Cora said. "Forget it."

She walked to the dining-room window and looked out at the old neighborhood. A feathery rain had started to fall as she had pulled up to the house in a Yellow cab, a bandanna over her blond hair, wearing a plain wool coat and her oldest shoes. The street outside, washed now in smoky rain, depressed her. It seemed smaller in an over-all way as compared to her early memories of it. The windows in the apartments across the street seemed tiny, dingy. When she turned away from the window she nevertheless felt truly at home. Her mother was in the kitchen, shelling peas, and a kettle was boiling on the stove.

"How long can you stay?"

"I have to go back to the Coast day after tomorrow," Cora said.

"I didn't mean to cause any trouble just now," her mother said, "I mean when I talked about that Gordon fella. But I was just wondering if what they say in the papers is true, that you and him is gonna get married."

"I don't know, Mom. We might."

"Is he a religious Jew?"

"What do you mean?"

"I mean how are you gonna get married? In the church?"

"I don't know, Mom. I suppose so. Anyway, it's not about to happen, so let's just forget about it."

"All right," her mother said. "I just want you to be happy, you know that. I mean Pauline is happily married and sure, poor Joe is only a good-natured, hard-working slob, but they've got two fine kids and they're getting along just swell. I want you to do as well."

Cora stared at the steam forming on the cold glass of the kitchen window. It was both good and bad, being Margaret Monihan again.

"I'm doing fine," she said. "I've got three mink coats, a house of my own in Bel Air, and the studio is giving me a big raise starting next month. Who the hell would help out around here if I was like Pauline, married to a bartender?"

"I keep telling you not to send me a penny," her mother said.

"I know," Cora said, "and it's pretty asinine, isn't it? You know you can use everything I send you."

"Well, just as long as you don't leave yourself short," her mother said.

"I don't. What time are Pauline and Joe coming?"

"About six, I guess. They won't stay long after dinner. Couldn't get a baby-sitter, I guess."

"How's Pauline feeling?"

"Oh, fine. Her back bothers her a little like it used to, but nothing serious. Oh, did I tell you Matty O'Brien died?"

"No," Cora said. However rarely she visited home, always there were the reports of deaths of old people Cora could scarcely remember. Her mother still read the death notices every day. She seemed slightly disappointed if she did not recognize the names of any of the deceased.

At six o'clock Pauline and Joe and their daughters burst in, all laughter and loud talk and firm handshakes and kisses and awkward jokes. There were the first few uneasy minutes as always, the family wondering if she had changed too much to be one of them any more, Cora wondering if they had forgotten how she really was.

"Well, how is it out there in the land of the silver screen?" Joe cried, smiling stiffly.

"Oh, just the same, I guess," Cora said.

"We saw you in *The Sailor and the Blonde*," Joe said. "Pretty hot stuff!" She felt embarrassed at his wink.

Uncle Tom came in shortly after six-thirty, looking tired and much older than Cora had remembered him, his dark gray cardigan sweater grimy and frayed at the cuffs. A stubble of white whiskers lay upon his lined cheeks and his blue eyes looked weak and wet. When he kissed her he smelled of tobacco and beer.

"Why didn't you let me know where you were?" he demanded. "I'd have gone down and picked you up. No sense wasting good money on taxi cabs when I can drive you around. Listen," he said, "I'm off tomorrow. You want me to drive you any place?"

"No, thanks, Tom," Cora said. Through the living room window she could see his car, an old Plymouth, parked outside, its paint devoid of sheen, one window cracked.

For dinner they had corned beef and cabbage, boiled potatoes, cauliflower, sliced tomatoes, pumpkin pie, and coffee. The sills of the windows in the dining room were dusty and the wallpaper was soiled, but the table service was spotless.

"I'll bet you don't get good food like this out there in Hollywood," Uncle Tom said, smacking his lips. "All they give you out there is orange juice and fish and things like that. At least that's all I got out there in 1932."

"Times have changed," Cora's mother said.

"I know," Tom said, "but home cooking is home cooking. You want some more corned beef, Marge?"

"No, thanks."

"Pauline?"

"Don't mind if I do," Pauline said.

"I could go for a little more myself," Joe said.

The youngest child spilled half a glass of milk and Pauline leaped to the kitchen for a rag.

"Here," her mother said, "have more cabbage." Before Cora could protest, a second helping of cabbage was dumped onto her plate.

"Have more corned beef," Tom said.

"She said no, Tom," Cora's mother explained.

"Well, give her more anyway. She looks skinny to me." As he laughed the look of his imperfect false teeth made Cora want to pat his arm.

After dinner they all sat in the living room on the Sears Roebuck furniture and tried to keep the conversation going. It was difficult. At last Cora began asking about old friends.

"Whatever happened to Sally Whatsername?" she said.

"The tall one?" Pauline said.

"Yes."

"Oh, my God, she married a Dago and they live in Seattle now, I think."

"And Tom Conlon?"

"The one you were sweet on?" her mother said.

"Don't be silly," Cora said. It was strange, she thought. One week ago at this very moment of the night she had been lying in Ty Curtis' bed, crying and trying to get drunk because after he had made love to her he had said, "My dear, you've got quite a problem there."

"What are you talking about?" she had said.

"You know what I'm talking about," he said. "Unless you're more naïve than I thought. Tell me, frankly, do you really enjoy sex at all?"

She had tried to slap his face, unsuccessfully. And now here she was sitting with her family, feeling schoolgirl embarrassment because she had asked about a long-ago, almost forgotten love and her mother had spoken to her in a teasing tone.

"He got married to a girl from Peoria," Pauline said, moving the conversation along gracefully. "He lives on the North Side now and they have five kids, I think."

"Whatever happened to Gloria Scanlon?"

"What didn't?" Joe laughed.

"Oh, she was all right," Pauline said. "She was a little wild and all, but she finally settled down after the war, after her first husband was killed."

"She did?"

"Yeah. She lives over around Halsted somewhere," Pauline said. "She got married again, to one of big Jack Dugan's boys. They live over around Halsted somewhere."

"No," said Tom; "they used to, but I think they moved. Over farther east. And they're mighty damn sorry, I'll tell ya. The whole neighborhood is overrun with niggers."

Cora looked at the children, playing on the floor; she expected someone to chide Tom, but the conversation flowed on. What from her viewpoint had appeared to be a sudden jagged rock in the stream was invisible to the rest of them. The talk surged past the word "nigger" as it had past "Dago."

"When *you* gonna get married out there?" Tom said suddenly.

"Why, I don't know," Cora said. "There are so many fellows it's pretty hard to make up your mind out there, you know." Defensively she had been driven to make a joke of her answer.

"Let's see," Tom said, bumbling on, innocently. "Pauline, how old are you now?"

"Thirty," Pauline said. They all knew that Cora was one year older. Only her public believed she was twenty-five.

"Listen," her mother said. "Anybody want to watch the television?"

"Ah, there's nothing on any more," Tom said, "except a lot of goddamned cowboys."

Pauline's oldest daughter, aged five, said, "What's a goddamned cowboy?" and they all laughed.

Cora sat for a while, listening to the rest of them talk, looking at Joe and wondering how it was with Pauline when he made love to her. Two children. Could you become pregnant without achieving—oh, of course. She whispered the word "stupid" to herself. She thought of Ty Curtis and worked over her old anger. Mr. Sophisticated. Big talker. Call a spade a spade. Quite a problem there, my dear girl. She had thought it might happen with him. There had been flowers. Champagne. Poetry. The deserted swimming pool with the lights underwater. Violin music on the invisible hi-fi. Her schoolgirl visions of Ty on the screen, Marge Monihan's adolescent Chicago schoolgirl crush on Ty Curtis. It had all added up to something—but not quite to what she had wanted. And of course with Mike it never had come close. He was patient. Understanding. Loving. Helpful. Cooperative. Self-sacrificing. She had said to him, aching to increase her passion, "How can you wait so long?" and he had given her his big, good-natured smile and held her very close. And none of it had done any good. During the long months Mike had gradually become thoroughly abandoned physically, experimental, almost embarrassingly so. It had not helped. As for "Handsome Bill Keith," that was a true laugh. Dates arranged by the studio. The Sailor and the Blonde. And the Sailor in actual life reserving his affections for real sailors or busboys or anything except women.

The studio pawings had not helped. The furtive attempted kisses at line rehearsals. The insinuations from married actors, agents,

producers, writers. The blunt propositions. Why could she not handle
it like the other women? The ones who got married, the ones who
were able to laugh it off, the ones who loved every minute of it, the
ones who pretended to enjoy it. She had tried that once but been
caught at it. Humiliating. She smiled now, remembering that she had
never really had much ability as an actress, in bed or before the
camera. Pauline's children looked fat and shiny on the floor.

"Those are gorgeous shoes," Pauline said.

"Thanks," Cora said. "Not too expensive, really. I'll send you a
pair if you'd like."

"Where in the name of God would I wear them?" Pauline
laughed.

"Why, what do you mean, Paul?" Joe said. "We could go dancing."

"Not in those shoes," Pauline said. "I'd fall down."

Pauline and Joe and the children left shortly after eight o'clock.
The house seemed remarkably quiet after they had gone. Cora, her
mother, and Tom sat in the kitchen, drinking tea.

On the radiator Cora noticed a stack of movie magazines. She
picked up a handful and put them on the table. Her face smiled back
at her from two of the covers. She selected a copy of *Photoplay* and
turned to the story about herself. There was a picture of her getting
off an airplane in Rome, a picture of her skiing with Ty Curtis (faked
in a studio), a color picture of her on the lawn of the house in Bel Air,
another color picture of her in a tight green knitted bathing suit,
lolling by her pool.

"It's a pity your father isn't here to see you now, Marge," Tom
said, sniffing.

The kettle sighed, seeming far away. A dog barked in the
distance. From the next block the sound of a streetcar clattering
through the night came through the substance of the walls.

"My God," Tom went on softly, speaking as if to himself,
"imagine Billy Monihan's daughter a movie star. What a good laugh
he'd get out of that. He had a wonderful sense of humor, ya know."

"I remember," Cora said.

"Tom," her mother said, "do you remember the night when the
man in the next building came home drunk and got into our place by
mistake and put his groceries down on our dining-room table?"

The two of them laughed heartily, stirring their tea.

Cora looked at the next magazine. The story about her was titled
"Cora Lane, Favorite Sweetheart of the GI's." A wartime story.

Cheesecake. There it was: the big picture, the shot of her standing long-legged on tiptoe, in what looked like a man's pajama top. That picture had been largely responsible for her success. A pinup favorite with millions of service men. A psychiatrist at a party in Hollywood once had gotten a bit drunk and aid, "My dear lady, have you any idea of your importance as a sex symbol to our troops? Have you any idea of the number of men who have looked at your picture before turning out the lights and then assaulted you in their dreams?" Someone at the party had interrupted the conversation at that point, to Cora's complete relief; but often during the years since that night she had thought of herself in just that way, as a sex symbol, as an object desired by millions of men. She had had a dream one night that millions of men, one after the other, had made love to her and that once or twice a face had loomed up for a moment that seemed to belong to someone who had brought her almost to the point of complete satisfaction, but . . .

"Is this Gordon fella a nice guy?" Tom was asking.

"Oh, yeah," Cora said. "Very nice. Kind of like that guy I used to go out with for a while, the one from the University of Chicago, remember?"

"I remember," her mother said primly.

They fell silent.

"This is good tea," Tom said after a moment.

"Yes," her mother said.

The clock over the sink ticked noisily.

"I wonder if it's still raining," Tom said.

"I think it stopped," Cora said.

A car backfired far down the street, the distant report emphasizing the silence in the steamy room.

"Be a late spring," Tom said.

"Guess so," said Cora's mother.

Cora sighed.

"You want to stay here tonight, Marge, or do you have to go back downtown?"

"Oh," Cora said, "I guess I'll stay here."

"Fine," Tom said, "I'll clear my pipe and newspapers and things out of the back room."

Lying awake just before midnight, listening to the whisper of cars gliding by in the dark wet street, Cora felt at home and out-of-place, a child and a mature woman, a saint and a sinner. After a while she heard her mother in the toilet, heard her whisper sadly,

"Oh, glory be to God," as she yawned and staggered back to her room.

Still awake at one in the morning, Cora got up, lit a cigarette, and read through more of the movie magazines, staring avidly at the more provocative pictures of herself. Her favorite, she thought, was the shot of her in the tight green bathing suit, lying in the sun by the pool, at the house where she lived in luxury and alone, the house in Bel Air.

THE PIGEON

■ ■ ■

Mrs. Patchford was passing Brooks Brothers when she saw the pigeon.

The day was gloriously autumnal, although on Madison Avenue Mrs. Patchford could only perceive the fact by reason of the briskness in the air. There were no trees visible and she was able to walk scuffingly through no fallen leaves, to tramp across no browned grass. There was just the sharp, winy bite in the air and the exhilarating chill of it against her ankles.

Overhead the sky, showing in regularly edged rectangles of pale blue, was bracing and footballish, but Mrs. Patchford did not lift her head to look at it. Instead she peered in an interested and intense manner into the face of each person who walked past her.

This was a custom of hers of which she was rather proud. One day she had been walking past the Sherry-Netherlands with Polly Gordon and she had suddenly whirled and grasped Polly's arm and said, "There's Harold Stassen!"

"Who?" said Polly. "Where?"

"Harold Stassen," Mrs. Patchford hissed. "There, going into the hotel. Oh, you missed him!"

"Well," said Polly, "I guess I did, all right. That's too bad."

"It's funny you didn't see him. He walked right past us on your side. You practically touched him. Weren't you looking at him?"

"No," Polly said. "I guess I'm not very observant about things like that. I never notice anybody on the street."

"I can't understand being like that," Mrs. Patchford said disapprovingly. "*I* notice everything. I look at automobile licenses and

103

children playing and people's faces and everything. You miss a great deal when you don't *see* what you're looking at."

Polly had admitted that she was probably right and from that time on Mrs. Patchford, who until the Harold Stassen incident had never really formulated her philosophy of observant pedestrianism, became acutely aware that she was possessed of an innate and long-dormant gift worthy of further cultivation.

It was not an unusual thing therefore that of all the people who had walked by the pigeon during the time he had been standing in front of Brooks Brothers only Mrs. Patchford brought the full power of her attention to bear upon him.

She was in a pleasant and expansive and slightly adventurous mood anyway. It was just a few minutes before eleven o'clock in the morning and she had just come from her doctor's office where the results of a series of tests of one kind and another had been made known to her.

"You're in great shape, Eleanor," Dr. Curtis had said. "Fit as a fiddle."

She had walked out of the office and started to hum something airy before she had even got off the elevator. The brown spot on her forearm had been worrying her for over three months, and then there had been the thing with the gall bladder. But now Curtis had wiped the slate clean and life was wonderful and she was eagerly looking forward to the stop at Bonwit's and then after that the visit to the hairdresser's. She would now, she considered, let Jeanette touch up the gray spots and try a deeper shade of red. When she thought of what Peter would say about her hair she giggled.

It was just at the moment she giggled that she saw the pigeon.

He was a small bird standing alone on a ledge about two feet above the sidewalk just to the right of Brooks Brothers door on the Madison Avenue side.

Unlike most of the pigeons of the St. Patrick's Cathedral covey he was not gray but tan, with streaks of white and deeper brown.

It was not the fact that he was huddled on the stone ledge that intrigued Mrs. Patchford, for the pigeons of Manhattan are an extraordinarily cool and reserved breed and they walk and fly among the bustling human and vehicular traffic with a great deal of aplomb. What made her stop in her tracks and look down at him was that he had not moved an inch as she brushed past him.

"Well," she said, "hello, there."

The bird regarded her calmly although he did not look at her eyes. He looked straight ahead so that he was looking at her knees.

"What's the matter?" she said, as if talking to a strange child.

The pigeon hobbled clumsily away from her and came to a halt after having traveled a distance of about eighteen inches along the ledge.

"Why, you poor little thing," Mrs. Patchford sang lovingly, "are you sick? Is your little wing broken?"

She put out her hand experimentally and again the pigeon shuffled out of her reach. He seemed to walk with a rather rolling gait, although she could not be certain if his awkwardness stemmed from a physical injury or simply from the precariousness of his cramped and slanted perch.

"Why," she said, "you're deathly ill; that's what's the matter with you. You've fallen and broken your wing or your little leg and you just don't know what to do, do you?"

The pigeon did not answer her.

"Here," Mrs. Patchford said, "come here." She was reacting to the situation out of the capacity for deep compassion and maudlin sympathy which was a part of her emotional make-up, and she was not entirely certain of what she would have done had the pigeon hopped into her extended hand.

He did not do so.

"Well," she cooed, "if you won't come here I don't know what I'll do with you, I just don't."

She straightened up and thought of walking on, but somehow the bird's plight kept her rooted to the spot.

"Don't worry," she whispered, bending down again. "You just stay right there and I'll go in here," pointing at Brooks Brothers window, "and get somebody to take care of you."

With a satisfied smile Mrs. Patchford walked resolutely into the store. On her left a young man in a gray flannel suit stood with his hands on top of a glass counter. He smiled at her.

"Good morning," he said.

"Good morning," Mrs. Patchford said in a confidential tone.

"Could I help you?" the young man said.

"Yes," Mrs. Patchford said. "There's a pigeon outside."

"I beg your pardon?"

"I was just wondering," Mrs. Patchford said, still confidentially, leaning toward the man over the counter, "I was just wondering if you had a telephone here."

"Why, yes," the man said, withdrawing almost unnoticeably. "I imagine it would be all right . . . if you wanted to use it, that is."

"Oh, no," Mrs. Patchford said, "I don't want to use it. You see, there's a little pigeon outside and he doesn't seem to be feeling well."

The man chuckled briefly for no apparent reason and then stopped suddenly and looked carefully at Mrs. Patchford.

"What's the matter with him?" he asked, looking about the store.

"Why," she said, lifting her eyebrows, "that's just it. I don't know. He seems to have been injured, but I don't really know what's the matter with him."

"I see," the man said, running his upper front teeth down hard over his lower lip and frowning.

A somewhat older man with steel-rimmed glasses sidled up casually next to Mrs. Patchford.

"Can I help?" he asked, looking at the younger man.

"Maybe," the man in the gray flannel suit said. "This lady wants to make a phone call about a pigeon."

The older man smiled for a moment and then looked serious again.

"A phone call, you say?"

"Yes," said Mrs. Patchford. "I was just telling this gentleman that there's a sick pigeon outside on your window ledge. I thought something should be done about it."

"Certainly," said the older man. "Just what was it you had in mind?"

"Why, I don't know, really," Mrs. Patchford said, shrugging. "I thought maybe someone should call the SPCA."

"I see," the man said thoughtfully. "But isn't the SPCA for dogs and horses and things like that?"

"I'm not at all sure," Mrs. Patchford said. "But there should be somebody you could call." She had raised her voice just a bit.

A third man walked up. He was plump and businesslike. "Everything all right?" he said.

"Yes, Charlie," the man with the steel-rimmed glasses said. "This lady just came in to tell us about a pigeon outside."

"What about it?"

"I've just told these gentlemen . . ." Mrs. Patchford began tiredly.

"Did you say a pigeon?" the new man asked.

"Yes," said the young man in the flannel suit.

"Who saw it?"

"This lady."

"Anyone else see it?"

"No," said the young man.

"No," Mrs. Patchford said. "I just came in this minute. It's outside, you see, on your ledge. I really wouldn't have bothered you but it *is* your ledge, after all, and I thought—"

"Maybe," the new man said, "we'd better all go out and take a look."

"I really don't see what good that would do," Mrs. Patchford said, with some condescension. "There's nothing to look at except this little pigeon and he seems ill, that's all. Why doesn't somebody call the SPCA?"

"We'll be glad to, madam," the plump man said, looking at her curiously. "Now just where did you think—just where did you see the pigeon?"

Mrs. Patchford turned with the merest trace of irritation and pointed to the display window behind her.

"He's right out there," she said, tightening the muscles at the corners of her mouth.

Unaccountably the young man behind the counter laughed. The others glared at him openly. He looked down and began straightening some wool-knit ties that lay on the glass counter.

"I think," said Mrs. Patchford, "that perhaps we'd *better* go take a look at him."

"Why, of course," the plump man said, shuffling in the direction of the door. The young man came out from behind the counter, the man with the steel-rimmed spectacles moved forward, and two salesmen from another part of the store moved in on the group.

Behind Mrs. Patchford's back the young man looked smugly at the two newcomers and lifted his right forefinger to his temple. He rotated the finger briefly and then pressed it to the side of his head.

Mrs. Patchford swept grandly out onto the sidewalk, followed by the five men.

"Now, then," she said grimly.

The men gathered in a small knot on the sidewalk and looked at her silently.

"It's right here," she said, directing a finger at a point on the blank, deserted ledge.

"Why," chuckled Mrs. Patchford, "that's funny. There's nothing— he's not here." She whirled frantically and searched the sidewalk, the entire store front, the curb, and the sky overhead.

"Looks like he flew away," the plump man said, looking sadly at Mrs. Patchford.

"But I can't understand it," she said. "I thought he couldn't fly."

"Well, you know," the plump man said softly, "sometimes they can."

"Yes," said Mrs. Patchford. "Well, good morning."

Behind her someone, she thought, laughed; but she could not be sure.

She had planned to buy only a skirt at Bonwit's but now she went in and bought three dresses and a pair of expensive gloves.

Afterward she had a headache and did not go to the hairdresser's at all.

THE INTERVIEW
■ ■ ■

When Sarah Brigham walked into the room she experienced a flicker of disappointment. It was a nice room but not quite what she had expected.

"Just make yourself at home," the maid said. "I'll tell Miss Prentiss you're here."

"Thank you," Sarah said, removing her gloves. Behind her, the maid fussed for a moment with an ashtray, then stepped out of the room.

"It's been rather chilly," Sarah said.

The maid came back into the room.

"Beg pardon, ma'am?"

"Oh," Sarah said, "I thought you were still here."

"Yes," said the maid absently. "I'll tell Miss Prentiss."

"Thank you," Sarah said, taking her glasses out of her handbag.

She removed her coat, placed it over the back of a chair, and looked about the room. After a moment she walked to the mantelpiece and picked up a large framed photograph of Josephine Prentiss. The maid re-entered.

"Miss Prentiss said to make yourself at home. She'll only be a minute."

"Thank you," Sarah said. "Have you been with her long?"

"No, ma'am. Only a minute."

"No, I mean—have you been employed by Miss Prentiss for a long time?"

"Oh, yes, ma'am. For a long time."

"I suppose it's quite exciting," Sarah said, "working for such a famous person."

"Yes," the maid said. "I suppose it is."

"Incidentally," Sarah said, smiling, "I'm not just being nosy. I've come to interview Miss Prentiss."

"Oh, that's all right."

"I'm going to write a story about her," Sarah explained.

"That's nice," the maid said. "There's a lot of stories about Miss Prentiss."

Lighting a cigarette, Sarah Brigham asked. "Are you happy working for her?"

"I guess so. She pays me good."

"I mean is she easy to get along with? Sometimes you can tell a great deal about a person just by the way they treat their . . . by the way they treat those who work for them."

"I suppose so," the maid said. "Yes, she's good to me. My sister gets all her old clothes."

"Your sister?"

"Yes," the maid said. "She's a thirty-eight. I'm too big. I used to be able to wear her things . . . but not any more. Not since my husband died."

"Oh?" Sarah said.

"I was smaller then. He always insisted."

"Just how did you happen to come with Miss Prentiss in the first place?"

"It was when she was working in *Springtime in Vienna*. My sister was her wardrobe mistress. She was married then."

"Your sister?" Sarah said.

"No, *Miss Prentiss*. That was the year she divorced Mr. Fontaine. They used to work together, you know."

"Yes," Sarah said, "I know."

"Twelve years it's been," the maid said, sitting down in a large chair.

"Did you know Mr. Fontaine?" Sarah said.

"Oh, yes," the maid said. "He was an easy man to know. He drank a lot."

"So I've heard," Sarah said, getting out her notebook.

"He used to cause Miss Prentiss quite a bit of trouble," the maid said, sighing. "People didn't understand him, exactly. We always had to explain him away."

Sarah rose and walked to a wall-to-wall bookcase. "Does Miss Prentiss find time to do much reading?" she said. "She has a wonderful library here."

"No," the maid said. "She reads the papers . . . and the Bible . . . and astrology magazines and Pogo. That's about all."

"Who's reading that book on the table?" Sarah asked, and at that moment Josephine Prentiss made an entrance, sweepingly.

"Hello," she shouted, advancing toward Sarah. "So sorry I've kept you waiting."

"That's quite all right," Sarah said, offering her hand. "I'm Sarah Brigham."

"Yes, of *Woman's Home Companion*, isn't it?" Josephine appraised her visitor: small, eager, plain, no make-up.

"Ladies' Home Journal," Sarah said.

"Of course. Mildred, have you offered Miss . . . er . . ."

"Brigham," Sarah supplied.

"Have you offered Miss Brigham a drink?"

"No," the maid said. "I didn't think."

"What would you like, dear?" Josephine said.

"Oh, it really doesn't matter," Sarah said.

"Make us martinis, Mildred," Josephine said. "Several of them." The maid left the room.

"Mildred's a dear," Josephine said softly. "A little peculiar, but a dear."

"Yes," said Sarah. "We've been speaking. She's very fond of you."

"Quite," Josephine said, settling herself in a large chair and waving a welcoming hand at the sofa. "Now, let's see. Just where would you like to start?"

"Well," Sarah said, "the Kramer office provided me with pictures, a biography, some other material, but I'd like to just, you know, chat with you for a while. I'd like to have you tell me all about yourself. It's the little personal touches that interest the reader."

"Well, let me see . . ." Josephine said, looking at the ceiling, anxious to begin discussing herself. She enjoyed being interviewed. "I've always wanted to be an actress, I suppose. I remember the year my family moved over here from Calcutta . . . my father was a missionary, you know."

"Yes, I'd heard."

"Well, I remember the year we all moved back here. The poor dear was in such bad health that they called him back and set him up in Boston. I remember the day he took me on his lap and looked me in the eye and said, 'Twinky . . .' He always called me by that ridiculous name," Josephine giggled.

"My father had a funny name for me, too," Sarah said.

Josephine Prentiss was almost imperceptibly taken aback. "Oh, did he?" she said.

"Yes."

"What was it?" Josephine asked politely.

"Snuggle-puff," said Sarah.

"Oh," said Josephine. "How . . . quaint!" Then, regathering speed, she said. "Well, my father looked me in the eye and said, 'Twinky, no matter what you do, as you go through life, remember this one thing—'"

The maid stepped into the room and said, "I think we're out of gin."

"Nonsense," Josephine said. "Some arrived this morning. It's probably out in the back hall."

"Oh, all right," Mildred said. "I'll look."

"Now, where were we?" Josephine said, looking at the Gimbels label in Sarah's coat as it lay over a nearby chair.

"You were telling me about your father," Sarah said.

"Oh, yes. Well, Daddy was a dear. You should have heard him preach a sermon. I tell you he could really put the fear of God in your heart, God bless him! He was a fine figure of a man. Tall, straight, touch of gray at the temples. My mother adored him."

"Is she . . ." Sarah asked, "are they both. . . ?"

"Dead?" Josephine said. "Yes. I'm alone now. Have been for quite a while. But I carry on. There's a great deal to live for. Did you see my last play?"

"No, I'm afraid I didn't," Sarah apologized. "I saw you in *The Fourth Commandment*, though. You were wonderful."

"That's what they all said. I *was* rather happy in the show, come to think of it. I believe I was in love with Stanley White at the time."

"Do you mind if I mention that in the story?" Sarah asked.

"No," Josephine said, "I suppose it's all right. It *was* in all the papers, although I wish Walter hadn't used that dreadful picture of me. I looked a million years old. It was taken the year they were wearing their hair like this, you know . . ." She gestured with her hands to her hair ". . . and I looked like Margaret Sullavan after she'd been soaked in water for three weeks. Dreadful, just dreadful. But, my dear, Stanley was a darling. An absolute darling. Ah, me . . ." She was lost for a moment in reverie.

"I always loved him myself," Sarah said. "He reminded me of a boy I went to high school with."

"Oh, did you?" Josephine said. "I mean . . . did he?"

"Yes," Sarah said. "The boy's name was Roland Culver. He was from Boston, too, come to think of it. I don't suppose you . . ." She paused.

"No," Josephine Prentiss said.

The maid entered with a silver tray. "Here are the drinks, Miss Prentiss." She served Sarah and Josephine martinis from the tray.

"Thank you," Sarah said, taking a sip.

"Thank you, Mildred," Josephine said, drinking rather thirstily. "Oh," she said. "I needed that. Just put the tray here, dear."

"Yes, ma'am," Mildred said, placing the tray and cocktail shaker on the coffee table in front of the sofa.

"Now, let me see," Josephine pondered. "What was I saying? Don't you take notes?"

"Sometimes," said Sarah, "but I prefer to just listen. I have a good memory."

"I see," Josephine said. "Well, anyway, my father (he was from Dublin, you know) he built our home with his own hands, the poor dear. The home in Calcutta, I mean. Oh, he had help, I suppose, but he directed the work himself. After Sissy (that's my sister), after Sissy and I were born he built a wing on the house instead of buying the organ that he'd wanted for such a long time. And then when Mother fell ill he built another wing. He was always doing something constructive. Well, we eventually lost the place . . ."

"How?"

"I don't know, exactly," Josephine said. "Perhaps it just flew away. That's just a little joke of mine. Yes. Well, anyway, when we came to America, Sissy and I were just two poor little waifs all alone in the great big city of Boston, and I remember Daddy took me on his lap the first night we spent in America, and said, 'Twinky, Mother is very ill, and it's just you and Sissy and myself from here on in, sweetheart.'"

"Oh," said Sarah, warmly, "did *your* father raise *you*, too?"

"I beg your pardon?" Josephine said.

"My mother died when I was fairly young," Sarah explained.

"You poor dear," Josephine said.

"I'm sorry. Go on."

"Yes. Well, Sissy and I were entered in a private school in Boston and I'll never forget the first day we showed up at the school. All the other children were quite wealthy and had just adorable clothes. Poor Sissy and I wore those horrible long black stockings that came up over our knees and I'll never forget, when we walked into the room (we were late, I think), and when we walked in all the other children laughed at us. They laughed and laughed and laughed, damn their ugly little hearts. It was dreadful. Poor Sissy burst into tears, I remember, and ran out into the hall, with me right after her."

"Oh, that's . . . tragic," Sarah said, touched.

"Yes," Josephine admitted, "it was. Sissy wouldn't go back to school for a week, but I'd be damned if they could keep me away. Oh, I was crying inside, too, but I wouldn't let on. I wouldn't give in and let those little snobs know how they'd hurt me!"

Sarah finished her drink.

"Here," Josephine said, "let me put a head on that for you." She poured Sarah and herself two more drinks. "Oh, my dear, the stories I could tell you."

"What was your mother like?" Sarah said.

"An angel," Josephine said. "An absolute angel. And what an actress! She, my dear, was the only real talent in our family. Oh, my father was magnificent, and I've had my modest success, but my mother . . . There, my dear, was the greatest thing since Duse. She had my father around her little finger. Never raised her voice, but she controlled him absolutely. And tears . . . You've never seen anyone who could cry like my mother. Phony tears, usually . . . crocodile tears . . . but she could call upon them as a weapon, a most effective weapon. I'll never forget the time (Mildred, bring some more martinis, dear), I'll never forget the time I was working in my first show, rather a long time ago, I'm afraid. Anyway, I had told Mother I had a very important role, the part of a great lady, because Mother wasn't too keen about my getting into show business to begin with, but she finally had decided that if I could possibly become a star, a very important star, that, well, it might be all right. Well, I had told her I had practically the lead in this production, and I made her promise that she wouldn't come to see the play on opening night. Well, I didn't even make my entrance until the middle of the second act, and when I did I simply walked up to a man standing under a street lamp—I don't think you'd remember the play—I walked up to this man and said, 'Pardon me, but do you have a cigarette?' I remember my hair was stringy and I was wearing a tattered skirt, with a split up the side. A pathetic little prostitute is what I really was. Well, my dear, I delivered this one line and then stood there, looking out over the footlights smoking a cigarette and flirting with this man.

"He ignored me, actually. Walked right away from me. Well, I'm standing there and suddenly my heart turned right over in my body. There, sitting in the first row, was my mother. The man, I forget who it was now, turned to me and said, 'Run along home, little girl. I think your mother is looking for you.' Well, my mother gasped! You could hear her all over the theater. And then she started to cry, and I started to cry. I don't even remember walking off the stage, I was so ashamed. I refused to come out of my dressing room until everyone had left the theater and I didn't go home for two days." Josephine Prentiss' eyes were tear-filled now at the memory.

"Was your mother angry?" Sarah whispered.

"No. That's the tragic part of it. The poor dear was terribly displeased, of course, but she wouldn't let me see it. She was ashamed of me, and I was ashamed of myself, but God bless her, she threw her arms around me when I walked in and kissed me and held me and told me that she was very sure that one day I would be the very greatest actress the theater had ever known."

With cocktail shaker refilled the maid entered. She walked to the coffee table and filled both glasses.

"Thank you, dear," Josephine said.

"Miss Prentiss," said little Sarah Brigham emotionally, "you *are* a great actress. I hope you'll forgive me. My eyes seem to have clouded up." She laughed with embarrassment.

"Thank you, dear," Josephine said. "You're very sweet. Well" (they lifted their glasses toward each other), "*c'est la guerre.* Did you say you were from Boston?"

"Well, partly," Sarah said. "We lived there for a few years. When Mother died we moved to Chicago."

"I see," Josephine said. "I loved Boston . . . with its winding streets and its straight people."

"That's a wonderfully descriptive line," Sarah said. "I think I will make a note of that." She fumbled in her purse, took out a note pad and pencil and jotted a few words.

"Do you think," said Josephine, "that the readers of *Woman's Home Companion*—"

"*Ladies' Home Journal.*"

"Of course. Do you think your readers would be interested more in little stories about me than they would in my comments about the theater?"

"Well, I imagine we can use some of both. Just say anything that comes into your head . . . the way you have been."

"Does it seem warm in here to you?" Josephine said. She opened her dress a bit at the neck and fanned herself with a handkerchief. "Mildred, darling, would you open a window or create a draft or something? These autumn afternoons are very much like . . . *summer* afternoons . . . aren't they?"

"A little," agreed Sarah, sipping her martini.

"Well," Josephine said, "let me see. Oh, yes. My first play. Let me see, it was back in nineteen . . . well, the date isn't important."

"It is to me," Sarah said.

"It's not to me," Josephine said.

"Very well," Sarah said, sipping her drink.

"I'll never forget that play," Josephine said. "I think that was the company . . . Yes, of course. It was *The Willow Tree*. Ralph Forbes or somebody was in the cast. No, it was Ralph Graves. I remember I had a love affair with the boy who died in the third act. You wouldn't remember his name. I remember I brought him home for dinner one night. He was tremendously wealthy. His father owns half of Canada or something. Anyway, I was mad about him, simply mad. I called Mother in the afternoon and told her I was bringing him home to dinner and when Richard . . . that was his name . . . when Richard and I arrived it was dreadful. Everything went wrong. First of all, my father answered the door in his stocking feet and suspenders."

"How dreadful," Sarah said.

"Yes, terribly," Josephine said. "We were trying to be so fancy, you see. Well, my mother had forgotten to tell Daddy about my bringing Richard home and it turned out that Daddy had invited his brother to dinner. It was his black-sheep brother. He was always getting into scrapes and Daddy was always getting him out of them. Well, this night Uncle Fred was a little drunk and, oh, my dear, I'll never forget it. He sat at the table and twice he belched right out loud and poor Mother, God bless her, the poor angel, was so embarrassed for herself and for me that she dropped the roast when she brought it into the dining room and she didn't know what to do, the poor darling. Daddy picked it up and took it back to the kitchen, and if it was just us we would have eaten it, but with Richard there we didn't know what to do. I think we just had soup and then Uncle Fred got into an argument with Richard and Richard went home. I was so terribly in love with him, you see, but I never had the heart to . . . speak to him . . . much . . . after that day. He married someone else, a society girl, a few months later."

Sarah blew her nose sniffingly. "Oh, dear," she said, "I'm so sorry. I don't know why I'm acting like this. It's just that you tell these stories as if they had just happened yesterday, Miss Prentiss, and I . . . I don't know. Something very much like that happened to me once and you just seemed to strike some kind of responsive chord. I'm so ashamed." She finished her drink.

"Nonsense, my dear," Josephine said. "A good cry never hurt anyone. I think you're a darling, acting like this. I really do."

"The boy in my life when I was about that age," Sarah passed on, ". . . the age you were in that story, I mean . . . was a very wealthy boy whose father owned the building we lived in in Chicago. Harry Ryan was his name. He played football, and I was the editor of our college paper. I remember I interviewed him one day and he invited me to have dinner with him. I . . . I wore braces on my teeth at the time, and even then I had to wear these horrible glasses . . . and I waited for him for two hours and then—"

"There, there, dear," Josephine said, patting her shoulder. "Don't you worry. Those football players are never worth it. Not a bit of it, you poor darling."

"Oh, I don't give a damn *now*," Sarah said, "but he never showed up. I didn't hear from him at all after that. Ohhh, God. The only reason I'm explaining all this is that you'll understand how close your stories strike to home. You've had such a tragic life, evidently."

"Yes, I have," Josephine confessed.

"And sometimes it just seems that life is so terribly full of tragedy for so many of us that . . . I don't know . . . sometimes you wonder what is the purpose of it all."

"Daddy knew what the purpose was, the poor angel. He raised Sissy and me to love and to fear God and to do the best we could for the most people."

"He must have been a fine man," Sarah said warmly. "I haven't been to church in years."

"That's too bad, my dear. It can be a great comfort. A great comfort."

"Oh, do you go?" Sarah said.

"No, not since Daddy died."

"Why not?"

"I don't know, really. I have nothing against it. I just seem to be up so late on Saturday night."

"I suppose your personal life must be very exciting . . . parties and things," Sarah said, trying to brighten the mood.

"Well," said Josephine, "there aren't so many parties, but . . . quite a few . . . things."

"When was it you met Mr. Fontaine?" Sarah said.

"Oh, Henry?" Josephine said. "Quite a few years ago. We worked together in *The Lost Chord*. We were married while we were touring. I think he proposed in Buffalo . . . and then in Cleveland . . ."

"That's where you were married?"

"No, that's where he backed out."

"Oh," Sarah said.

"He changed his mind in St. Louis and we were married in Los Angeles. Henry wasn't a bad sort, the poor dear, although he drank a great deal."

Sarah rose unsteadily and walked to a tray of cigarettes on a lamp table. "Where is he now, do you know?"

"No," Josephine said. "He floated away about seven years ago. Last I heard he was in Honolulu or Cuba."

"What was he doing?"

"I think he had gotten into Rum . . . or vice versa."

Sarah laughed heartily. "When you met him, was it love at first sight?" she said.

"I don't think so. You might say his interest in me was purely paternal."

"Paternal?"

"He wanted to become a father."

"Oh," Sarah said, returning to the sofa. "It all sounds so romantic and exciting. Sometimes I get so sick of *my* life. By contrast it seems so drab, so dull. The same thing day after day. I'd love to be like you—to live dangerously, as the saying goes—to do something . . . to be somebody's mistress or something." She emptied her glass and poured herself another. "Tell me another of your stories."

"Well, let me see," Josephine said. "Oh, yes. I did want to tell you about the time when Sissy and I were looking for work on Broadway. We took a little room in a dingy hotel just off Times Square, and day after day we tramped the streets, looking for a walk-on, a small role, anything. Sissy, the poor dear, as I remember didn't even have a decent coat. We had this one nice coat between us; Mother had made it, as I recall. That's right. My mother made it. It was heavy red wool with a black velvet collar and it was really darling. Well, when we were looking for work in some cheap show or in a small agent's office we could walk in together because Sissy's old brown coat was good enough for that sort of thing, but when we were trying to make an impression on somebody *important* the poor little waif would have to stay home in that dingy little room in that run-down hotel (I remember the bellboys were unspeakable), and there she'd sit, the angel, looking out the window, looking up Forty-seventh Street till she'd see me coming back, and I'd look up at her, sitting up there on the third floor looking down at me (she was only about sixteen at the time) and, honestly, it would break your heart to see that dear little face, with those big brown eyes, looking down like a puppy. Yes, for all the world like a dear little puppy that had been left behind. And then if I'd found something I'd smile and nod, 'Yes,' and by the time I'd gotten upstairs to the room she'd be delirious with joy. And if I hadn't been able to find anything I'd shake my head, 'No,' and we'd sit up there in that damned dingy room and hold onto each other and cry. And then I'd let her put on the red wool coat with the black velvet collar and she, poor angel—I remember it was just a little bit too large for her—she'd put it on and out she'd go, and I'd sit in the window and watch her as she went off up the street with her pretty yellow hair gleaming . . . and her little face lifted eagerly and so bravely. Oh, my dear, it," crying, "it's so sad to think of it now. I tell you—"

"Where is Sissy now?" Sarah asked breathily.

"She's living in Denver," Josephine said, sighing. "Her husband is head of one of the Sears-Roebuck stores there or something."

"Oh, it's all so very touching," Sarah said. "How brave you are, Miss Prentiss. How very brave to fight your way up out of poverty and sickness and tragedy to your present position. This is going to be a marvelous story to write. I can't wait to get to my typewriter. . . . Does your maid have any more martinis ready?"

"There's more in here," Josephine Prentiss said. She poured from the cocktail shaker, filling Sarah's glass and then her own.

"I can't wait to sit down and begin working on this thing," Sarah said. "The material is perfect. Just fascinating. I suppose you've been telling these stories all your life and you're a bit tired of them, but to me—"

"Oh, not at all, my dear. I get quite carried away hearing them myself, I really do. We actresses need only an audience, you know. We thrive on attention and approval and adulation."

"Oh, I understand perfectly," Sarah said. "In fact, I haven't felt at all as if this has been an interview, if you know what I mean. Sometimes it has seemed more like a . . . a performance . . . and I've felt like a spectator. Then again I've felt as if I were chatting with an old, old friend—I hope you'll forgive me."

"Don't be silly, dear. There's nothing to forgive."

"I suppose I've been drinking a bit too much," Sarah said. "I usually don't act like this."

"Nonsense. It's good for you. I remember one time when—"

"You see, I usually don't drink much at all. It's so . . . funny."

"Of course," Josephine said. "As I was saying, I remember the time when Daddy and—"

"Oh, your *father*," cried Sarah. "He sounds so much like my own!"

"Is that right?"

"Yes, terribly, the poor thing. Our mothers were nothing alike. Your sounds like a saint, but my mother was a . . . a . . . she ran a speak-easy."

"A speak-easy?"

"Yes," Sarah said, making a face. "I hated her. Does that sound awful? She was beautiful and exciting and everything that I'm not, and she was cheap and coarse, too. For all her faults my father adored her. She ruined his life."

"Dreadful," said Josephine, looking on dully.

"Yes," Sarah insisted, "it was. We lived up over a restaurant on the South Side (my father sold shoes and was trying to write a novel on the side), and my mother had an affair with a man who owned the restaurant and the two of them decided to open a speak-easy . . . it was in the first days of Prohibition, you see. My poor father had a lot of respectable friends, poor people, but respectable, and finally he got so embarrassed when they would come around that he stopped inviting them. He would just sit up in the apartment at the dining-room table at night, with his pathetic little papers and things spread out in front of him, trying to write something worthwhile. He never did though. He had no talent whatsoever, the poor angel. But he was only happy, I think, when he was up there trying to write something, sitting there amongst his dictionaries and thesauruses and clippings and rejection slips—and then my mother would come upstairs with that unspeakable man—and the two of them would drink and carry on right in front of my father. Ohhh." She recoiled at the memory. "And right in front of me. I couldn't ever bring boys home because of all the fighting and drinking. I remember one time a boy walked me home from school, and I liked him very much, and when we got to the back gate out in the alley I don't know what went through my mind but I didn't want to say good-by to him and go upstairs alone. I wanted to keep him with me. I guess I was in love with him . . . so

I said, 'Would you like to come upstairs for a Coca-Cola or something?' and he said, 'Why, yes, I suppose I would,' so I said, 'Well, all right, come on up,' and we walked up the back stairs, and I thought my mother would be out (my father was at the store. It was a dingy little store near the Stratford Theatre, just up a ways from the corner of Sixty-third and Halsted Street—I don't think you'd know just where—But it was right next door to a candy store and my father used to bring me home little things from the candy store sometimes, pink and yellow bonbons). Well, anyway, this boy and I walked up the back stairs. We were holding hands and laughing and for a minute I thought he was going to kiss me while I was standing there putting my key into the door, but I guess he saw my braces and changed his mind or something . . . but there we were, laughing and having a really wonderful time. He was so tall and thin and sweet and shy, I just loved him. I was never happier and then I opened the back door and the lights were out in the kitchen and we both stepped in and . . . ohhhh—" She sobbed uncontrollably.

"There, there, now," Josephine said. "What happened? It'll do you good to go on."

"We stepped into the kitchen," Sarah said thickly, "and I turned on the light over the table and there on the *floor* was my mother, lying right there on the linoleum, drunk! With her kimona open and nothing to cover her body. Lying right there on the linoleum, you understand—in the kitchen—half-naked . . . like a wild animal . . . and there were broken bottles all around. I guess she and that man had had a fight or something, but there she was . . . Oh, God! It was awful. I wanted to die. I told the boy right there while he stood there looking at me and then at her . . . I told him I was sorry and that I wanted to kill myself. I wanted to run to him and put my arms around him and beg him to take me away, far away, to someplace where it was warm and green and the sun was shining—but I couldn't ask him to do that. We were just two children in school and he was so pathetically embarrassed." She laughed a little hysterically. "I remember he even laughed, he was so embarrassed. He tried to laugh it off! He laughed a little and said, 'Oh, don't worry, Sarah. It's all right. My father drinks a little too. It happens in the best of families. Think nothing of it.' And then he said, 'Well, I guess I'll be running along,' and when I saw him backing out of the kitchen like a big, confused puppy I wanted to hold him, to make him stay. I needed something to hold onto, I guess. It was so confusing. Because at the same time I wanted him to go away and never come back. I didn't

ever want to see him . . . ever again. Or else I wanted to run away
with him . . . but before I would have gone . . . I wanted to walk
over to that drunken *slut* lying on the linoleum, snoring, and stamp
on her face with my heels. I wanted to kill her! Oh, God . . .
God . . . God . . . God . . . God." There was a long pause while
the two women sat, not looking at each other, each absorbed in her
own thoughts.

Mildred entered, whispering. "Was there anything the matter,
Miss Prentiss?"

"No, Mildred," Josephine said, "nothing. We . . . we've just
been sitting here, conducting an interview, Miss Brigham and I.
Everything is fine."

Sarah, gathering herself together: "I'm so sorry, Miss Prentiss. I
guess I've overstayed my welcome."

"Why, no . . ." Josephine started to protest.

"No, it's all right," Sarah said. "I have to be running along
anyway. You've given me a great deal of material, and I can fill in the
rest from the biography. I think I need a bit of fresh air." She rose and
put on her coat and gloves. Then she put the hat on so that it was
rather askew. Her purse was hanging open. "I don't remember when
anything went to my head like . . . those martinis," she said. "I do
hope you'll forgive me. I've got to get back to the office now."

"Do you?" Josephine asked. She felt a little drunk.

"Yes. I'm expecting a gentleman caller there. He's taking me to
dinner. Thank you very much, Miss Prentiss. If there's anything else
I need I'll—" She broke off and walked out of the apartment.

"Mildred," said Josephine Prentiss quietly, "I have been
upstaged."

THE SAINT

■ ■ ■

Martin lay on his stomach, feeling the unyielding rock pressing flatly against his ribs. The desert sun had baked the dull stone during the morning and now, late in the day, the stored-up warmth, relaxing the tension of his muscles, almost tempted him to sleep.

His beard matted damply under his jaw; through it his interlocked hands supported his chin. Squinting against the reflected light slanting up off the desert floor, he looked down at the road that passed along a small defile beneath his position, waiting. It had been over an hour since anyone had passed along the trail and he was becoming impatient for the sight of another human. Squirming with some pain up into a kneeling position, he threw his head back and stared fiercely at the sky. Then he smiled and said as loudly as he could, "Oh, Almighty God, please deign to send someone along the road, for I am desolate in my—in my—" For a moment Martin considered how he might gracefully end his prayer, but at last, feeling himself unequal to the task, he broke off and prayed for a few minutes silently. The prayers that were thought rather than spoken were easier to handle. He could not stutter within the privacy of his mind and if a word failed him, if an idea was developed obscurely, the realization never was crystallized so that he had the impression that his unspoken thoughts had a great dignity and symmetry that his more formal vocal entreaties could not equal.

Rising stiffly, he walked to the overhanging rock that had been his roof for the past fortnight and there, in a sliver of shade, began to eat the few dates he had left. The sugar in them was immediately sucked off into his weakened system and revived him somewhat, but at the same time it gave him a terrible thirst with the result that he

123

had to climb down the hill to the road and then walk half a mile to the nearest well to refresh himself. Twice along the way he toyed with the idea of giving up his hermit's existence, but each time the possibility occurred to him he regarded it as a temptation of Satan and prayed vigorously for strength, which, it seemed, was thereupon vouchsafed.

At the well he publicly offered his blessing to two women who were filling goatskin bags. They regarded him silently as he called down upon them the beneficence of heaven and then, having completed their work, nudged a small donkey and departed without saying a word to him.

After he had drunk his fill he hurried back off down the road, walking swiftly so as to catch up with the women. After a few minutes he came within sight of them and called loudly, "Do not worry about your water jugs, for it has been said, 'Take no thought for your life, what ye shall eat or what ye shall drink, nor yet for your body what ye shall put on.'"

The women turned, glanced back fearfully, and increased their pace somewhat:

"Behold the fowls of the air," Martin shouted, "they sow not, neither do they reap, nor gather into barns, yet your heavenly Father feeds them."

One of the women turned without slackening her speed and said, "Peace, brother."

"I did not come to bring peace," Martin shouted, "but a sword; and to set brother against brother and daughter against daughter and father against mother."

The women walked on in the hot sunlight, Martin following them at several paces.

"I have given up all that I owned," Martin said.

"Good for you," said the taller of the two women.

"A rich man cannot enter the Kingdom of Heaven," Martin said.

"So we have heard," the woman returned.

"Resist thee not evil," Martin said, speaking somewhat more softly, "but whosoever shall smite thee on thy right cheek, turn to him the other also."

The women did not answer.

"Let your light so shine before men that they may see your good works and glorify your Father, who is in heaven," he intoned.

The donkey whinnied softly and ambled slowly on through the dust.

After a few minutes Martin stopped in his tracks and raised his voice to its former volume. "Do you not intend to heed what I am saying?" he cried.

"We are busy," said the tall woman, "and we must return to our homes and families."

"Woe be unto you," Martin shouted, stamping his foot. "Woe be unto you because—because—" but he could think of no words of his own to express the contempt that welled within his heart; he could create no phrases to match the sentiments that seethed inside him. "An eye for an eye and a tooth for a tooth," he screamed at last, at the disappearing figures. "The angels will—will descend and cast you into the fire—and there shall be weeping and gnashing of teeth."

Tears began to stream from Martin's eyes as the mixed feelings of impotent rage and love for God boiled in his breast.

"My God, my God," he cried, "why hast Thou forsaken me?"

A hawk circled silently high overhead, gliding on boiling air. When Martin at length began to walk again, this time off to his hermit's retreat, it veered away and disappeared.

When he had climbed back up to his flat rock he could perceive, at a great distance, the figures of the two women and their beast.

"Witches," he cried after them, and the desert rocks echoed his voice, "thou shalt not suffer a witch to live!"

Picking up a stone, he threw it after them, futilely. "And thou shalt stone him with stones that he die," he said. At last, tiring, he lay down full length on the warm rock and cradled his head sideways on his folded arms that he might rest but still be able to survey the road. He thought about the women for several minutes and eventually came to concentrate on the tall one, who had had lustrous, dark eyes, and a full mouth. He saw her as the personification of evil and wished that he might encounter her again, at the well or anywhere, in order that he might denounce her publicly or, better yet, strike her with his fist in the name of the Lord, punish her physically for what he imagined must be her many and colorfully varied sins.

He would beat her to her knees, he considered, and then, while she pleaded for mercy, rip her sinful garments from her body that her shame might be exposed to the merciless eye of the sky. Squinting slightly, looking sideways now, he could almost see her lying in the dust of the road below, her clothing in disarray, her bosom heaving in remorse and fear, her eyes turned toward him in supplication. He could almost see her lifting her hands to him, catching hold of his robes, pitifully pulling herself close to his body, pressing her detestable warmth against him.

It was then that Martin gave a great shout and, rising, began to pull off his own garments. In a moment he stood naked under the blazing sun, stomping up and down and crying wordlessly to the heavens. In this state, he considered, he might romp in the pure innocence of Eden, undefiled by the skins of lustful beasts, unhampered in his sheer pulsing desire to be at one with nature and the hum and slide of the universe. Looking afar, he could no longer clearly see the women although he could still faintly make out that something moved along the trail in the distance, raising a pale puff of smoky dust. Suddenly he was consumed with a wish to see them again and, leaping from boulder to ledge to slant of ground, he clambered down to the trail and began to run after the women. "They toil not," he screamed, "neither do they spin, and yet Solomon in all his glory was not arrayed—"

At that moment Martin came to a full stop and over his browned face there came an expression of horror. His eyes glared fiercely at the horizon and then at the sky and then down at his wiry body, and at that moment he began to writhe as well as to claw at the flesh of his stomach and thighs with his fingernails. His mind a tornado of lust and sensitivity to the blueness of the sky, the warmth of the sun on his body, the lazy grace of a passing vulture, the soft lavender of the distant mountains, he sobbed half-words of prayer and tender carnal sentiment.

After a while a smile came over his features, although his eyes were still wet with tears, for he knew now for the first time in a long time what he had to do. There were the long, seemingly endless hours and days of fasting and prayer and doubt and then there came the blinding moments of certainty and strength. This was one of them. Turning away from the women, he ran back toward his home among the rocks, toward his meager cache of belongings, his walking stick, his water bag, his extra sandals, his outer cloak, and his knife.

"Oh, yes," he cried, "it has been made clear to me. The Scripture tells me plainly." He laughed triumphantly as his body slithered whitely up the low hill. Once, as he fell, broken desert rocks scraped his pale skin cruelly. He suffered the pain with a feeling of glory and threw himself headlong again that he might again be tortured. A worthy sentiment, he considered, but it was only delaying the supreme act, the culmination of all his years of prayer and trial.

He had sinned, clearly and beyond question of doubt, in thinking

of the woman. His mind had been delirious with pleasure at the idea
of her nearness and his body had contorted and wrestled with itself in
a frenzy of guilt and excitement. There remained nothing now but to
complete the act, to solve the problem, expiate his sin, drop the
curtain on his drama.

Another moment and he knelt trembling, reaching into the
shadow of the stone that protected his few belongings. The knife was
partly rusty and its sharpness left something to be desired, but it
would serve. It would have to. Destiny could not be delayed.

"If thy right hand offend thee," Martin shouted to the silent
desert, "cut it off!"

At that he knelt and placed his right forearm against a round
stone. Thanking heaven that he was left-handed and could bring his
entire strength therefore to bear, he jabbed the point into his right
wrist and then brought the blade flat against the arm and pressed
down as firmly as he could, shouting the while to distract his
concentration from the pain. Surprisingly, there was very little. The
job was done more readily than he had expected and when at last
he had fulfilled the letter of the law he stood naked, staring up into
the blank, terrible, cloudless blue of the universe, blood pouring from
the end of his arm, turning his head from side to side, looking up the
way a child might stand in its crib after a fright in the dark, looking
longingly for a parent to enter, to pick it up, to comfort it and offer it
the love that comes from strength.

"I HOPE
I'M NOT INTRUDING"

■ ■ ■

The first inkling they had was when the woman at the other table held the hand of the man who had just stood up. "Don't tell me," they heard him say, freeing his hand, and then he began to walk toward them.

"Oh, God," Gus said, "here we go again."

As he approached, walking with that great dignity that only the slightly intoxicated are able to muster, the man smiled thinly. When he reached their table he stood stiffly, waiting to be addressed. They all kept their heads down and began talking again.

"I don't see that the dress itself mattered so much," Gus said. "It's just that we discussed the whole thing yesterday. I *told* her she looked better in something tight and clinging, ya know? And so tonight, wham, here she comes back again with the same dress that started the trouble."

"I didn't think it was the *same* dress," Gordon said.

"Well, if it wasn't it photographed the same, so my point is still good."

"You say you mentioned it to her?" Gordon's wife said.

"Sure," Gus said. "After the show the other night we had coffee. I did like twenty minutes on the dress bit and she says fine, she'll take care of it, and then tonight we're right back where we started from."

"We should have caught it in rehearsal," Gordon said.

"Oh, I noticed it all right," Gus said, "but I didn't want to bother you while you were busy, and then too sometimes she'll rehearse in one dress and work in another, ya know?"

129

"Excuse me," said the man standing in the aisle. They all looked up and pretended to be surprised that he was there. He looked about forty-five, Mid-western, well-to-do. His suit was gray, conservative. His glasses were rimless. He looked like a speaker at a Kiwanis luncheon. He did not appear to be at all embarrassed.

"Excuse me," he repeated, "I hope I'm not intruding."

"Not at all," said Gordon.

There was a pause.

"Gordon Lester?"

"That's right," Gordon said, feeling for his fountain pen automatically. Perhaps an autograph would . . .

"I saw your show tonight."

"That's fine," Gus said. "Just fine. We hope you enjoyed it. Now, anyway, Ruth, when I told Billie she ought to get down to see Florence Lustig or somebody about some dresses, why, she thought—"

"I'm from Baltimore," the man said.

Gus stopped talking and looked at him. "All right," he said.

Gordon and Ruth put their heads down and concentrated on their scrambled eggs. Gus looked vainly for the headwaiter.

"Saw the show tonight at the hotel," the man said. "On TV, that is."

"Was there something we could do for you?" Gordon said.

"Why, no, nothing in particular," the man said, "although there *is* something I'd like to talk to you about. My wife and I watch the program all the time and I—listen, I hope I'm not intruding or anything."

"It isn't that," Gus said, "but if it's a business matter or something, Mr. Lester would be happy to have you get in touch with him at the office."

"Oh, I don't want to bother anybody during working hours," the man said. Then he turned and pulled an empty chair toward the table. "May I sit down?" he said.

Ruth stared at Gordon helplessly. Gus pursed his lips. "Certainly," he said.

"Fine," the man said, seating himself. "I'm from Baltimore. Arnold's the name. J. K. Arnold."

Gus nodded.

"Your name?" the man said.

"Mr. Werner," Gus said.

"Have a little proposition for you," the man said.

"Fine," Gus said, taking out a pencil, writing a number on a piece of paper. "Look, this is the number at the office. Give us a call any time after one in the afternoon. Be happy to talk to you."

"Tell you the truth," the man said, "I'm leaving in the morning. Besides, you fellas probably have enough to do putting your shows together without me taking up your time. Here's my card."

"Thank you," Gus said, taking it.

"Yes, sir," said the man. "We get a mighty big kick out of your program there, Mr. Lester. A *mighty* big kick. I tell my wife I'll divorce her if she doesn't stop staying up every night to watch you, but she says she don't care. She just loves that damn program. Tell you the truth, she loves it a darn sight more'n I do. Meaning no offense, you understand, but some nights are better than others."

Ruth bristled, putting down her fork.

"Gordon," she said, "have you heard from Agnes?"

"Why, no," Gordon said. "Just that letter we got around Christmas. Nothing since."

"That's funny," Ruth said. "She's usually very good about writing."

"Say, listen," said Arnold, "I'm not interrupting anything here, am I? I mean I came over here on a business proposition."

Gus leaped at the bait.

"Fine," he said. "Then you just give us a call at this number any afternoon after about one or one-thirty and I'll be happy to take care of you. I'm Mr. Lester's manager."

"Oh, yeah?" said the man.

"That's right."

"Well, that's all right," the man said, "except for the little fact that I happen to be leaving town in the morning. But I'll get right down to business here. I've got an idea that I think you might be very, *very* interested in, Mr. Lester."

"Thank you," Gordon said, because he could not think of anything else to say.

"We watch you every night down there, by God," the man said. "You're a much younger-lookin' fella than I thought you were, judging from TV, I mean. It don't do you justice."

"Thank you," Gordon said.

"No, sir," the man said. "On TV you look kinda fat, but in person you look a lot better."

Ruth turned, craning her neck trying to catch the attention of a captain.

There was a pause.

"You were saying something about a business matter," Gus said softly.

"Oh, yes," the man said. "That's what I wanted to talk to you folks about, but I certainly didn't want to intrude on your little gathering here."

They all looked at their plates.

"It's just," the man continued, "that I don't think you TV fellas ever look down your nose at a little commercial business, do you?"

"No," Gus said.

"Well, fine and dandy," the man said, "because that's the area I'm talking in."

"Maybe you'd better take it up with the network," Gordon said, "if it's that sort of thing. We just *do* the program, we don't *sell* it."

"Maybe *you'd* better take it up with the network," the man said, showing the first sign of truculence. He withdrew another card from his vest. "My card," he said, handing it to Gus.

"You already gave me one," Gus said.

"That's all right," the man said. "All the better."

Ruth gasped with audible impatience.

"Like I say," the man said, "I'll be leaving in the morning but I'll be at the Waldorf till about eleven-thirty. I think it might be a very good idea if you boys had the network call me about this little matter."

"All right," Gus said.

"I mean, I don't want to impose or anything, but you fellas are in the same kinda business we're all in, aren't you? The business of making a buck?"

"That's right," Gus said.

At this admission the man evidenced vast satisfaction. "Well, then," he chuckled, "you just have them call J. K. Arnold in the morning at the Waldorf and everything'll be just fine. Got a few ideas that might help that program of yours, Gordon-boy."

He rose to his feet, swaying slightly.

"My apologies," he said grandly, "to the lady. Mrs. Lester, is it?"

Ruth smiled confirmation.

"Fine," he said. "Very happy to meet you. See you TV or movie fellas out with a pretty girl, ya don't know *whose* wife it might be."

At this moment Ruth happened to catch the eye of the head-waiter. She looked at him sternly, then nodded toward Arnold. The waiter made an apologetic face, stepping forward.

"May I help you, sir?" he said to Arnold.

"No, you may not," the man answered. "I was talking to my friends here."

"All right," said Gus, getting as much finality into his voice as possible. "Thanks for the information. You'll hear from us."

"You know Gordon Lester?" Arnold suddenly demanded of the captain.

"Certainly, sir."

"Well, take good care of him and his friends here. They're all right. Ol' Gordon ain't the *funniest* guy on television, but he *does* have the prettiest wife."

Laughing softly, Arnold retreated.

Gus carefully tore his two cards into small pieces.

Back at his table Arnold addressed his wife rudely. "Come on, Sal. Let's hit the road."

"Sit down till the check comes," his wife said. "I hope you didn't bother them over there."

"Bother?" Arnold said. "Are you joking? Nobody is ever bothered when you offer 'em a chance to make a buck. Say, that reminds me, I gotta go back there and get Lester's autograph for the kids."

"Jack, sit down, will you?"

"All right. All right. I'll sit down. Say, captain."

"Yes, sir?"

"Tell Mr. Lester to step over here on his way out, will ya? I want to get his autograph for my niece and nephew."

THE STRANGERS

■ ■ ■

We are all shocked and made unhappy if we see a jackal devour a rabbit, yet at this moment white teeth are sinking into furtive fur and tearing panicked flesh in all the jungles of the world and we are unaffected by the knowledge.

We wince if we hear that in the saloon on the next block a man was cut with a knife, but across the world men are daily cut to pieces and we are unmoved. Distance lends unreality.

We teach that our mothers and fathers must be honored and we honor them not. We are accustomed to coveting our neighbors' goods and our neighbors' wives. We are not even certain which day *is* the Sabbath day, hence we have difficulty keeping it holy. We find it, ordinarily, impossible to fall in love with God. All of us make something of a habit of bearing false witness against our neighbor. One of the rare occasions on which we will not bear false witness against him is when we are able to broadcast some damaging truth about him.

Those of us who do not commit adultery are almost without exception those who have not the opportunity. The rest are largely those who have not the inclination.

We say it is wrong to kill, but we kill cockroaches and pigs and hamsters and daffodils and burglars and Jews and Negroes and intruders and time and initiative and joy or anything that is convenient for us to kill.

Two of us pulled into a gas station outside of Indio, California, one day in late summer. It was about two days after Dan Scanlon had left New York.

The two were Mormons: Homer Snow and his wife Betsy. They

135

had been visiting with Betsy's relatives in San Diego for three weeks and now they were driving back across the desert on their way to their home in Provo, Utah.

Homer was a bishop in his church but he was also a dentist. The title *bishop* does not mean quite the same thing to the Church of Jesus Christ of the Latter-day Saints that it means to the other churches of Christendom, so it was not unusual that Homer wore no ecclesiastical robes and that he pulled teeth and also sold a little insurance on the side.

The Mormons are a thrifty and respectable people and Homer had saved a considerable amount of money during the twenty-four years he had been married to Betsy. He owned the two-story building in Provo in which he had set up his professional offices, and since his time was largely his own he was able each year to take a month's vacation.

He was as rangily tall and easygoing as his wife was small and shrewish. And yet, for all his good nature and for all her calculating determination, Homer was the boss and Betsy meekly did his bidding.

They had raised four children, put them through high school and college, and seen them all happily married. One of the girls had taken a job in Dallas and married a semi-Baptist and fallen away from the church, but this was the only black mark on the Snow's religious record.

They were well liked in Provo and though they had accumulated some riches and learned a fair amount about the rest of the world, they clung tenaciously to their faith and observed all its admonitions and restrictions. They did not drink coffee, tea, or Coca-Cola and Betsy had never tasted liquor of any kind, although once in a great while if Homer happened to be out of town alone and among strangers he would take a drink.

They had a large radio in their front room and they subscribed to *Time*, *Collier's*, and *Reader's Digest*, yet they still believed that Christ would return in bodily form to the earth during their lifetime.

During the war they had stored away vast quantities of canned peaches, pears, Spam, Florida orange juice, flour (in glass jars), blackberry jam, peas, baked beans, applesauce, soups, and pineapple, for the church had passed along the word that a famine might soon fall upon the land and that the Saints would therefore do well to provide themselves with as many of the edible necessities as they thought would store well without spoiling. There was some embarrassment among the faithful when Washington let it be known that to hoard was unpatriotic; but by simply not thinking about the conflict of interests, very often most of the Saints were able to go about their business and do whatever else they could to help the war effort.

Homer got along quite well with the non-Mormon members of his community, although he could not abide the Catholics because of their conceit and their belief that they were the one, true fold.

Of all the non-Mormons he had met and discussed religion with, only the Catholics seemed to have a faith as strong as his own. He attributed their success and their alarming increase to the direct help of Satan, although he often thanked God that Utah was still largely a Mormon state. He was alarmed about the problem of communism but he was secretly pleased about the war between Moscow and Rome. He considered that it was the will of God that two such powerful forces for evil should expend so much of their energy against each other.

Stopped now outside of Indio, he hooked the scratched bronze nozzle of a water hose over the mouth of the open radiator of his 1951 Dodge. A faint wisp of steam issued from the open pipe, and as he leaned over to look down its length the smell of hot oil assailed his nostrils.

"Help you?" said the station attendant.

"Yes," Homer said. "Give me five regular."

The attendant moved around to the back of the car as Homer sprayed the honeycombed radiator front with water to wash away the bugs and cool off the motor.

"Want to get out and stretch your legs?" he said to Betsy.

"No," she said. "I'm all right." Scattered bits of hair stuck wetly to the back of her neck and she fanned vaguely at her chest with a limp handkerchief, but Homer had known that she would not get out of the car and go into the station to keep cool. Betsy enjoyed being a martyr, and Homer was so used to her attitude by now that he would have been emotionally jarred if she had suddenly changed. She had sacrificed much to raise her children, had learned to sew exceptionally well to save money on clothing, and had seen to it that the children had had many of the "advantages" that she had been denied. It never occurred to her that, now that the children were out on their own and she and Homer had more than enough money, she no longer had any need to deny herself.

She wore no make-up, she had never owned a fur coat, she

mended her own stockings, and she had never taken a penny from any of the children.

She sat primly, looking out at the dry desert foliage and the empty, hot sky. Homer had lowered the hood of the car and she could look straight ahead again. Heat waves wrinkled and waved the objects that she regarded, lizardlike, through the windshield, and after a few moments her eyelids became heavy and she dozed slightly sitting there in her mussed lavender cotton-print dress.

She had not slept well the night before in the motel in Pasadena. She had wanted to stay at a hotel, but Homer had preferred the convenience and the savings that a motor-court stop represented.

All night long cars had whispered by on the highway outside. She had lain in the twin bed by the window, tossing and turning and muttering, "Goodness," and "Land."

She finally had fallen asleep shortly after midnight and thereafter awakened fully only twice, but when she had gotten up in the morning she had groaned and said, "I didn't sleep a wink. Not one wink."

"You snored," Homer said.

"I did not," she said, walking into the too-small bathroom.

Lying in his underwear in the unfamiliar bed, listening to her washing her face and flushing the toilet, Homer had known a flicker of desire and had felt himself briefly. Sitting on the side of the bed he thought for a moment of Sarah, his receptionist, for it had been at least ten years since he had actively desired his wife, and though Sarah was married he still could not keep himself from looking at her sometimes as she moved efficiently about the office.

Fortunately for his peace of mind, desire came upon him very rarely. He stood now, scratching his stomach and yawning and said, "It's only eight-thirty. I thought it was later."

"Time we were on our way," Betsy said.

"Remind me to pick up some postcards for Davey later, will you?"

"Yes. We can get them when we stop for breakfast."

Homer had little use for Betsy's people in San Diego but he loved his nephew, Davey Udall. Davey was five years old and blond and affectionate, and Homer made it a point to send him a little postcard message now and then. In San Diego or "Dago," as Homer rakishly learned to call it, he would take Davey for long rides or for walks along the waterfront. They would stop and talk to men fishing and Homer would buy Davey ice-cream cones and tell him stories about Utah.

Pulling out of the gas station, he kept the car in second gear.

"Why are you driving so slowly?" Betsy said.

"Looking for a place to buy postcards," Homer said.

He saw another gas station joined to a grocery and novelty store and pulled the car off the highway and up into the shaded gravel near the building.

In a moment he was back in the car, smiling.

"Got some nice ones," he said. "One with a little Indian boy riding a jackass."

"That's nice," Betsy said.

They drove along the highway at slightly more than sixty miles an hour, not speaking. Occasionally a car would whip past them, edging Homer over to the right a bit, and he would shake his head and say, "Crazy fool," or "I hope he gets there on time."

That night they stopped in Phoenix at the home of Homer's brother, Joe. Joe was older than Homer by four years, and he ran a used-car lot.

"Why don't you folks stay over a few more days?" Joe said the next morning, standing on his front lawn, leaning against their car.

"Oh, you know," Homer said. "Betsy's anxious to get back and everything. We'd like to, but I'm afraid we'll have to wait till next time around."

They had an appointment anyway.

"Well, take care of yourselves," Joe said, backing off and waving, stooped-over, as Homer gunned the motor gently.

"You too," Betsy said, waving a loose hand.

"Write," Joe said.

"You bet," Homer called back.

There were mirages before Homer on the highway now as he sped north out of Phoenix. Dips in the road ahead appeared to be full of water and the numbing heat of the desert pressed down upon the car, made the motor run hot, and dried the throats of Homer and Betsy.

They felt sleepy and Homer turned on the radio. He tried to find a newscast but there seemed to be nothing on but cowboy or jazz music and interminable commercials. Betsy flicked a button and silence filled the car, broken only by the steady hum of the tires on the hot pavement.

"Just a little love," sang Homer, "a little kiss. I would give you all my life for this . . ."

Shortly thereafter, about the time Homer ran over a rabbit, Dan was turning off Highway 66 and pushing his car steadily toward Phoenix. He had been on the road for three days and he was nervous and jumpy.

The first night out of New York he had driven on the Pennsylvania Turnpike and got lost for over an hour trying to get out of Pittsburgh.

A stupid gas-station mechanic had given him the wrong directions just before an important junction, and he had found himself getting deeper and deeper into the Allegheny hills above Pittsburgh, on a narrow road that became more desolate with each passing mile.

Below him in the valleys strange flames glowed in the night and layers of blue smoke hung thickly over the landscape.

Irritably he screeched to a stop and shouted to a boy on a bicycle, "Is this the way to Wheeling?"

"No, *sir*," the boy said, laughing.

"Goddammit," Dan shouted, whipping the car around. "Son-of-a-bitch!" He had driven at least twenty-five miles out of Pittsburgh and now, on the way back to town, traffic unaccountably piled up in front of him and he could not make time. He drove all night to make up for the delay and did not sleep until almost noon the next day.

When he woke up in the dingy motel in the small West Virginia town, he felt dizzy and sick to his stomach. A shave and shower picked him up, but he was disgusted to see that it was after six o'clock and already beginning to get dark.

He drove all night again, squinting at the lights of oncoming cars, stopping now and then to drink a Coke or have a hamburger and coffee while the car was being filled with gasoline.

At first he had eaten good steaks and heavy desserts and tipped lavishly, but now as he stood under the dim neon-blue light of a tiny gas station in Missouri, counting his money, he was startled to observe that there were only thirty-nine dollars in his wallet.

He thereafter ate less expensive food and began taking peanuts and packaged cookies with him in the car and using regular instead of ethyl gasoline.

He stayed at the cheapest motels he could find and counted his money again and again and finally figured out that he had lost a twenty-dollar bill somewhere along the way.

Now and then he would pass hitchhikers standing like patient statues along the road or under lamp posts at lonely intersections. Some fear made him refuse to pick them up. It was strange. Now that he was a motorist, now that he had money (somewhere, if not in his pocket), now that he had a big car with shiny exterior and a powerful motor, now that he rode like a baron unarmed in a strange forest, he was not inclined to stop or to think of how his speeding past affected the stolid, lonely people who stood with thumbs lifted by the side of the road.

He had possessions and he did not want to risk them. It was just one minor example, but it illustrated perfectly the difficulty of being truly Christian.

It was the same old thing: the truth and the exception. The ideal and the expediency.

He listened on the car radio to a disc jockey playing Stan Kenton records and passed lonely figures in the night.

He had been a hitchhiker once and had stood angrily in gutters and beside ditches. He could still remember the feeling, still recall vividly muttering threats and orders at passing cars. Hitchhikers, he thought, with their veiled shoutings and demands, were like poets who are forever standing on verbal hilltops with their shirts open, shouting instructions to the elements:

"Roll on, thou deep and dark blue ocean, roll!"

"Blow, blow thou wintry wind!"

"Stop, you mother-grabber, stop for me!"

He saw himself clearly, standing by the highway in Arkansas (or had it been Texas?), when he had run away from home years before.

Standing by the side of the road, he alternately prayed and swore as car after car passed him by. Sometimes after half-a-hundred cars had gone by, tires whining on the pavement, he would make little efforts toward improving his appearance. People were afraid of hitchhikers. Perhaps he looked too dirty, too threatening. He removed his hat, folded it flat, and shoved it up under his sweater, along one side. Then he took out his broken comb and combed his hair. His handkerchief was wrinkled and filthy, but he rubbed it on his face to remove some of the dirt. There was a chill in the air and his jacket was zipped up tight under his chin, but it would be better, he thought, if it were open at the neck and neatly folded back at the collar to show a little of his shirt. With the zipper lowered a few inches the air lay cold on his neck, but he knew that he looked a little better, a little less threatening. Without the hat more of his face was visible and as cars approached now he smiled, tried to look innocent, harmless, friendly, casual.

A car was approaching and he slicked down his hair with one last pat, then moved out onto the road to make sure the driver could see him. He opened his eyes and smiled idiotically as he lifted his right hand. The car did not slow down.

The rush of air as the car hurtled past made his eyes water, and a sudden rush of anger forced the corners of his mouth down.

"Lousy son-of-a-bitch!" he said, looking at the disappearing rectangle that grew smaller far down the highway. "Lousy son-of-a-bitch!"

After a moment his anger subsided, but a feeling of sullen resentment remained. To hell with all the people with cars, the lousy, selfish bastards! It wouldn't cost any of them a cent to stop and give him a lift. No skin off their noses, the selfish bastards. He wished he had a gun. It would be great to give the next bastard that came along a good square chance to stop. Wave at him nice and friendly and show him the old thumb, and then if he didn't stop whip out the gun and blast the son-of-a-bitch off the road.

His mouth turned down again as he fancied himself pumping bullets into the back of a car, the back of the driver's head, seeing the vehicle careen and wobble off the road, seeing it turn over and burst into flame. The dirty, lousy bastards. It would serve them right. If he had a car he'd be glad to stop for them. Why wouldn't they show him the same courtesy? What the hell; they weren't any better than he was. Lousy hillbillies, they weren't as *good* as he was. Who the hell wanted to ride in their goddammed rattle-traps anyway? All he wanted was to get the hell out of that neck of the woods for good!

He zipped his jacket up tight under his chin again. Why the hell should he catch cold to please a bunch of stupid hillbillies?

He walked along for a while, disdaining to even turn and face the cars that continued to speed past him. For perhaps twenty minutes he stalked along, kicking at rusty beer cans and stones, muttering epithets.

The throaty, grinding rumble of a truck sounded behind him distantly and he turned, feeling hope again in the instant. Some truck drivers shrugged apologetically, pointing to the "No Riders" sign pasted on their windshields. They seemed like nice guys and it wasn't their fault if they weren't allowed by their companies to pick up hitchhikers. Others just didn't give you a tumble and they could go to hell. But a lot of them stopped. Truck drivers, mostly, were good guys. Maybe this one would stop.

He stepped out onto the road and lifted his hand, his head cocked eagerly, his ears tuned to pick up the slightest change in the roar of the motor that might indicate that the truck was slackening speed. It seemed to be a giant Mack, he thought, as it loomed larger.

He peered intently at the cab, wavered, then condescended to wear the simpering smile again, trying to see the driver, establish contact, read his expression.

For a moment he could tell the man at the wheel had lifted his foot from the accelerator and then, miraculously, the juggernaut was slowing down. His heart leaped up and his smile was genuine as he trotted up to the side door. Two Negroes regarded him without expression through the open window.

"How far you goin'?" one of them said.

"As far as you are," he answered.

"Okay," said the driver. "You can ride in back." He trotted to the back of the truck and pulled himself up. The back was walled and deep like that of a coal truck, but when his eyes reached the level of the rim he saw it was piled high with what looked like dirty cotton.

As the driver gunned the motor tentatively, he flung himself over the tail of the truck and sank deep into the cloudy pile of fiber.

"Hey," he shouted at the men in the cab, clambering forward, "what is this stuff?"

"Cotton seed," shouted the man next to the driver. The rest of his words were drowned out by the grinding of the motor as the truck gathered speed again.

Riding in the back, he squirmed around till he was spread-eagled, his face to the sky, luxuriating in the resilient softness of the load of fiber-stuck cotton seeds. The drone of the motor, the yellow-streaked, late-afternoon clouds, and the blue of the sky were all he could sense of the world as he stretched and lolled on his magic carpet. The air was still chilled but he did not care, snuggled in the cotton. He wished that he could ride thus forever and he felt guilty at the bitterness that had been in his heart. This was really beautiful country and from his royal vantage point he now surveyed the Southern sky and the tips and branches of trees with a warm and appreciative feeling. He drunkenly reveled in the comfort that had fallen his lot, turning over on his stomach, flexing his muscles, yawning loudly, rolling onto his back again to lose himself in the bare, limitless beauty of the sky. For perhaps a quarter of an hour he lay like a drunken oriental potentate till, literally overcome by comfort, he relaxed completely and slept.

Recalling the feeling of warmth now, he smiled sleepily and reflected with slight sadness over the passing of youth's ability to appreciate pleasure in its own peculiar, delicious, rawly sensitive way.

But still he did not pick up any hitchhikers. Perhaps it was just as well.

Coming through Oklahoma he was eating more peanuts, drinking more Cokes and chocolate milk, and eating less real food. The money problem now was acute. He considered stopping and wiring ahead to Helen for money, but that would have meant waiting for twelve or eighteen hours in some out-of-the-way spot while she answered him, and so at last he decided to gamble on making the money last.

That night he did not go to a motel at all but slept in the car, twisted stiffly on the front seat. Actually it was after dawn when he pulled off the road and stopped and curled up and went to sleep. When he awakened his mouth felt bone-dry and bitter.

He had had a dream about Elaine and as he began to clear the shrouds of sleep from his brain, he tried to remember what he had been dreaming about.

It had seemed that he had been walking with her by a body of water, perhaps an ocean. They had walked along, hand in hand, on broken, furrowed earth that fell away and sloped down sharply, among rocks, to the water line.

He had stepped out onto the rocks and then been terrified to see that the water was washing the dirt away from among them. He was at last left high and dry on one tall, thin columnar rock that teetered in unstable sections beneath him. Elaine was somewhere near and he recalled having tried to hold her to him, put his arms around her, and to put his hands on her body, but then she had receded and he had been terror-stricken again at the precariousness of his position.

When he was fully awake the memory of the dream left him, although he was left with a quivering, early-morning desire for a woman.

He pulled himself up to a sitting position and sat half dazed with his eyes closed, trying to pull himself together.

He looked at his wrist-watch and discovered that he had slept only a little over three hours. It was fully fifteen minutes before he could summon up enough energy to step out of the car and flex his muscles.

The morning air felt cool and refreshing on his face, and to stir up the blood in his head he rubbed his cheeks and chin vigorously with both hands, feeling the beard stubble sliding under his fingers.

His mouth was sour and he spat again and again and inhaled deeply to clear it out. With trembling fingers he took a package of gum out of his pants pocket and put two pieces in his mouth. The sugar was immediately sucked into his system and helped a little to wake him up more completely and the flavoring in the gum made him less displeased with his mouth.

Cars slipped by at long intervals in the cool morning air, and he waited for a few minutes till the horizon was clear on all sides, then stepped away from the car a short distance and urinated, shivering.

When he got back behind the wheel of the car seemed hot and stuffy again, for the sun was well up in the sky and beginning to burn off the cold air that had accumulated on the desert during the night.

Half an hour later he stopped at a roadside market and bought a pound of juicy purple grapes for breakfast.

He also stopped for gas and washed his face with cold water, and when he got back in the car he was whistling a little, although he was still very tired.

For three days he had tried not to think of what he would have to do when he got to Los Angeles. At times he would think of the prospect of marrying Elaine and settling things once and for all and he would feel excited and happy, but then after a few minutes he would begin to worry and wonder about what Helen would say and what the children's reactions might be and he began to wonder how he would break the news to his mother.

Then he would turn on the radio and try to become absorbed in a newscast or a soap opera.

Although he was hurrying to Elaine, things had not, it seemed, changed so much after all, and the knowledge saddened him.

He had left New York in a mood of some defiance and conviction, but he had not been able to sustain the bravado, and now he could pull it back only by fits and starts. Sometimes a simple physical longing for Helen would overcome him and he found that he was able to convert the feeling into a sort of strength, a sort of armor for the battle that he feared lay ahead.

"Perhaps," he said to himself, "when I get there Elaine will tell me she loves someone else. I'll feel bad for a while, but then maybe that will make everything all right and I can go back to Helen."

Then the squirrel cage would begin turning again, and pros and cons would tumble back and forth in his mind so rapidly that he could not get them into any sort of order at all.

But some of the time he had the idea in his mind that he was going out to Los Angeles to marry Elaine and he felt pretty good about the whole thing.

After all, Helen was happy with Randy. Maybe everything would be all right.

He began driving faster now on the road coming south toward Phoenix, although parts of the road were twisted and dangerous. His brain felt numb again and he began to get drowsy, but at each possible stop he would step down hard on the accelerator and say, "Just a little farther and then I'll pull up." For perhaps twenty-five miles he pushed himself past stop after stop, thinking each time that the next place would be more inviting. Once he found himself slowed to a crawl by two giant trailer-trucks that were held to a snail's pace by a slight incline in the highway.

He tried to pass them, but the road ahead was either curved or blocked by oncoming cars, so at last he settled down to the speed of the trucks and crept along behind them, frustrated and furious for several minutes.

Finally an opportunity opened up and he swept past the two juggernauts and resumed his former high speed.

The road wound its way into mountainous country now and he was glad, for the flat land made for monotonous driving. He blinked to clear his head and rest his eyes and began holding the steering wheel more firmly as fatigue assailed him again.

Shortly after noon he began talking to himself and said, "Go just fifteen more minutes and then stop at the very next place you come to. You have to stop and go to the toilet, rest, and have something else to eat."

He nodded, by way of agreeing with his decision, and began going just a bit faster so as to squeeze the last possible mile out of the time limit he had set for himself.

The speedometer needle now showed that he was traveling between seventy and eighty miles an hour, although he did not realize he was going that fast. The car handled beautifully and hugged the road well on the long, gradual curves that unfolded before him through the mountains.

The scenery was striking, although because of his fatigue he appreciated it only rather dimly. The sky was desert-blue, cloudless, and hot, and the mountains were clearly etched in great, jagged, purplish masses against its background. Close by the road stately saguaros loomed out of the desert floor, and a million heavy rocks lay baking at the foot of the mountains from the surfaces of which they had been wrested by time and gravity.

The vistas were so far-reaching, the distances over which the eye could sweep so vast, that it seemed to Dan, when he looked away from the road, that he was crawling at a pallbearer's pace and would never cover the long, wild, empty stretch to the next mountain range.

In the mountains now there was much static on the radio and he finally could not stand to listen to it.

In Los Angeles at that moment Helen was bathing the baby, kneeling beside the tub in the front bathroom, saying, "That's it, sweetheart. Close your eyes while Mama gets the soap off your face and then we'll have a niiiccee nap, won't we?"

Randy was at a Safeway store, shopping for the week's groceries, and Michael and Patrick were with him, helping push the wheeled basket down the aisles, asking him to buy Wheaties so they could send in the box top with a quarter and get a magic-code ring.

In Beverly Hills Elaine was having lunch with her mother, sitting in the kitchen, wearing a slightly soiled pink housecoat, saying, "Who called early this morning?"

"I think it was Jack whatshisname," her mother said. "He said he was only going to be in town for two days. I told him you'd call back. He's at the Ambassador."

"Thanks," Elaine said, pouring herself a second cup of coffee.

Dan was holding the car steadily on the road now, his mind numbly calm, almost happy. He was wondering if the next stop would be a good place to eat. The fifteen-minute period was almost over.

He shook his head once to throw the dark specter of sleep out of his brain, and then began squinting carefully, trying to drive with his eyes half closed and his head tilted back so that he could see the road quite clearly under the lids. He felt warm and relaxed. As he was coming up out of a slight dip in the road his head nodded, forced down as the car climbed the incline out of the dip, and it was then that the other car bore down upon him. He did not know that he was driving in the center of the road, straddling the white line, and he was never to know it.

His speed did not slacken, but the driver of the other car jammed down violently on his brakes and grabbed the steering wheel hard when he saw Dan's Buick dead ahead.

The other car started to pull away to its right, but it was too late to help; the autos hit together, not exactly head on, for the other car had angled itself a little to one side, but with tremendous force nevertheless.

The top of Dan's head hit the windshield squarely and his chest was pushed back against the seat, driven back by the steering wheel which buckled in his hands and lifted his legs off the floorboard, breaking them.

The man in the other car was thrown against his windshield at a slight angle and his steering wheel hit him a glancing blow, breaking his arms. The woman beside him was dashed into the windshield as forcibly as if she had been shot out of a cannon, She died in the instant.

Lizards and rabbits and buzzards scuttled in terror among the hills as the deafening roar of the impact echoed across the desert floor and bounced back off the mountain walls.

The Buick stopped almost squarely where it had been hit, twisted halfway around so that it was facing off the side of the road; the other car rolled over three times and came to rest among the cactus and tumbleweed that edged the highway. It lay on its right side a full thirty-five yards from the Buick, and when steam stopped pouring from its radiator an ominous silence fell over the scene, broken only by the soft whipping of the wind as it slipped among the desert brush.

Three minutes later a Pontiac with Michigan license plates stopped and a man got out and looked first at the Buick and then at the other car.

He walked fearfully over to the Buick and looked in.

"Holy God," he said and then broke into a run and got back in his car and raced off at high speed. Not far down the road he skidded to a stop at a gas station. Leaving the door of his car open, he ran into the station, knocking down a little girl who was playing by the door.

"I'm sorry, sweetheart," he said, picking her up. "Listen, is there a phone here?"

"Yes," said a tanned elderly man with short-cropped white hair. "What's the matter?"

"There's been an accident. An awful one. Right back up the road. You better get help, quick."

"Lord, God," said the elderly man, stepping out quickly from behind a counter, "that's the second one this month."

He took the phone off the hook and spoke loudly into the mouthpiece when he had gotten an operator on the line.

"Get the highway police, quick," he said. "Another accident up the road here. Yeah, this is Charley. Tell'em where, will you? Wait a minute." He turned to the man at the door. "Where was it? North or south of here? I didn't notice which way you drove up."

"Up that way," said the man, pointing, "Oooh, it was awful."

"How many people?" asked the old man, hanging up the phone.

"I don't know," said the other. "I only looked at one of the cars. That's all I had to do."

"It's awful," said the old man. "Just awful. Makes you kind of sick."

"Yes, it does," said the younger man and suddenly he ran outside and went behind the building and vomited.

After a few minutes he went into the station washroom and rinsed out his mouth, and then felt the need for a pickup and went back inside and had a bottle of root beer.

In a few minutes a highway patrol car whined past the station at great speed.

"There they go," said the old man.

"What happened?" asked the child.

"Nothing, honey," the old man said. "You go on and play. Your ma'll be back soon."

Another car stopped outside and a man and woman got out and walked briskly into the station.

"Has somebody called an ambulance?" the new man asked.

"Yes," said the proprietor. "It's all taken care of. The highway patrol just went out."

"We just saw them," said the woman, "but they'll need an ambulance, too."

"Must be one on the way," the old man said. "They got a radio in the police car."

"Oh, dear," said the woman. "What a sight."

"Yes," said the man from Michigan, "it was awful. I saw it a few minutes ago. Awful." He screwed up his face at the memory.

"Don't know what people mean, driving fast," said the old man.

"It's just awful," the man from Michigan repeated.

"You want to go back there, honey?" the new man said to the woman who stood behind him.

"No," she said, shuddering. "No, sir!"

"All right," he said. "Let's move on."

"Good-by," the old man said. "Thanks for stopping in."

"All right," said the new man as he left, closing the door.

"Just last month," the old man said. "One of them big trucks. Burned right up. Now this. I don't know what's going on these days."

"Yes, it's awful," said the man from Michigan. "Makes you sick."

Back at the scene of the wreck a dozen cars had stopped and pulled off the road. The highway patrolmen had put out flares and a small red flag. Some of the passing drivers were out in the road in their shirt sleeves, ready to wave off on-coming traffic, willing to help if they could. Women sat in several of the cars, fearful.

"Looks like a head-on," one of the patrolmen said to the other.

"Yep. I've called for the ambulance. May take a few minutes."

The taller of the two took out a pad and pencil and began making notes.

"The Buick has New York plates," he said. "What's on the other car?"

"Utah plates," his companion said.

"A mess for the families, handling it long distance."

"Yeah."

"They all dead?"

"Pretty sure. This guy is, that's for certain. And the woman looks done for. Might be a chance for the driver of the Dodge, but I doubt it."

"Son-of-a-bitch," said the tall patrolman, shaking his head from side to side. "What can you do?"

"Yep," said his companion. "All right, you people there, keep over to the side. Over! Over! We've got to keep traffic moving through here, goddammit!"

"What happened, officer?" said a small man with a loud sport shirt and dark glasses.

"What do you think?" the patrolman said scornfully. "Keep out of the way there."

The small man stepped nimbly away and took a three-dimensional color camera out of a small leather case that hung by a strap over his shoulder. He walked carefully around the Buick and took three or four pictures, then walked down the road to the overturned Dodge and took two more. In a short time he had gathered a small group around him and set himself up as an authority.

"Must have happened right over there," he said. "You can see the Buick was going south."

"Is that right?" said a woman, pushing her hair out of her eyes.

"Yes, that's the way I figure it," the man with the camera said.

THE SCRIBBLER

■ ■ ■

Stanley Moss was a small man. He was getting bald. He was forty-seven years old. His wife had great contempt for him.

"You're a lousy fag, practically," she said to him once.

He had struck her then.

She was so surprised she wept and then that night they had made love. It had been like it was when they were first married. It had been strange.

But other than that one night, they had not had a good relationship for many years. Florence was five years younger than Stanley. She was almost fat, but she was attractive in a cheap way. Her hair was peroxide-blonde and her nails were always kept red, although they were not always clean. She wore a lot of perfume and liked to drink beer. The combination of the smell of beer and the smell of perfume made her irresistible to many of the men she met in bars.

They lived in a run-down but not too unpleasant building on the West side. Stanley worked at Macy's in the basement hardware section. Sometimes he would get so angry thinking of Florence that he would stand behind this counter looking at the blades of kitchen knives, and sometimes he would grip the handle of a sharp knife and make an ugly face. He was basically, though, a mild man.

One hot Friday evening in late summer he came home to find the apartment empty. The bed had not been made and there were dirty dishes in the sink.

He watched television for a while and then went down the street to Riker's and had dinner, which consisted of Irish stew, apple pie, a glass of milk, and a cup of coffee.

When he got back to the apartment there was still no sign of Florence.

He walked over to the phone table and dialed a number.

"Hello, Dora? This is Stanley. Fine, thanks. Dora, is Flo still with you? She said she'd be home at seven o'clock. What? Oh, that's funny. No, it's nothing important. She probably just got tied up somewhere. Yes. All right. Thanks, Dora. 'Bye."

He hung up viciously, looked at his watch, rose, and paced the floor. Lunging for the phone, he dialed another number. After a moment:

"Hello, Charlie. How are you? This is Stanley Moss. Yes. Say, I don't suppose you've seen *Mrs.* Moss, have you? Sometimes she stops in with her sister in the—oh? About how long ago? I see. What? No, nothing's wrong. I *thought* she might have stopped in at your place for a drink, that's all. Yes. All right, Charlie. Thank you."

At that moment he heard a scuffling sound from the hall outside the apartment and the sound of a woman's laughter. Stanley walked toward the door, pressed his ear to the door, and listened. In the hall Florence was saying:

"Mickey, you're a dear . . . an absolute dear. I'll take those things from you as soon as I find my key."

He could hear her fumbling.

"Oh, goodness, Mickey, you'll have to forgive me, sweetie, I don't seem to have a bit of change on me."

The elevator man said, "That's all right, Mrs. Moss."

"But you worked so hard carrying those big old heavy bags for me. Why don't you come in a minute and wait while I find some change?"

"No, really, it's okay. I'm glad to do it . . . for *you.*"

"Well, aren't you a doll! If there's anything I can do to return the favor, Mick, don't fail to call on me." She laughed tipsily, amused that her teasing had embarrassed him.

"Good night, Mrs. Moss," Mickey said.

"Good night, Mickey." She laughed again to herself. Her face was relaxed, gay. As she opened the door and saw Stanley her face froze.

"Where've you been?" Stanley said.

"I've been out. Where've *you* been?"

She walked past him, through the dining room, into the kitchen. He followed at her heels.

"I've been here, waiting for you. What's the big idea?"

"Oh, leave me alone!" She put the groceries on the kitchen table.

"What do you mean . . . leave you alone?" Stanley said. "I expected you'd be here at seven o'clock. I expected I'd be given my dinner tonight. Is there anything wrong in that? What do you think I am anyway?"

"Some time when you've got a few hours to spare, I'll tell you!"

"You've been drinking again."

"Thank you, Sam Spade."

"I called Charlie's. He told me you were there this evening . . . for a long time."

She removed her coat. She was wearing a tight sweater. "He did, eh? Well, it's nice to know who your friends are."

"Florence, what's the matter with you? What do you suppose men think of a woman dressed like that, sitting at a bar in the middle of the afternoon?"

"I *know* what they think . . . and it's a damn sight more interesting than what *you* think."

"Don't talk like that, Florence!"

"I'll talk any way I want."

"Haven't you any pride?"

"Not as much as I had when I married you. What good does it do me to sit around this dump in the afternoon all dolled up? Do you ever tell me I look nice? Do you ever show me a good time? A woman has a right to things like that and if you can't give me what I want, there's lots of guys who can!"

Stanley clenched his fists. "I'm sorry, Florence, but sitting in a saloon isn't my idea of a good time."

"Oh, it isn't mine either, but what else is there? You think I have any laughs sitting around here at night, watching you mope around with your books and papers? Where's the can-opener?"

"It's over there. I was going to make myself some soup, but I went to Riker's. Florence, I . . . I'm sorry if you're not happy with me, but you shouldn't associate with the kind of people you meet in bars in the afternoon. You don't know what kind of men you're liable to meet."

"Don't I?"

"No. And what was the idea of falling all over the elevator boy?"

"Falling all over who?"

"You heard me. 'Mickey, you're a dear.' Calling an elevator boy *sweetie*. It's disgraceful!"

"What's disgraceful about it? He was very nice. He carried my groceries for me, and I didn't have any change."

"But your *attitude* . . . I was listening and it made me sick to my stomach! You know, Florence, you're a very exciting woman. Some time you're going to get a little too friendly with one of these elevator boys or delivery men and you're going to be sorry."

"All right. Let that be our thought for the day. I'm a very exciting woman. Stanley, you know what *you* are? You're a square! A genuine, A-number-one, gilt-edged *square*. Get me the coffee." He took a can of coffee from a cupboard and handed it to her.

"Aw, Florence, I don't want to argue with you. Why don't you kiss me when I see you in the evening, like other wives do?"

"Cut it."

"What's the matter?"

"Nothing's the matter. I'm just not in a mood to be pawed, that's all."

"I hope you felt the same while you were sitting at the bar this afternoon."

"You've got a vicious mouth! Get me a drink!"

"Don't you think you've had enough already?"

"Get me a drink!"

"All right." He took a bottle and a glass from the cupboard.

"And stop making all those unfunny comments about what I do on my own time. Before I married you you were more than happy to stand in line and wait your turn, mister . . . don't forget it!"

"But you're my *wife* now!"

"Stop reminding me!" The front door buzzer rang. "I'll get it," Florence said. "Keep an eye on the stove."

She walked into the front room, drying her hands. When she opened the door a Western Union boy was standing in the hall.

"Mrs. Florence Moss? Sign here," the boy said.

"Wait a minute," Florence said. She walked away from the door and reached up to the top of a glass-front chest that stood in the hall. "Stanley, is that change purse still up here?"

The boy eyed her as she exposed part of her leg in reaching up. He whistled softly. She smiled at him over her shoulder, took down a small coin purse, and extracted a quarter which she handed to the boy.

"Thank *you*, ma'am."

She closed the door.

"Florence!" Stanley said. "*Must* you flirt with everything that wears pants?"

"Don't tell me you're getting jealous of Western Union boys?"

"It isn't that I'm jealous, Florence. It's just that . . . well, that's no way for a lady to act."

"Thanks for the compliment."

"Who's the wire from?"

"I think this is a scene from that new picture called *None of Your Business*." She opened the envelope and read the message. "If you must know it's from Dick Kramer."

"I didn't know you'd been seeing him."

"I haven't been seeing him. He just says he'll be in town tonight or in the morning. Business trip or something."

"Does he want to see you?"

"Of course he wants to see me."

"Oh. Well, don't let me stand in your way."

"Look, stupid, Dick Kramer is a much older friend of mine than even *you* are. He's a darling, and if he has time I intend to see him. There's no harm in that!"

"If he's such an old and good friend why didn't you marry him when you had the chance?"

"Oh, stop! That's all water over the dam."

"Florence, why must you think that every man in the world is your personal property? Sometimes I think you're sick. I actually do."

"I am. Sick of you. Did you get the papers?"

"No. Why?"

"Give me some change. I'll send Mickey for the *News* and *Mirror*."

He handed her some change from his pocket. She walked to the door and opened it. At the doorway she stopped, speaking back into the room. "Is there anything else we need? Any beer or anything? As long as Mickey . . ." She broke off. She was staring at the wall just to the right of the door.

"What's the matter?" Stanley said, his throat tightening.

"Who did this?" Florence said.

"Who did what?"

"It's disgraceful! Where's there a pencil with an eraser on it?" She found a pencil in her purse and began to erase something on the wallpaper. "What kind of dump is this getting to be, anyway? she said. "People drawing on the walls."

"What are you talking about?"

"Come here and look at this! You'd think this was the back of a barn someplace . . . the pictures people think they can get away drawing."

He walked out into the hall. There was a smudged obscene drawing on the wallpaper.

"What's this over here? This writing?"

"It says, 'Lord, help me. Please. Before it's too late. Johnny.'"

"Was this here before?" Stanley said. "When you came in?"

"No. Or if it was . . . I didn't notice. Why?"

"Oh, nothing."

"Well, I'll rub it out with . . ."

"No, wait."

"What for?"

"I'd like to know who did this, wouldn't you?"

"Yes."

"You're sure it wasn't here when you came in?"

"I don't know. I don't think it was."

"I knew something like this would happen."

"What are you talking about? Some punky kid scribbles a picture on the wallpaper. What do you mean you knew something like this would happen?"

"Florence, a *kid* might scribble something dirty on a wall, but this writing . . ."

"What about it?"

"Only a psychopath would write something like that!"

"What are you talking about? It says, 'Lord, help me. Please. Before it's too late. Johnny.' I don't even know what it means."

"I don't either. But it sounds kind of familiar."

"You've seen it before?"

"No. I read something. I can't seem to . . . that case in Chicago a few years ago. Remember? There was this guy who would scribble a message on a wall or on a mirror every time he'd kill a woman."

"You trying to frighten me?"

"Don't be ridiculous. I don't like the looks of this. We'd better call the police."

They walked into the apartment and closed the door.

"No, wait. This is silly. You can't call the police just because somebody scribbles on your walls."

"You don't seem to get the point, Florence. We can erase what's on the wallpaper. That doesn't matter. What does worry me is that some unbalanced character . . . for all we know, a potential murderer . . . has been lurking out here in our hallway. Is there any writing anywhere else in the hall?"

They both walked out into the hall again and looked about.

"No. It just seems to be in this one place."

"Maybe we can handle this ourselves. Is there anyone who works in the building named Johnny?"

"Yes," Florence said.

"Who?"

"The night man. But it couldn't be him. He's a thousand years old."

"I guess you're right. Has anyone delivered anything here today? Did anything come from the delicatessen this morning? Anything from a department store?" Stanley was enjoying himself.

"No. Yesterday there was something. A man checking the light and gas meters."

"If only you could remember whether or not this scribbling was here when you came in a while ago. If it wasn't . . ."

"Then it must have been—oh, no. Not Mickey. His name's Mickey. Not Johnny!"

"I knew something like this was going to happen, Florence. You and your tight skirts and your sweaters . . . I warned you!"

"Shut up! This is no time for I-told-you-so speeches. You're supposed to be so smart. Do something. Figure this out!"

"I don't see how it could have been Mickey either. Although a man would hardly sign his own name to a thing like this. It could have been the boy with the telegram. Looks like whoever wrote it was fairly tall."

"That's right."

"See. I'm only five-seven, and if a tall man did the writing it would be up here like it is. What did the boy look like?"

"How do I know?"

"You certainly were friendly enough with him."

"Oh, stop. Look, why don't I just ring the buzzer and call Mickey and ask him if—"

"No, that's no good. If he did it he'll just deny it . . . then we'll never know. I still think I ought to call the police. Maybe they could check for fingerprints."

"Maybe. Maybe it could be one of the maintenance men."

"Maybe. Are any of them tall?"

"One of them is. But I've never spoken to any of them. They don't know me."

"I doubt that. What did the man who checked the meters look like?"

"He was cute. I mean he was . . . oh, I don't know. What difference does it make what he looked like?"

"What I want to know is, did he look odd in any way? Did he act suspicious? Did you flirt with him?"

"I gave him a cup of coffee. We talked for a minute. You call that flirting?"

"When the woman is you, yes!"

They walked back into the living room and closed the door.

"Well, I hope you're satisfied," Stanley said. "It could have been the meter man or Mickey or the doorman or the Western Union boy or even Dick Kramer."

"Oh, now you're being asinine."

"It's possible. Maybe he just sent the wire as a gag. He could already be in town. I never did trust him anyway."

"He wouldn't do a thing like this. He was a little wild, I'll admit, but not like this."

"Didn't you split up with him because of some trouble he got into about a girl?"

"Yes. I'd forgotten about that. But it couldn't be. Unless it's a prank. Only this isn't very funny."

The door buzzer grated harshly. Florence and Stanley stood rooted, looking at each other. The buzzer sounded again.

"Don't answer it," Florence whispered.

"No, wait. I'll tell you what. You answer it and I'll stand right behind the door. You'll be perfectly safe. I just want to get a line on who it is."

"I'm afraid."

"You're perfectly safe. I'll be right here. If *I* answer the door, I may frighten them away. If it's our man he might give himself away, if *you* answer."

A knock was heard at the door. Florence, ashen, advanced toward it.

"Who's there?"

The Western Union boy said something muffled behind the door.

"Go ahead. Open it," Stanley whispered.

The door opened.

"Another telegram, lady. Sign here."

"Thank you."

"Looks like you're pretty popular tonight. Here, you want to use my pencil?"

Stanley stepped out from behind the door. "I'll take that."

"Hey, what's the idea?" the boy said.

"You the boy who was here a few minutes ago?" Stanley said.

"Yeah. What's the matter . . . you want your tip back?"

Stanley stepped out into the hall. "I just want to see something." With the boy's pencil Stanley scribbled briefly on the wall.

"Mac, you're signing in the wrong place."

"Very funny, son. Did you do this writing on the wall?"

"What?"

Stanley said to Florence, "It looks like the same kind of lead . . . I can't tell for sure. Your name is Johnny, isn't it?"

"I don't know what you're talking about," the boy said. "My name is Wilbur."

"Somebody drew a dirty picture on the wall here! And somebody wrote something. See it? Did you do it? Did you?"

"Stanley, take it easy," Florence said.

"Lady, what's this guy talking about? If you two won't sign for that wire, it's nothing to me. I'm gettin' outta here." He retreated to the elevator door.

"All right. Get out! And don't come back. And don't act so friendly with this lady next time . . . you hear?"

Stanley and Florence walked back into the living room.

"There's no sense acting like that. You had no reason to frighten the kid like that."

"Why not? He frightened *you*, didn't he?"

"But you had nothing to go on. He didn't seem like the type."

"No. Who *is* the type? Who is the type, Florence? The type to get funny ideas about you into his head? The type to follow you home and scribble nasty things on the wall outside your apartment? Tell me that if you wouldn't mind? Who is the type?"

"Ah, shut up. The way you're making a Federal case out of this we'll never find out who we're looking for!"

"Florence, I love you."

"What?"

"Don't look at me as if I just said something shocking. Maybe you don't care . . . but I love you. And *because* I love you I worry about you. I'm trying to protect you, to take care of you."

"Stanley . . . you're jealous."

"Don't read lines at me, Florence. Of course I'm jealous."

"Why, baby," she said, "I never realized you had it in you. You're jealous as hell."

He tried to kiss her. She accepted a kiss on the cheek. "What's the idea? Don't you like the way your husband kisses?"

"Ah, shut up!"

Stanley was shouting now. "You have no right to talk to me like that. Don't do it again or you'll be sorry!"

There was a knock at the door. Stanley and Florence stood motionless. It was Mickey, the elevator man. "Mrs. Moss! Mrs. Moss!" He knocked again.

"Don't move," Stanley said. He walked to the door and opened it. "What do you want?"

"Oh, hello, Mr. Moss. I—uh—"

"You thought my wife was here alone?"

"No. I knew you were here. I could hear you yelling out in the hall. I just came up to . . . I mean . . . well, the Western Union kid who was just here, he said he thought there was something wrong . . . so I—I just got off the elevator to check and I heard you yelling, that's all."

"Well, Mrs. Moss and I are very grateful to you, but there's nothing the matter."

"Well, that's fine. I just wanted to be helpful, that's all. Didn't want to cause any trouble. You know, if there was something wrong . . . I just wanted to be Johnny-on-the-spot."

"Mickey," Stanley said, "how did this scribbling get on the wall?"

"Where? Oh. I don't know. I'll send somebody up to clean it up right away."

"Don't bother. Before we have it cleaned off I think we'll have the police look at it."

"Oh, I wouldn't do that. Probably just some punky delivery boy or something with a new pencil. No sense gettin' anybody in trouble over a little thing like that."

"All right, Mickey. Thank you." Stanley closed the door.

"I can't believe it was him," Florence said.

"Why not? You know you appeal to him. You remember, of course, not fifteen minutes ago you were out in the hall practically flirting with him . . . deliberately asking for trouble!"

"You stop that crap!"

"You slut!"

"Watch it, Stanley. Watch it with the name-calling. I don't like it!"

"Don't you realize, Florence, that these men whose emotions you play around with are made of flesh and blood, just like I am? Don't you realize that if you give one of them the come-on he's liable to react in an unusual way. They know you're a married woman; they know they can't step into your life; so don't you realize that a thing like this is the most natural result in the world of—of what you've been doing?"

"I haven't been doing anything!"

"Stop lying! Stop lying in your teeth when I know you're lying. I know where you spend your afternoons. I know what you think of me. And now, a thing like this. It's more than a man can stand, Florence!"

"Who's asking you to stand it? Why don't you just shut up and leave me alone? If you want to accomplish something to show me what a big strong man you are, then go out and find out what bum did that scribbling. Don't just stand here and shout at me . . . what is *that?*"

"Don't try to order me around, Florence. I'll find out who did that scribbling. Don't worry about that. I'll find out and you'll find out, too. They say once a man does a thing like that he'll do it again. The urge will come over him again, Florence, if it has once already . . . don't worry about that. He'll show his face again."

"So all right. So fine! But in the meantime, stop talking to me like I was an idiot. I don't have to take your abuse!"

"Oh, yes you do. You're my wife, so I own you. And I'm very jealous of you and I don't like the idea that other men can joke with you and flirt with you and for all I know make love to you when you don't like to have me touch you. Not that I ever really want to, of course."

"I've heard about enough of that!"

"No, this is once you're not going to shut me up, Florence. Because you're afraid now. And the reason you're afraid is because there's somebody out there who may be able to do you harm, so you need me, you see? You need me. So you can't shut me up. You've brought this about yourself, you see? There's no one else to blame. I'm your husband and I've got a right to talk to you this way." His voice was high, ringing.

"Stanley, stop. That's enough!"

"No, it's not nearly enough. I should have done this a long time ago. I won you once. I never have been able to understand why I've had to win you time and time again, but now I understand. That's what you want. You don't want weakness. You admire strength. You despised me for being a gentleman and you sat with bums in saloons.

Well, have it your way, Florence. You'll submit to me now. I want you."

"Take your lousy hands offa me," Florence shrieked. "You hear? Take your lousy fag hands offa me!" She started to say something about his having hands like his mother's and that was when he hit her.

He hit her first with the flat of his left hand and then punched her in the side of the head with his right. She kicked him in the shins and then he killed her with a large bread knife that he had bought at Macy's at a discount.

Somebody heard the fight and called the police. When they came Stanley was standing quietly in the hall, weeping, scribbling something on the wallpaper.

THE BLOOD
OF THE LAMB

■ ■ ■

Slater had been dozing, with his seat belt still buckled around him, for perhaps ten minutes when he felt someone tapping his elbow.

It was the man next to him in the aisle seat, the small, wispy-looking man with the gold-rimmed glasses.

"I beg your pardon, sir," the man said, smiling. "I thought perhaps you might enjoy having some reading matter." Slater looked down and saw that he was holding out a pamphlet.

"Thanks," he said. "Thanks a lot." The pamphlet had a white cover on which was printed *The Blood of the Lamb*. When Slater saw that it was a religious tract, he experienced a slight flicker of embarrassment without being able to understand the reason for the feeling. For a moment he sat half-turned toward the man, expecting a continuation of the conversation, but the stranger had taken a pencil from his inside coat pocket and was busily occupied in making a notation on a small piece of paper.

Slater looked at his watch and then out the window. Flat-bottomed clouds were shelved with seeming firmness about three thousand feet below the plane; above, all was blue infinity washed in sunshine. At that moment one of the stewardesses passed along the aisle carrying a paper cup full of water, and automatically Slater turned, admiring the trim fit of her gabardine skirt. When his head had ninety-degreed to the left he suddenly became aware that the stranger was looking at him. Clearing his throat, he reluctantly opened the pamphlet.

The heading on the first page was "An Open Letter to Men of Good Will." As he read, Slater became conscious of the little man's breathing and then, by pretending to check the air vent overhead, he glanced to the side without turning his head and saw that the man's eyes were fixed on the open page.

"Since men of science and men of politics," the pamphlet said, "have created a physical detonation and an A-bomb-ination unto the Lord, we offer as a panacea for the ills of the world the news of an H-bomb: a Heaven-bomb. Not very long ago it became abundantly clear to those with eyes to see and ears to hear that Satan was on the loose and sat in the palaces of the world. However, it has been written 'the Devil is mighty but God is almighty,' so those of us who have been or are willing to be or are not opposed to being washed in the Blood of the Lamb have faith that we will be lifted up and made safe even in the midst of the coming holocaust."

"Amen," the stranger whispered softly in Slater's ear.

Slater said, "Oh, God," moving his lips but making no sound. Only twenty minutes out of New York, almost three hours before the plane was scheduled to land at Chicago and here he was, trapped by a religious fanatic.

Having nowhere else to turn, he returned to the pamphlet.

"'The wrath of men worketh not the righteousness of God (Jas. 1:20),'" he read. "'Be not afraid of them that kill the body (Luke 12:4) . . .' but desire only to drinketh of the Blood of the Lamb and ye shall be saved. For I say unto you that whosoever shall make an a-bomb-ination in the sight of the most High shall not avail himself of the graces of the Lord's at-one-ment (atonement)!"

Slater closed the booklet and pinched the bridge of his nose.

"What's the matter, brother?" the little man said.

"What?" Slater said, a nervous itch spreading across his chest.

"Aren't you receptive to the message of the Lord?"

"Yes," Slater said, "it's just that I—I'm somewhat tired and the print is a bit small for my eyes."

"Better stick with it, brother," the man said, "there isn't much time."

"Much time for what?" Slater asked, feeling a vague uneasiness above and beyond the simple embarrassment the conversation was calculated to arouse in him.

"In the world ye shall have tribulation," the man said. "John, sixteen, thirty-three."

"Yes," Slater agreed lamely, "I guess you shall."

"So?" the man said.

"So what?" Slater said.

"Oh, Lord, be merciful," the man said, looking to the ceiling. "Brother, I am trying to give you a friendly, fair warning. Prepare your soul."

Impatient, Slater considered pretending to want to go to the lavatory and then seeing if he could change his seat. But looking back and forward through the plane's length, he could see that all the seats were occupied. It was the damned holiday traffic, he recalled; he'd even had difficulty getting accommodations on the flight at all. Gritting his teeth, he said, "Prepare my soul for what?"

"For the crash," the man said, smiling fiercely.

For several seconds Slater stared at the pamphlet, then out the window, then at the hostess flashing her teeth between red lips at the front of the plane. His mind was filled with impressions, half-thoughts, and halting plans, but for some reason he could not find voice. At length he cleared his throat.

"Did you hear me, brother?" the man said. "I'm giving you the word of the Lord out of the goodness of my heart."

Slater started to say, "Thank you," and then silently cursed himself.

"There is not a just man upon the earth, that doeth good and sinneth not," the man said, "Ecclesiastes seven, twenty."

"I suppose that's right," Slater said. "Frankly I'm not as familiar with the Bible as I might be."

"Who is?" the man said, genially enough. "That's why I've been sent to do the work of the Lord and spread the glad tidings of the Heaven-bomb."

"What bomb is that?" Slater asked.

"Fear not," the man said. "The trumpet shall sound and the dead shall be raised. But I'm pleased to hear, my friend, that you are interested. I spoke to some of the other passengers in the waiting room and they ignored me. But soon," he said, and his lip curled with a ferocious sneer, "their blood will wash the expression of contempt from their sinful faces."

"What do you mean by that?" Slater persisted, feeling compelled to make sense out of the man's message, wanting to clear up the aura of threat that hung over his words.

At that moment the other stewardess loomed above them with a clip-board and a pencil. "Name, please," she said, smiling at Slater.

"Henry Slater," he said, wanting to speak to her about the man but not knowing how to start.

"Your name, sir?" she said to the stranger.

"Percy Warren," the man said, "Tulsa, Oklahoma. Would you care to have some interesting reading material, young lady?"

"Why, yes, thank you," the girl said, opening her eyes wide as if speaking to a child. "Thank you so much." She took the tract and tucked it into the pocket of her jacket. Slater was surprised to see Warren reach a speckled, blue-veined hand into her pocket and extract the pamphlet. "Here," he said, "you'd better read that pretty quick, while there's still time."

The girl's mouth opened blankly and then she said, "Certainly, sir, just as soon as I've finished here." She looked at Slater with a slight smile as if to ask if his companion were making a joke, and Slater took advantage of her concentration to frown and carefully touch his right forefinger to his temple in a sort of smooth movement with a follow-through so that the man would not notice.

The girl evidently got the idea of his message. "Let's see," she said, "you're getting off at Chicago; is that right, Mr. Warren?"

"The dead, small and great, shall stand before God," Warren said, "and they shall be judged according to their works."

The girl smiled automatically, turned with no apparent haste, and walked slowly forward to the pilot's cabin.

For perhaps a minute nothing happened. The monotonous drone of the plane's motors began to induce in Slater an almost hypnotic calm. Perhaps, he thought, the whirring in Warren's head had run down. Perhaps he would not speak again. Another half-minute passed. It was like the sensation, familiar to parents, of waiting for a peevish baby to fall asleep, each passing uneventful second seeming to be a tiny triumph.

Suddenly the man leaped to his feet and began passing out pamphlets to people up and down the aisle. "And the dead shall be judged out of those things which were written in the books, according to their works," he shouted, his face wreathed in an unaccountable smile. At the far end of the plane somebody laughed and, closer, a woman gasped in fear.

Slater, now released by the man's movement, leaped to his feet and stepped into the aisle. Momentarily he considered taking the man, whose back was to him, by surprise, striking him a Judo blow on the back of the neck, the way he had learned in the Marines. But it would be ridiculous. Warren had made no threatening gestures. To attack him would be unjust. A man on the other side of the aisle tapped Slater's arm.

"He with you?" the man said.

"No," Slater said.

"What's the matter with him?"

"Damned if I know," Slater whispered. "He's nuts."

"Isn't somebody going to do something?" a woman behind them said.

"What do you suggest, lady?" Slater said.

"I don't know," the woman said, huddling back against her window as if to get out of harm's way.

At that moment the two stewardesses bore down upon Warren from the front of the plane.

"Mr. Warren," Slater heard one of them say, "I'd like very much to hear more about your—about your booklet. Did you write it?"

"I am a witness unto the Lord," Warren said loudly. "The Lord is the hand. I am the pencil."

"That sounds very interesting," the other girl said. "Why don't we go back to the lounge and talk about it?"

"Just a moment," Warren said. "I've got to give all these people the message and the warning."

"All right," said the first girl. "Listen, why don't I just give you a hand? Here, I can pass some of these out to the people up front."

"Why, that would be fine," Warren said, taking a short stack of booklets from his pocket. "You people up there pay attention to the young lady, you hear?"

"They hear," the girl said. "Of if they don't, I'll tell them."

The man across the aisle spoke out of the side of his mouth. "You've got to hand it to those girls," he said. "I wouldn't have known *what* to do with the bastard."

"Yeah," Slater said, in complete agreement. But there was still the matter of the warning. A warning against what?

"Here, Marge," the first girl said to her companion, "why don't you help by handing these out back that way?"

The second girl nodded, took half of the tracts Warren had given her companion, and moved to the rear of the plane, smiling at the passengers who looked up at her, lifting her eyebrows in a gesture of amused understanding as if Warren were only a naughty, exasperating child.

"Hurry up back there," Warren said, still standing in the aisle, toward the front of the plane. "Now, when you've all received your

books, please open them to page fourteen. For there it is written: 'For
if the dead rise not, then is not Christ raised.' First Corinthians,
chapter fifteen, verse sixteen."

"Ah, shut up and sit down," somebody shouted from behind
Warren.

He whirled as if stabbed in the back.

"What?" he screamed. "Do you refuse to hear the word of God?"

"My God," a woman said, near Slater. "Why did they do that?
Why did they have to open their mouths up there?"

Somebody made a shushing noise and all eyes focused on
Warren.

"Prepare to meet thy doom," he shouted. "You're all so smug and
so self-satisfied, aren't you, you whited sepulchers?" He pronounced
the word "suplukers." "Well, perhaps your hard hearts will be
softened and turned toward the Lord when I tell you that this plane
will never land!"

A woman screamed softly and a man's voice said, "Be quiet.
Listen."

"That's right," Warren said, laughing. "*Now* there's nobody
telling me to shut up, is there? Oh, no. *Now* things are a little
different, aren't they? Well, it's too late now to come crawling to me,
but, praise God, it's not too late to be washed in *the Blood of the
Lamb*."

Behind Warren the co-pilot appeared, walking fast. "What's
wrong here?" he said, his face frozen in an insincere smile.

"Wrong?" Warren screamed. "Nothing is wrong, my friend,
except in the hearts of this assemblage that are blackened with sin."

"Hadn't you better sit down, sir?" the officer said.

"Certainly," Warren said, surprisingly. "It doesn't matter
whether I stand or sit or what I do. What *is* important is that you all
get it through your thick, sinful skulls that this plane will never land
safely."

The co-pilot spun him around and snapped, "What do you mean
by that?"

"Why," Warren said, "it's simplicity itself. You know what the
plane is, don't you? And you know what to land means, don't you?
And you know what safely means, don't you? Well, let's hope you
understand just as clearly what it means to crash in flames of wrath!"

"Why do you say we're going to crash?" the officer demanded,
making a pointless effort to lower his voice, to keep the passengers
from hearing.

"Because, you idiots," Warren shouted, "there's a time bomb in my suitcase."

The co-pilot raced to the empty seat and grabbed Slater. "Where was he sitting?" he said.

"Right here," Slater said, stepping to one side.

Together they looked under the seat and in the rack overhead. They found nothing except a cheap straw hat.

"Christ, I thought maybe he had a small bag," the co-pilot said, racing back to Warren, grabbing him by the shoulders. "Listen, you, I'm going to ask you just once. Is your suitcase in the baggage compartment?"

"Where else would it be, you tool of Satan?" Warren shouted, smiling triumphantly.

"You men keep your eye on this bird," the co-pilot said, heading for the cockpit. "We're going back."

"You'll never make it," Warren chuckled.

Slater noticed that a woman near Warren had taken out a rosary and was praying half audibly, her lips moving. Warren spied her and cackled, "Six-sixty-six!"

"Should we rush him?" a baldheaded man said.

"What the hell good would that do?" Slater said. "We're in no danger from him; it's the damned bomb."

"Just remain in your seats," one of the stewardesses said, moving along the side. "The captain is radioing for instructions and landing clearance. We'll get back down as fast as we can."

At that moment the plane went into a steep bank and Warren stumbled, falling onto the lap of an elderly woman who screamed and shoved him back to a standing position.

"Would you please sit down, sir?" one of the hostesses said to Warren. "You might get hurt like this."

"That's a great one," the baldheaded man said.

"The wages of sin is death," Warren shouted. "Don't waste your time being angry at me, dear friends. I pray you, make good use of the last few remaining minutes to make your peace with God. Why is it that the world always reviles those of us who bring the glad tidings? They killed my Christ and ye would kill me, would you not, if your hands were not at this moment paralyzed with fear."

The baldheaded man ripped out an oath and ran forward at Warren, striking him a blow in the face. Warren fell backward and rolled along the aisle as the plane suddenly lost altitude in a sickening, slanting drop. The hostesses restrained the baldheaded man and Warren got to his feet. "That's it," he said, smiling. "That's what your vaunted civilization has brought you after all these thousands of years. Well, it's all right. Revile me. Spit upon me. Kill me if you will; but if you do, remember you die shortly thereafter yourself with murder on your soul. The Lord has a special love for martyrs, for their blood mingles with his own. Oh, praise God and drink the Blood of the Lamb."

The baldheaded man, breathing heavily, went back to his seat, white-faced.

"Ladies and gentlemen," the voice of the captain said over the loud-speaker, "please remain calm. We're going to try to land soon, perhaps at Philadelphia. Fasten your seat belts, please. We'll do our best."

"What the hell good are seat belts at a time like this?" somebody said.

The co-pilot, his tanned face seeming paler now, came down the aisle again and walked up close to Warren.

"This bomb," he said, half-whispering, "when do you have it—I mean, when do you think it's supposed to go off?"

"That's for me to know and you to find out," Warren said smugly.

"Listen, man," the co-pilot said, bringing his face close to Warren's. "I don't want any trouble with you. I mean personally. I happen to be a Christian. My grandfather was a Baptist minister and my father was a simple, Godfearing farmer. As one Christian to another, I'm asking you—what time is that bomb set for?"

For once Warren was silent.

The passengers passed the word back, telling about the co-pilot's clever approach. His calm self-control helped to reduce slightly the feeling of hysteria that had been about to take over the ship.

After a long pause the officer again said, "Tell me, sir, at once."

"All right," Warren said, looking at his watch. "I'm usually a little slow. What time is it now?"

"It's exactly two-forty-six," the co-pilot said.

"Then," said Warren, "that bomb is going to go off in fourteen minutes."

The officer pushed past him and raced to the front of the plane with the information.

Unfortunately Warren's announcement had been overheard and within seconds everyone aboard had learned that the deadline was three o'clock. Somebody tearfully asked if Daylight Saving Time had any connection with the matter, and for a brief moment hope flickered up and down the cabin like an almost visible force, only to be dashed out when Warren pointed to his wrist watch and said, "Repent ye. Death shall be your lot in thirteen minutes."

For the first time Slater became aware that there were no children aboard. Unable to force himself to comply with the order to fasten seat belts, he sat cross-legged on the arm of Warren's still vacant seat, his feet in the aisle. Two women were crying but most of the passengers seemed stunned into silence.

Looking at them, Slater found his heart torn in two directions. Part of him was filled with anger. He wanted, like the baldheaded man, to strike out, to avenge. The other part tried to concentrate on the fact, the idea, of death. Strangely, a feeling of unreality softened what might otherwise have been his terror. He thought of Ellen and the children, picturing them as they must be at this moment, the children in school, the wife shopping or doing something with a vacuum cleaner or a paring knife. Then he thought of them receiving the news of his death and at that picture he winced and actually turned his head away, as if by so doing he could blot out the prospect.

In a moment he found his thoughts taking a religious turn, but then he considered Warren's motivation and found himself unable to concentrate upon his personal identity as a man and a creature of God. There was the inclination but it was immediately followed by the reaction, the feeling that in doing what Warren had demanded, in praying, in abasing himself, he was participating in a bargain with a madman. He spent several minutes in this confused state, his thoughts at last broken by the captain's voice on the intercom.

"Folks, we're down to under two thousand feet and we may make an emergency landing. Again may I remind you to fasten your seat belts securely and to remain calm. I'll do all I can—to see that—that we get down all right."

Slater sat down now and fastened his belt. The only person standing was Warren, who swayed in the aisle near the front of the plane, muttering to himself.

A man at the rear said, "What time is it?" and when another voice said, "Two-fifty-one," a woman shrieked and began to sob.

Slater found himself staring at his watch, so that he eventually had to make a firm, definite effort to pull his eyes away from the seemingly speeding minute hand. Looking out the window, he could see that they were quite low now. Trees, houses, and a few automobiles were plainly visible.

"Folks," the pilot's voice droned, "we're going to try to land at a private field just about five minutes away. We're going in very slowly and as soon as we touch down I'm going to have to reverse the props because the field is not the right length for a plane this size. It may be a little—a little rough . . . so I repeat, fasten your seat belts tightly and remain calm. There's nothing else you can do. If everything goes—when we stop we'll have to move fast. We'll open the escape hatch and we'll open the regular passenger door and you'll all have to jump for it. There'll be no passenger-loading ramp, but it's not too much of a jump and we'll give you a hand. Please leave the plane calmly and without pushing and shoving. Miss Ryan and Miss Simonetti will give you instructions at the proper moment. It is now two-fifty-three."

"Make your peace with the Lord, my friends," Warren cried benignly. "Thou shalt worship the Lord, thy God, and Him only shalt thou serve."

Every eye on the plane was turned toward him with hatred, but he seemed not to notice.

Below, the land looked frighteningly hilly to Slater, but the calm voice of the pilot had brought him a degree of extra courage. He checked his watch. Six minutes before the bomb was timed to explode.

The plane shuddered as the flaps extended to their fullest width and the pilot reduced speed, dropping another hundred feet almost too quickly.

"Which of you," Warren sang, "if you had your lives to live over again, now would not be a more willing servant unto the Lord, thy God? Which of you would not now gladly bargain to bathe daily in the Blood of the Lamb?"

When his watch said five minutes to three Slater conferred with the man across the aisle. "What time do you have?" he said.

"Four minutes to go by me," the man said. "I may be a few seconds fast."

Slater did not answer.

It seemed that two seconds later somebody said, "Three minutes to go." Unaccountably Slater found himself remembering the old jocular explanation of relativity, the line about kissing your girl for one minute seeming like no time at all but sitting on a hot stove for one minute seeming like eternity.

The plane lurched and stumbled lower in the sea of air, approaching bottom. Slater's fists were clenched, his palms wet.

"We're almost in, folks," the pilot announced. "We have no direct radio control with this field, but I believe they know we're coming in. I have—" he broke off.

"What's wrong?" a man said.

Nobody answered.

At that moment the plane shuddered sickeningly and lifted as the motors were gunned with a powerful roar. "There was a small plane landing on the runway," the pilot said, his voice sounding uneven. "We're going to have to go around and make another pass at it."

"My God," the baldheaded man said, "we'll never make it. This plane will have to make such a big turn we can't possibly get down before three o'clock."

Thirty seconds before three o'clock Slater found himself tightening into a knot, blinking his eyes as if waiting for a door to slam, for his face to be slapped, for a gun to go off, or a life to end.

The plane leaned far to the left as the pilot fought for altitude to make the second pass. The treetops looked remarkably close to the lower wing-tip.

"Holy God," Warren said, "we praise Thy name."

By Slater's watch there were fifteen seconds left. Ten. He braced himself, placing the soles of his shoes against the seat in front of him. Even if they blew up, perhaps at this low altitude they might skid in. He counted off seven seconds to himself and sat rigidly, squinting, feeling cowardly, his chest wriggling with fear.

"It's after three," somebody shouted.

The baldheaded man shouted at Warren, "You son-of-a-bitch," he said, "that thing was supposed to go off just now. Well, is it or isn't it?"

"Let every soul be subject unto the higher powers," Warren said meekly, looking faint.

The plane had gotten turned around and now was lumbering clumsily out of the sky. The landing was bad and jolting and when the props were reversed there was a sickening lurch forward, as if the tail was going down again hard and then at last they knew they were not going to crash.

Warren had fallen to the floor and now he was on his feet, but so was everyone else, despite the captain's plea for calm. They all jostled forward and when the co-pilot had opened the door they began piling out, the first to hit the ground turning to break the fall of the others. One man who had gotten out started to run from the plane but somebody said, "Come on back, you bastard, and help these women down."

Within two minutes they were all out and away from the plane except Warren, who stood forlornly inside the door, looking out and up at the sky.

"Come down out of there," the pilot shouted. "You'll be killed."

"No, I won't," Warren said, his hair lifting in the wind that whipped across the field. In the distance they heard the wail of a siren and now from both sides of the landing strip people began to approach.

"Keep back there," the pilot shouted. "There's a bomb on that plane that may go off any second. Keep back."

"What does he want to do," somebody said, pointing at Warren, "kill himself?"

Half an hour later two policemen put a ladder up to the side of the plane and dragged Warren out. At the local station, while they were telephoning for bomb-disposal information, he said, "You needn't bother. There's no bomb in my suitcase."

"What?" the man on the phone said, interrupting his call.

"I said there's nothing to worry about," Warren answered. "I just wanted to prove to those people how terrible it is that our generation has forgotten God. We have made an a-bomb-ination in His sight. Somebody had to bring us to our senses and announce the news of the H-bomb. The Heaven-bomb."

"All right, Pop," the policeman said. "You get in this cell back here and lie down. I think we'd better keep you away from the other passengers."

"Give them my love," Warren said. "Tell them we all are saved by the Blood of the Lamb."

POINT OF VIEW
■ ■ ■

After the word had gotten around town that the child's body had been found just off the main highway about a mile from Roy Davis' gas station, there were three or four people who remembered having seen *something* lying in the weeds off to the left of the road.

"I distinctly recollect," said Buddy Elder, "seeing some cloth or something or other as I drove in yesterday afternoon. Didn't stop, though."

"Wouldn't-a done any good if you had," someone said. "Kid was dead then twenty-four hours."

It was three days later that the sheriff picked up Lafe Washington as he lay drunk in his shack. Lafe was never too bright and he had been walking around town with the child's change purse practically in plain sight in his khaki shirt pocket, half-drunk and talking to himself. When they went to pick him up they found a blood-stained pair of denim trousers hanging on a nail.

Some of the white people of the town, what with it being Saturday night and there being nothing much to do but relax and drink and smolder, got into a rather ugly mood. There was even some talk of going down to the jail and dragging Lafe out. The colored people, too, surprisingly enough, began to mutter. In years past they would have kept their own counsel and never dreamed of concerning themselves with civic vengeance, but this particular crime had aroused an uncommon degree of hatred.

It was not acceptable to the people of the valley that any man should kill any child, and for once white and colored alike were seething, although not to an equal degree. There seemed no question in anyone's mind about Lafe Washington's guilt; the few who did

177

have qualms were relieved when early Monday morning it was announced that Lafe had made a full confession.

"Ah don' know why ah did it," he said, "but she gimme some sass, Mistuh Sheriff, and ah jus' hit huh. She started cryin' and then ah hit huh again." There were other details too sordid to relate, although for all that one was afraid to offend the sensibilities of the people Lafe might have recited them aloud to music in the town square; within twenty-four hours the details of the crime, horrible as they were, were exaggerated, blown up out of all relation to reality, almost savored over.

Monday morning the town was astonished to learn that Lafe Washington, who would scarcely have been thought to have the gumption, had escaped from jail.

When the news reached Gus Benton late that afternoon, he turned to the men around him and said, "Like to get my hands on the son-of-a-bitch. String him up's what I'd like to do."

"You ain't just a-woofin'," responded Martin Cole. "That would really be somethin' to do. That would show them bastards once and for all to keep their hands off our kind."

"Yeah," said Gus drawlingly. "Be a good lesson to all of 'em."

"You guys are nuts," said Sanford Davis, a small man and a careful one. "You ain't got no right to lay a hand on Washington. Two wrongs don't make a right."

" 'f that was your kid you wouldn't say that," Gus said. "You didn't see the child. I did. She didn't look so good."

"Well, don't get yourself all riled up, boy," Sanford said. "There ain't been no lynchin' 'round here for over twenty years and I don't figure they be one now."

"What you mean?" demanded Gus. "They been two in Georgia during the past—"

"I'm not talkin' 'bout the whole *state*," said Sanford, "I mean right here 'round the valley."

"You don't know *what* you talkin' about," Gus said.

The three men got in the battered Ford pickup that was owned by the lumber company Sanford worked for, and started on the road to Ludlow. Gus had a bottle and the three of them passed it around. About ten minutes out of town they came to a group of cars pulled over to the side of the road.

"Slow down," Martin said. "That's the sheriff."

A khaki-clad figure stood almost in the middle of the road, one hand upraised. When the truck stopped he walked over and put one foot on the running board.

"We're lookin' for Washington," he said quietly. "Heard he'd been seen through here. You boys see anything along the road as you came up?"

"No, sir," Gus said. "We'd like to, but we didn't see nothin'."

Another man walked up beside the sheriff. "He's somewhere between here and Ludlow," the man said. "You can be pretty sure of that. He wouldn't be back this way."

"I guess you're right," the sheriff said. "All right, let's fan out along this side of the road. We've got about two hours before it gets dark. If we don't find him we can come back tomorrow and try the other side."

When the two men stepped away from the truck Sanford gunned the engine.

"Where you goin'?" Gus said.

"Where you think?" Sanford said.

"Hold on," Gus said. "I wonder if they could use some help here."

"They don't need the likes of us," Martin said. "Let's keep movin'."

They sat silently for a moment, watching the sheriff as he moved away.

"There's twelve of us," he was saying to the man at his side. "That's not enough, but it'll have to do. Now remember—if there's any gunplay I'll handle that part of it. We just want all these men to fan out and beat the bushes. No telling where the bastard might be hiding."

"You hear that?" Gus said.

"Yeah," Martin said. "What about it?"

"There's gonna be some action around here for sure. Let's wait till they start out and then follow 'em. See if we can do any good."

"They don't want us," Martin said.

After a moment it seemed that the sheriff's men had all struck off into the brush. "Come on," Gus said to Sanford. "Pull over to the side. We got work to do."

Sanford eased the truck off the road and turned off the motor with only slight reluctance. The three men felt a nervousness in the stomach. Each of them wondered what he would do if he met Lafe in the woods.

"Lafe got a gun?" Sanford said.

"No," said a man who had walked up behind them, unheard. They whirled in embarrassment.

"You boys keep your eyes open," the man said as he turned off the road. "He's not armed but he's still dangerous." They watched his blue jacket moving away.

When the man had disappeared Sanford said, "Well? Let's go if we're goin'."

They shuffled off into the weeds at the side of the highway, where the ground dropped away from the cracked asphalt.

"Whoo-wee," Gus said. "I'd like to be the one to find that son-of-a-bitch. I'd fix him."

"You better shut up," Sanford said. "You're lookin' for trouble."

"Sure I'm lookin' for trouble," Gus said. "What you think we lookin' for? A Sunday-school picnic? I tell you, man, that kid had her little dress torn off and she was cut up bad. She's your kid you'd sure be singin' outta the other side of your mouth."

"I'd like to get *my* hands on him," Martin said. "There's too many people 'round here need a lesson anyway. Might do some good to get this goddamned Washington. Might show people a thing or two."

"Boy," said Sanford, "you're talkin' crazy."

Keeping their eye on the man in the blue jacket, they moved off through the woods, spreading out so that there was a distance of about fifty feet between them. Sanford was on the left, Gus in the center, Martin on the right.

Once, about twenty minutes after they had lost sight of the highway, something moved in the brush, and the three stiffened, listening.

"Must have been a rabbit," Sanford whispered hoarsely after a moment.

"Yeah," Gus said. He was disappointed. The woods began to look confusing to him. "Martin," he called, "you still see that guy the other side of you?"

"Yes," Martin said. "Not every minute, but I pick him up from time to time."

"Don't lose him," Gus said. "I wouldn't wanna have any trouble findin' my way back outta here."

"No problem," Martin said. "The road is just off to the right here a ways."

"Yeah," said Gus, "but it makes a right turn about a mile down and if we don't turn with it we gone be walkin' into some mighty deep timber."

Half an hour later Gus said, "Let's rest a minute."

"All right," Martin said.

"You still hear the rest of 'em?" Sanford asked, wiping his brow. He was unfamiliar with the back woods.

"No," Martin said, "but we're all right. We'll catch up."

"I'm pooped," Gus said, taking the pint from his jacket pocket. They passed the bottle around twice and then started walking again. After a few minutes Martin realized they were lost.

"Hey, man," he said to Gus, "I ain't see that fella in the blue jacket for about twenty minutes or so."

"Son-of-a-bitch," Gus said. "So we *are* lost. Damn, I shoulda worked that side myself."

They gathered together in a small, worried knot and looked for the sun but it had gone down, though there was still plenty of daylight.

"Boy," said Gus in agonized frustration, "I'd like to get my hands on that Washington now. Wasn't for him I'd be home now, havin' dinner."

"Me too," Martin said. "Like to kill the bastard."

"You ever seen anybody killed?" Sanford said.

"Seen 'em?" Gus said. "Man, I've killed 'em. I fought in Italy for twenty-three months. Killin' a guy ain't nothin'. Besides"—he spat out of the side of his mouth—"you forgettin' that Washington done whatever killin's been done around here. Whatever happens to him from here on in he's got comin' to him."

Sanford took another drink from the bottle that Gus had passed to him. "I guess you're right in a way," he said. He began to think of his own child, a nine-year-old boy. If anybody ever laid a hand on Billy, Sanford considered, he would be quite willing to commit murder. The alcohol began to warm up his brain and give him confidence. He no longer felt apprehensive about meeting Lafe Washington. Suddenly he knew he *hoped* to meet him. He passed the bottle on to Martin, who emptied it, then returned it to Gus somewhat apologetically. Gus threw it into the brush, swearing.

It was then that they saw Lafe Washington standing quietly, looking at them, beside a large tree.

For ten seconds nobody spoke or moved.

Then without a word Lafe broke and ran, disappearing into the brush. They took after him, trotting unsteadily.

"He didn't have no gun, did he?" Sanford said.

"No," Gus said, his lips turned down. "Don't you remember what the man said?"

"How we gonna bring him in?" Martin said.

"I don't know," Gus said. "All we gotta do now is catch the mother."

It was not difficult to keep on Washington's trail. They could easily hear him pounding through the trees, falling, breathing heavily, breaking twigs and small branches.

"Stop, you son-of-a-bitch," Gus called out.

They were surprised to hear Lafe cry out, "You leave me alone!"

"Ha!" said Gus. "We gettin' him now!"

For several more minutes the four staggered through the forest till at last Washington had a lead of only ten yards. From time to time they could clearly see his face, turned backward, the eyes flashing fear, the mouth wide.

"You *better* run, you murderin'——" Gus shouted.

Lafe stumbled into a tree, dropped, rose, and began to run again, wobblingly. Gus was now almost upon him, with Martin and Sanford not far behind.

With a desperate spurt of energy Gus closed the short gap between himself and Lafe and leaped upon the latter's back. The two fell heavily to the ground. Lafe rose but just in time to take a punch in the face from Martin. As he fell Sanford kicked him in the ribs and he whimpered.

"There!" shouted Sanford, thinking that all the fight was out of Lafe, but Washington suddenly lashed out with both feet and kicked him in the groin. Sanford doubled up, screaming with pain. "Ohhh," he shrieked, "God damn you!"

Gus, who had by now regained his feet, lunged at Lafe, knocked him off balance, and kicked him as he fell. Sanford began stomping on him as he lay thrashing in panic on the ground, and then Gus ran and picked up a skull-sized rock that was partly embedded in the loose earth at the foot of a tree.

"Ye get away from me," Lafe shouted. "Ah didn't mean to kill that little nigger."

The last thing Lafe Washington ever expected to see on this earth, as he sat white-faced on the ground, blue eyes rolling, blond hair matted to his bleeding forehead, was three strange Negroes coming at him with murder in their eyes, one of them holding aloft a heavy rock.

But that was the last thing he saw on this earth.

THE SUNDAY
MORNING SHIFT

■ ■ ■

I didn't like being assigned to the Sunday-morning shift. But I was the new man, so I had to take it. Like anything else, it wasn't so bad once you got used to it. It did mean you couldn't do much on Saturday nights, but sometimes, driving in from the ocean on a nice, cool Sunday morning with the streets deserted, and the fog lifting off the lawns and palm trees, it was sort of nice. You had the feeling you had the world all to yourself.

I remember on Sunday mornings Los Angeles used to look like it had in the old days, in the thirties, when there were a lot of empty lots and pepper trees growing wild and orange-juice stands and for-rent signs. The boom of the war years did something bad to Los Angeles as far as just simple living was concerned. The town had gotten overcrowded, more industrial, smoggier, pushier, noisier: more Eastern.

But on Sunday mornings it was, as I say, a lot like the old Los Angeles. Quiet. Peaceful. You felt like taking deep breaths as you drove along.

Of course, working the Sunday-morning shift, you couldn't go to church. But it was all right, in a way, because church came to you. You opened up the station at about ten minutes to six, said good morning to the janitor and the engineer, went to the record library, picked up the records you needed, if any, went to the announcer's booth, and that was about it. At six o'clock you signed the station on the air and it was pretty much of a snap from then till twelve, when the Sunday-afternoon man came on.

183

Weekdays you had to be on your toes every minute, what with playing records, doing newscasts, reading a million and one commercials and all, but on Sundays there were very few records to play, there was only one brief newscast at nine o'clock, and you didn't have to do any commercials at all. Not that there weren't commercials to broadcast. The time was all sold, from six to noon, to various churches around the town, but the gentlemen of the cloth did their own commercials.

Some of the other radio announcers used to kid me about working for KTLB. We were known as the Bible Station, which is certainly better than poking yourself in the eye with a sharp stick, but the other announcers meant it as a plain insult. You see, the rest of the week we did pretty much the same job as other independents in town: records and news. But during a slump just before the war old Charlie Young, who used to own KTLB, found the used-car dealers and supermarkets weren't buying much time, so out of desperation or something he cut prices a little and made some sales to a few of the clergy. The first boys to get on really had a field day, and then the rest of them began to buy time and before Charlie knew it he found himself with a pretty big church business.

When I say church, of course, I don't mean Episcopalian or Catholic or Methodist or anything like that. The outfits we had broadcasting on Sundays were pretty much Los Angeles-type churches, if you know what I mean, and if you've never lived in Los Angeles I guess you don't. For some reason LA has become the nut center of the world. I don't mean pecans and walnuts, I mean flippo-time. Nuts in the head style. Don't ask me why. That's one for the brainy people to figure out, but man, there are more weirdos walking the streets without keepers in LA than in any city I've ever lived in and I've lived in plenty, being a hack announcer. I've worked in Pittsburgh, Des Moines, Peoria, San Francisco, Santa Barabara, and Seattle. LA beats 'em all. People there don't seem to be like people in other places. Oh, that's an exaggeration, I guess. Maybe the majority of people are pretty much the same all over, but I guess it's just that the percentage of oddballs is higher on the Coast than elsewhere. You see an awful lot of health-food stores, revival tents, lecture halls where nobody in his right mind can figure out what the hell the lecturers are lecturing about, hospitals that medical societies keep trying to get closed up, and churches with names like Church of the Holy Triangle (Spirit, Love, and Health) and Church of the

Atomic Christ and Church of the Living Holy Ghost and things like that.

I think maybe one reason things are so peculiar along this line is that Los Angeles is a city where lots of people go to live after they've really finished living and don't know it and aren't quite ready to lie down and die. So they go out there and with all this free time on their hands and maybe being in their old age where their health isn't too good, they fall easy prey to the vultures that infest the city.

Anyway, a lot of these evangelists had bought time on KTLB and on Sunday mornings it was my job to put them on the air. An engineer would give 'em one of the studios, and from the announcer's booth I'd play an opening theme record (always some organ music) and read their introductions out of the copy book. It was always something like: "The Wilshire Boulevard Church of the New Prophecy is on the air! Yes, friends, once again it's time for one of your Sunday-morning visits to the Shrine of New Prophecy [with the organ music still going] and another inspiring sermon by Dr. Homer Crockett. With Dr. Crockett this morning you'll hear the choir in a medley of your favorite hymns of yesteryear. And now, Dr. Crockett."

Most of the ministers who had taken to the airways were pretty nice guys personally and, for all I know, they were as sincere as the day is long. But I said most. Couple of those boys were confidence men for the Lord for sure, and oddly enough they were more interesting, if you know what I mean, than the honest ones. I mean they were better speakers; they had better vocabularies. They could get themselves more wound up in a sermon. And they could pull in more money.

That's the purpose, of course, of broadcasting church services. It's not the only purpose, but it's one of the main ones and in a way it's perfectly easy to understand. You see, even on a small station radio time costs a lot of money. Most of these fellows ordinarily couldn't have afforded it if they tried to pay for time-costs out of what they took in with the collection baskets at their churches. Their real source of income was from all the folks out in what we used to call radioland. That's the reason why a few minutes of each broadcast period would be allotted to a frank appeal for funds. Some of the fellas used to ask for the money sort of bashfully, as if they were ashamed to have to bring the subject up. But not old Mort Fairview. How about that for a name? Dr. Morton *Fairview*. I don't know where he got it, but I bet he wasn't born with it. It was a good name for his purposes though. You had to hand it to him. He didn't overlook a trick.

He's the fellow I started to tell you about. In a way he made the Sunday-morning shift interesting. At least he saved it from being a total loss. He had several gimmicks that—well, let me tell you how he operated.

First of all, he bought the eleven o'clock time. More people awake than at six or seven. Then he didn't talk just simple Sunday-school stuff like most of the other clergymen who broadcast on the station. He'd get up plenty of steam. He'd take on Russia or the devil or sin or atheism or something and really tear it apart. He also used to buy newspaper space in the Saturday papers and advertise sermons entitled "Rome versus Moscow" and "666" and "The Vatican and the White House," but he used to go easy on the anti-Catholic stuff when he was on the air. He seemed to be the only one of the Sunday-morning bunch who realized that one way to get ahead in this world is to give people something to hate. You tell 'em there's something they ought to hate, and then you hate it right out loud to show them how, and then you tell the people to tear off a little piece for themselves, and then you all get to hating together and, man, you can really do all right if you know the ropes. That's the way Fairview used to work it.

I had to admire him. When he wasn't calling fire and brimstone down on some common enemy, he used to do the greatest sleight-of-hand with words you ever heard in your life. He practically used to convince me that what he was saying made a lot of sense till I would try to concentrate very hard on the meaning of his words and then I'd be aware that there was no meaning.

He was a natural-born salesman, was what he was. He would have made a great used-car man or a great Senator or a great football coach or a great anything. How he got with the religious dodge I don't know, but that's beside the point. He had the simple old gift of gab. After listening to him for about six months, though, I finally got on to some of his tricks. One of them was what I called the "How many ways can you say it?" routine. That isn't a very good way to explain it, so I'll give you an example. He'd be going along doing sort of a normal sermon for a minute or two and then he'd happen to land on a phrase like *The Lord is a rock* and he'd be off.

He'd say, "The Lord is a rock in time of storm. He's a rock in time of strife. He's a rock in time of darkness. He's a rock in the middle of the sea. He's a rock in the desert. The Lord is a rock to cling to, a rock to hide behind, a rock to rest upon, a rock to build upon, a rock to stand upon, a rock to count on, a rock to plant on, a rock to tower up, a rock to shine forth, a rock to give you strength, a rock to give you safety, a rock to give you protection, a rock to give you love, a rock to lift up, a rock to bring you peace." Man, he'd come on like a quarry for about five minutes with the rock routine.

Then he'd switch to something else: "The blood of the Lamb was shed for you. The blood of the Lamb was shed for me. The blood of the Lamb will wash you. The blood of the Lamb will cleanse you. The blood of the Lamb will feed you. The blood of the Lamb will revive you. The blood of the Lamb will thrill you. The blood of the Lamb will give you strength. The blood of the Lamb will nourish you. The blood of the Lamb will quench your thirst. The blood of the Lamb will soothe your pain. The blood of the Lamb will open your eyes. The blood of the Lamb will wash away your sins. The blood of the Lamb will make you free. The blood of the Lamb will put love in your heart. The blood of the Lamb will give you new understanding."

As the saying goes, it's a free country, and I'd be the last man in the world to clap a hand over the Doc's mouth, but if that's teaching people religion then that's what makes horse races. The Doc's sermons always sounded to me like they were written by the guy who wrote "Sh'Boom." Funny thing was, though, they sort of got to you, you know what I mean? Fairview himself was such a commanding guy that you just couldn't help getting carried away a little if you listened to him for a few minutes.

He'd bring three or four people with him to do a little singing, and after he'd get himself up to full speed they'd start with the "Yeah" and "Amen" routine and quite a lot of emotion used to come pouring out of that little Studio B.

Another thing I've always felt about the Doc is that he really ad-libbed all those sermons. Most of the other men used to bring scripts or notes or Bibles or something, but Fairview would just start talking and take it from there. "I met a man the other day," he might say, "and he said to me, 'Doctor Fairview, I'm sick. I'm sick of heart and mind and body. I'm sick of soul and I'm sick of bone and blood and marrow.'" I used to think that whatever it was that people said when they walked up to Fairview on the street it sure wasn't anything like that; but as I say, it didn't matter what kind of malarky Doc handed out, you just sort of went along with him. His eyes were so open and so blue and his face so red and good-natured and his hair was so white that, while you were looking at him, you just couldn't find it in yourself to doubt him or criticize him. It was only later that you looked at yourself in the mirror, so to speak, and realized that you hadn't come away with one single idea that you could put your finger on.

This one particular Sunday morning that I'm telling you about, though, the Doc really topped himself. I was sitting there in my swivel chair, with my feet up on the board, watching him through the glass panel of Studio B, listening to him and sort of dozing a little when suddenly he said he was going off the air.

"My friends," he said, "I have a shocking bit of news for you today. This program, which has brought the word of God to the people of this community for so many years . . . this program, which has brought so much comfort to so many troubled hearts, is going off the air. I had hoped I would never come to this moment, after all the wonderful support you grand folks out there in radioland have given me these past years, but this is the moment. This is my Gethsemane. This is my cross, and I must bear it. I have had a talk with the people who run this station. They are good people. They are fair people. They are upstanding American people. But they are not idle millionaires. They are not fools. They are ordinary people like you and me. People with families. People with bills to pay. Yes, a radio station has bills just as you and I do. They have to pay for the electricity they use. They have to pay salaries. They have to pay for typewriters and papers for scripts and janitors' salaries, and they have to pay for recordings and newsmachines and transmitters and broadcasting towers and millions of miles of wires and tubes and connections and plugs and sockets and parts of all sorts. This all takes money. That's why they can't afford to just *give* their broadcasting time away. I had a talk with them the other day and they told me they were very sorry, that they enjoyed my program and were very proud to be the station over which it was broadcast, but they said that as much as they sympathized with me, as much as they sympathized with my bringing the Word of God to the people of Los Angeles, they would, nevertheless, regretfully have to ask me to give up the time of this broadcast on next Sunday morning.

"For you see, my friends, these are troubled times we are living in. The cost of everything is going up. I don't have to tell you that. You know the cost of milk is up. The cost of bread is up. Rents are up. Everything is up. And my friends, the cost of broadcasting time is up, and I . . . I hesitate to say it . . . but it is a fact; I cannot afford it. That's right, my dear friends. I lay the facts before you. I cannot pay what it would cost me to buy one half-hour of time on this station next Sunday morning. I have spoken to the people who run this station and they were wonderful people, but after all they run a business. They cannot give away their commodity, time, any more than a butcher could give away meat or a lumberman give away wood, and still stay in business. So that's it, my friends. I am terribly sorry to have to say good-by to you after these many long years. I have gotten to know a great many of you personally these past few years. Some of you I have known by your letters, others by your personal visits to my Tabernacle. I have heard your stories, I have suffered with you in your time of strife, I have prayed for you in sickness and in all sorts of unhappiness. And now, in one terrible moment of time, all is lost. Nevermore are we . . . you and I . . . to know each other so intimately by the wonderful magic of radio that God in His goodness and mercy has deigned to give to a needy world to spread all manner of good and happy tidings. Ah, what a wonderful gift radio is, my friends. What a comfort it is to shut-ins, to the infirm, the aged, the lonely. What a godsend it is to all of us . . . to you and to me. For it has been by the miracle of radio, beloved friends, that I have been able to bring you the holy word for such a long time. But now, in one tragic moment, all this is swept away. In one sad announcement I am reciting the news of my doom. Or rather not my own doom but the doom of my work or my mission in life. But ours not to reason why. Perhaps God in His goodness and wisdom will show me the purpose behind the tragedy. Perhaps He will let me know for what cause I have struggled so long. I am sure He will. And yet perhaps I betray Him if I give up so easily. It is difficult to tell what to do, my friends. Perhaps I should turn to you. What do *you* think I should do? You, who have so often turned to me for advice, now *I* am turning to *you*. What poetic justice! And what a wonderful testimony to God's wisdom. How He shows us that we help ourselves best by helping others. Will you help me, my friends? Is it possible that is what God is doing this morning? Testing you as you sit there listening in Los Angeles and Glendale and Burbank and Santa Monica and Eagle Rock and in all the wonderful sections of this great city of ours? Is that His grand and glorious purpose? I do not know, my friends.

"*Is* He testing you? Will you help? Do you feel any call at all this morning? Do you feel that God is giving you a very special opportunity to help Him spread His holy word? Is there grace in your heart this morning? Is there love? Is there joy? Is there gratitude? Is there the love of God and all His creatures? Is there the love for the little creatures of this earth? The love for the little blue-eyed children who may be denied the word of God if they do not one morning hear it over this microphone? Is there love and compassion in your heart this morning? It is written . . . *faith, hope, and charity, and the greatest of these is charity.* You know your Bible. You know the word. Is there charity in your hearts this morning? This grand and glorious California morning with sun shining and the birds twittering in the trees. This morning when we all ought to get down on our knees and thank God for our many blessings. Why don't we do that? Why don't we do *just* that right now? Let's all get down on our knees right now, all over this great city, all over the ocean towns and in the mountains and in the valley. Are you on your knees in front of your radio right now? That's it. Kneel! Kneel before God! Feel His grace flowing into your heart right out of the radio. Isn't it a grand and glorious feeling? Isn't it grand? Aren't you grateful to the good God in His everlasting heaven? If you are, my friends, then perhaps there is yet hope. Perhaps there is a way whereby the word of God might yet be preserved in a heathen world. Perhaps the devil shall yet be banished from the temple and the moneychangers cast out into the byways in terrible disgrace. Right now, my friends, if you are on your knees, and I can see that you *are* all over this wonderful city of ours, right now lift your right hand to heaven and promise, make a solemn vow, if you really feel the call, to save this program. Yes! You can do it and you alone. Don't wait for the other fellow. You can't expect God to perform miracles because you've been lazy. You've got to do your part. Right now make a vow to help and then, God love you, get up off your knees and go to your writing desks and put a love offering in an envelope. Address it to the Reverend Dr. Morton Fairview, Station KTLB, Los Angeles. That's all there is to it, my friends. It's up to you. Will you do that? Will you help the Lord? If you will, right now, out loud say, 'Yes, Lord.'"

The people in the room with Fairview all said, "Yes, Lord."

"Then," concluded the Doctor, "we'll see. I can't promise anything. It's in God's hands now. He knows. And in a few days I'll know. I'll know if I'll be back here with you for another wonderful visit next Sunday morning. If you tune in and don't hear me, be not of faint heart. It means you did your part, but you got no help from your fellow citizens. The seed fell upon barren ground. No growth sprang up. But if, in the infinite mercy of the Lord, there is a wonderful outpouring of generosity here these next few days, then, praise God, I shall be back with you, my friends. For now I count on your prayers. Help me. I pray you. Remember the mailing address: Dr. Morton Fairview, Station KTLB, Los Angeles."

The Doc and his followers got out of the studio before I could say good-by to him or offer him my sympathies and I had to go yank some news off the ticker and introduce the next program anyway, so I didn't give him much more thought for the moment.

At twelve o'clock Jack Norton replaced me.

"Don't forget your lunchbox," he said as I was leaving the control room.

"Thanks," I said. "Say, it's too bad about old Doc Fairview."

"What about him?" Jack said.

"He's through as of today," I said. "Couldn't meet the ante. Said he was checking off as of this morning unless his fans come up with some last-minute scratch."

"Say, that's right," Jack said. "I forgot you've only been with us for about six months."

"What do you mean?"

"Man, Fairview does this thing all the time. Every seven or eight months."

"Maybe he needs the money though."

"Are you kidding?" Jack said. "He's got this time bought and paid for for the next twelve months. He makes a good steady income, but every so often the people get lazy with the five-dollar bills. He does the going-off-the-air speech to wake 'em up."

It was still Sunday morning when I got back in the car. There was some traffic now, but not much. I drove back out to the beach at a good clip. I wanted to take the kids on a picnic.

THE PUBLIC HATING

■ ■ ■

The weather was a little cloudy and here and there in the crowds that surged up the ramps into the stadium, people were looking at the sky and then at their neighbors and squinting and saying, "Hope she doesn't rain."

On television the weatherman had forecast slight cloudiness but no showers. It was not an unusual day for early September. It was not cold. People from all over town, about sixty-five thousand of them, were pouring out of streetcars and buses and subways all over the neighborhood surrounding the stadium. In antlike lines they crawled across streets through turnstiles, up stairways, along ramps, through gates, down aisles.

Laughing and shoving restlessly, damp-palmed with excitement, they came shuffling into the great concrete bowl, some stopping to go to the rest rooms, some buying pop-corn, some taking free pamphlets from the uniformed attendants.

Everything was free this particular day. No tickets had been sold for the event. The public proclamations had simply been made in the newspapers and on TV, and over sixty-five thousand people had responded.

For weeks, of course, the papers had been suggesting that the event would take place. All during the trial, even as early as the selection of the jury, the columnists had slyly hinted at the inevitability of the outcome. But it had only been official since yesterday. The television networks had actually got a slight jump on the papers. At six o'clock the government had taken over all network facilities for a brief five-minute period during which the announcement was made.

"We have all followed with great interest," the premier had said, looking calm and handsome in a gray double-breasted suit, "the course of the trial of Professor Ketteridge. Early this afternoon the jury returned a verdict of guilty. This verdict having been confirmed within the hour by the Supreme Court, in the interests of time-saving, the White House has decided to make the usual prompt official announcement. There will be a public hating tomorrow. The time: 2:30 P.M. The place: Yankee Stadium in New York City. Your assistance is earnestly requested. Those of you in the New York area will find—"

The voice had droned on, filling in other details, and then the newspapers went to press with the complete details and, in the morning, the early editions included pictures captioned "Bronx couple first in line," and "Students wait all night to view hating" and "Early birds." The pictures showed several people standing in line outside the stadium or sitting on blankets on the sidewalk, reading papers and drinking coffee to pass the time.

By one-thirty in the afternoon there was not an empty seat in the stadium and people were beginning to fill up a few of the aisles. Special police began to block off the exits, and word was sent down to the street that no more people could be admitted. Hawkers slipped through the crowd selling cold beer and hot dogs. An engineer stepped shyly to an open microphone, tapped it with his fingernail, and said, "Hello, Mac. Testing. One, two. Woof, woof."

At this there was a smattering of applause followed by a ripple of laughter. An airplane droned overhead in the leaden sky and a slight breeze whipped the flags at the far end of the field.

Sitting just back of what would have been first base had the Yankees not been playing in Cleveland, Frederic Traub stared curiously at the platform in the middle of the field. It was about twice the size of a prizefighting ring. In the middle of it there was a small raised section on which was placed a plain wooden kitchen chair.

To the left of the chair there were seating accommodations for a small group of dignitaries. Downstage, so to speak, there was a speaker's lectern and a battery of microphones. The platform was hung with bunting and pennants.

"Remarkable," said Traub softly to his companion.

"I suppose," said the man. "Effective, at any rate."

Traub allowed his eye to wander from the platform to the bull pens, out over the brilliantly green playing field to the center-field bleachers. The crowd was beginning to hum ominously, like a lion audibly considering the possibility of going out to kill meat. Here and there cow bells rang out; sitting about twenty yards to the left Traub could see two Shriners standing up, addressing those in their immediate vicinity. He could not hear what they were saying.

At two minutes after two o'clock a small group of men filed out onto the field from a point just back of home plate. The crowd buzzed more loudly for a moment and then burst into applause. A military band struck up a brisk march, and two or three of the men in the group on the field could be observed to be making an effort to keep in step.

The applause had stopped before the group reached the platform. The men carefully climbed a few wooden steps, walked in single file across the platform, and seated themselves in the chairs set out for them. Traub turned around, rubbernecking, and was interested to observe, high in the press box, the winking red lights of television cameras.

"I didn't know you televised the thing," he said.

"Certainly," said his companion. "On all networks. I think at one time only one network carried the event, but the program simply annihilated the competition, no joke intended, and they finally hit on the idea of having all the stations carry it. Only sensible way."

"I guess that's right," said Traub. "Still it all seems a little strange to me. We do things rather differently."

"That's what makes horse-races," said his companion.

Traub listened for a moment to the voices around him. Surprisingly, no one seemed to be discussing the business at hand. Baseball, movies, the weather, gossip, personal small talk, a thousand-and-one subjects were introduced. It was almost as if the attempt to avoid a mention of the hating were deliberate.

"Think you'll be all right when we start?"

His friend's voice broke in on Traub's reverie.

"What?"

"Think you'll be okay when we get down to business?"

"Oh, certainly," said Traub. "Certainly."

"I've seen 'em keel over," said the other.

"I'll be all right," said Traub, shaking his head in admiring disbelief. "But I still can't believe it."

"What do you mean?"

"Oh, you know, the whole thing. How it started. How you found you could do it."

"Beats the hell out of me," said the other man. "I think it was that guy at Duke University first came up with the idea. The 'mind over matter' thing has been around for a long time, of course. Everybody from Christ to Mary Baker Eddy has had a crack at it. But this guy, I forget what his name was, he was the first one to prove scientifically that mind can control matter."

"Did it with dice, I believe," Traub said.

"Yeah, that's it. First he found some guys who could drop a dozen or so dice down a chute of some kind and actually control the direction they'd take, at least control it to a small extent."

"I'm familiar with the experiments," said Traub, anxious to show that he was not in complete ignorance. "I believe the dice fell into a tray that was divided into two sections."

"Right," said his companion. "Anyway, some people could make a few more dice slide down into the right half of the tray, say, than chance would allow. After a few years they found out that the secret was real simple. The guys who had this particular power were nothing but the guys who *thought* they could do it."

"In other words," said Traub, half-smiling, "faith can move mountains."

"That's about the size of it," said the man. "Of course not many people could convince themselves they really had the knack of the damned thing, so nothing much was ever done with it. Then one time they got the idea of taking the dice into an auditorium and having about two thousand people concentrate on forcing the dice into one side of the tray or the other. That did it."

"Really?"

"You betcha. Why, hell, it was the most natural thing in the world when you think of it. It was so simple everybody just over-looked it all those years. If one horse can pull a heavy load so far, it figures that ten horses can pull it a lot farther."

"Remarkable," said Traub.

"Anyway, that did it. They had them dice fallin' where they wanted 'em to go about eighty per cent of the time. Then some wise boy got the idea of trying a little mass hypnosis on the crowd before they tried the experiment, and it worked even better. Seems there'd been some in the crowd who didn't think they could do it, ya know. They were cuttin' the average way down. Well, when this boy got the people all excited, why, man, they really had themselves a crap game!"

"When did they first substitute a living organism for the dice?" Traub asked.

"Damned if I know," said the man. "It was quite a few years ago and at first the government sort of clamped down on the thing. It's still under strict Washington control, you understand."

"Of course."

"I was just a kid at the time but I do remember that the SPCA and some of the papers got wind of some of the things they were monkeyin' around with and there was a lot of gab back and forth there for a while."

"What happened?"

"Like I say, the government stepped in and put a stop to all the malarky. There was a little last-ditch fight from the churches, I think. But they finally came to realize that this trick was something you couldn't stop. It couldn't be called evil any more than fire or electricity or atomic power could be called evil, even if they kill a lot of people."

"I see."

"So, as I say, that's about all there was to it. Six months after Congress passed the law forbidding capital punishment, they started the public hatings. It's worked just fine."

"Is this an unusually large crowd?"

"Not for a political prisoner. Some regular old rapists, murderers, some of them don't pull maybe more than twenty, thirty thousand. The people just don't get stirred up enough. They just don't have enough hate in them and if you ain't got enough of that, man, you might as well stay home."

"I suppose so," said Traub.

The sun had come out from behind a cloud now and Traub watched silently as large map-shaped shadows moved majestically across the grass.

"She's warming up," someone said.

"That's right," a voice agreed. "Gonna be real nice."

Traub leaned forward and lowered his head as he retied the laces on his right shoe, and in the next instant he was shocked to attention by a guttural, maniacal roar that was loosed from the crowd's throat. The floor beneath his feet vibrated at the sound as his head snapped up. He looked at the field.

At the far end, in distant right-center field, three men were walking toward the platform. Two were walking together, the third was slouched in front of them, head down, his gait unsteady.

Traub had thought he was going to be all right, but now, looking at the tired figure being prodded toward second base, looking at the bare, bald head, he began to feel slightly sick to his stomach.

It seemed to take forever, but at last the three tiny figures reached the platform and the two guards jostled the prisoner up the stairs and toward the small kitchen chair.

When he reached it and seated himself the crowd shouted with renewed vigor. Then a tall, distinguished man stepped to the speaker's lectern and cleared his throat, raising his right hand in an appeal for quiet.

"All right," he said, "all right."

The mob slowly fell silent. Traub clasped his hands tightly together. He felt slightly ashamed.

"All right," said the speaker. "Good afternoon, ladies and gentlemen. On behalf of the President of the United States, I welcome you to another Public Hating. This particular affair," he said, "as you know, is directed against the man who was yesterday judged guilty in United States District Court here in New York City, Professor Arthur Ketteridge."

At the mention of Ketteridge's name the crowd made a noise like an earthquake-rumble. Several pop bottles were thrown, futilely, from the centerfield bleachers. They landed nowhere near the platform.

"We will begin in just a moment," said the speaker, "but first I should like to introduce the Reverend Charles Fuller, of the Park Avenue Reformed Church, who will make the invocation."

A small man with glasses stepped forward, replaced the first speaker at the microphone, closed his eyes, and threw back his head.

"Our Heavenly Father," he said, "to whom we are indebted for all the blessings of this life, grant, we beseech Thee, that we act today in justice and in the spirit of truth. Grant, O Lord, we pray Thee, that what we are about to do here today will render us the humble servants of Thy divine will. For it is written: *the wages of sin is death.* Have pity on this wayward soul who is about to be committed back into Thy personal care, O Lord. Search deep into his heart for the seed of repentance, if there be such, and if there be not, plant it therein, O Lord, in Thy goodness and mercy."

There was a slight pause. The Reverend Fuller coughed and then said, "Amen."

The crowd, which had stood quietly during the prayer, now seated itself and began to buzz again.

Traub nudged his companion.

"Tell me," he said, "do these things ever misfire?"

"Not that I ever heard of," said the other. "Why?"

"Oh, no particular reason," said Traub. "I was just wondering."

"No, this hatred is a pretty effective thing," said the man, lighting a cigar. "Like I said before, it's a wonder it took such a damned long time before they figured it out."

"I guess it is."

"They started it, I think, kicking around the old story about people dying of broken hearts and that sort of thing. Folks just wasting away when they lost loved ones. That kind of stuff. Then somebody combined it with these experiments with the rats and monkeys and there you were."

"The power of rejection is something, all right," agreed Traub. "I guess this thing is rooted in Freud, too, eh?"

"Freud, Shmeud," said the man. "It don't take no big-dome to tell you that a kid breaks up if his mother kicks him out or gives him a rough time. You take away love and anybody will be hurt, but you replace affection with some nice, powerful hatred and brother, you've had it!"

"Reminiscent of voodoo," said Traub.

"Guess it is," said the other.

"But you know," said Traub, "it just occurred to me; it isn't the mechanical plausibility of the thing that frightens me. It's the public spectacle of it that—"

"Better cut that kind of talk," said the man. "What do you want people to do? Mail in their hatred? You gotta *be* there. You gotta be right on the scene. You gotta keep whipped up. And what the hell's so unusual about a public execution? For thousands of years that's about the only kind there were. Burning at the stake, lynching, the firing squad. Hell, even after they started with the electric chair and the gas chamber you could still see the damned thing if you wanted to, like if you were a newspaperman or something. This passion for privacy at executions is a pretty new idea and as far as I'm concerned it was started by either a bunch of pantywaists or by guys who were afraid they were killing innocent men."

On the platform the speaker was again addressing the crowd.

"All right," he said. "You know why you were invited here today. You know that we all have a job to do. And you know why we have to do it."

"Yes!" screamed thousands of voices.

"Then let us get to the business at hand. At this time I would like to introduce to you a very great American who, to use the old phrase, needs no introduction. Former President of Harvard University, current advisor to the Secretary of State, ladies and gentlemen, here is Dr. Howard S. Weltmer."

A wave of applause vibrated the air in the stadium.

Dr. Weltmer stepped forward, shook hands with the speaker, and adjusted the microphone.

"Thank you," he said. "Now we won't waste any more time here since what we are about to do will take every bit of our energy and concentration if it is to be successfully accomplished. I ask you all," he said, "to direct your unwavering attention toward the man seated in the chair to my left here, a man who in my opinion is the most despicable criminal of our time, Professor Arthur Ketteridge!"

The mob shrieked at this mention of Ketteridge's name. A woman seated near Traub fainted.

"I ask you," said Weltmer, "to rise. That's it, everybody stand up. Now. I want every one of you . . . I understand we have upward of seventy thousand people here today . . . I want every single one of you to stare directly at this fiend in human form, Ketteridge. I want you to let him know by the wondrous power that lies in the strength of your emotional reservoirs, I want you to let him know that he is a criminal, that he is worse than a murderer, that he has committed treason, that he is not loved by anyone, anywhere in the universe, and that he is, rather, despised with a vigor equal in heat to the power of the sun itself!"

People around Traub were shaking their fists now. Their eyes were narrowed; their mouths turned down at the corners.

"Come on," shouted Weltmer. "Let's feel it! Work it out of yourselves. Work out every bit of hatred you've stored up, not only for this man but for anyone. Work it all out, use up all the hatred, the hatred that ordinarily is unproductive, even sinful, but that today has a fine and good purpose. Let us feel it. Let it burn out of your eyes."

Traub was on his feet and under the spell of the speaker he was suddenly horrified to find that his blood was racing, his heart pounding. He felt anger surging up within him. He could not believe that he hated Ketteridge. But he could not deny that he hated something.

"On the souls of your mothers," Weltmer was saying. "On the future of your children, out of your love for your country, I ask you, I demand of you that you release the inhibitions that are damming up some part of your animal power to despise. I want you to become ferocious. I want you to become as the beasts of the jungle, as furious as they in the defense of their homes. They would kill to defend their own. Would you?"

The "yes" that followed took Traub's breath away. It pounded against his ears like the sound of cannon.

Weltmer's voice was getting louder.

"Do you hate this man?" he demanded.

"Yes!" shouted the mob.

"Fiend!" cried Weltmer. "Enemy of the people! Do you *hear*, Ketteridge?"

Traub watched in dry-mouthed fascination as the slumped figure in the chair straightened up conclusively and jerked at his collar. At this first indication that the power of their venom was reaching home, the crowd rose to a new peak of excitement.

"We plead," said Weltmer, "with you people watching today on your television sets, to join with us in hating this wretch. All over America stand up, if you will, in your living rooms. Face the East. Face New York City, if you will, and let anger bubble up in your hearts. Speak it out, let it flow!"

A man beside Traub sat down, turned aside, and vomited softly into a handkerchief, swearing the while. Traub picked up the binoculars the man had discarded for the moment and fastened them fuzzily on Ketteridge's figure, twirling the focus knobs furiously. In a moment the man leaped into the foreground. Traub saw that his eyes were full of tears, that his body was wracked with sobs, that he was in obvious pain.

"He is not fit to live," Weltmer was shouting. "Turn your anger upon him. Channel it. Make it productive. Be not angry with your family, your friends, your fellow citizens, but let your anger pour out in a violent torrent on the head of this human devil," screamed Weltmer. "Come on! Let's get it over with!"

Traub was in the moment at last convinced of the enormity of Ketteridge's crime and that was when Weltmer said, "All right, that's it. Now let's get down to brass tacks. Let's concentrate on his right arm. Hate it, do you hear. Burn the flesh from the bone! You can do it! Come on! Burn him alive!"

Traub stared unblinking through the binoculars at Ketteridge's right arm as the prisoner leaped to his feet and ripped off his jacket, howling. With his left hand he gripped his right forearm and then Traub saw the flesh turning dark. First a deep red and then a livid purple. The fingers contracted and Ketteridge whirled on his small platform like a dervish, slapping his arm against his side.

"That's it," Weltmer called. "You're doing it. You're doing it. Mind over matter! That's it. Burn this offending flesh. Be as the avenging angels of the lord. Smite this devil! That's it!"

The flesh was turning darker now, across the shoulders, as Ketteridge tore his shirt off. Suddenly, crying out in a loud voice, he broke away from his chair and leaped off the platform, landing on his knees on the grass.

"Oh, the power is wonderful," cried Weltmer. "You've got him. Now let's really turn it on. Come on!"

Ketteridge writhed on the grass and then rose and began running back and forth, directionless, like a worm on a griddle.

Traub could watch no longer. He put down the binoculars and staggered back up the aisle.

Outside the stadium he walked for twelve blocks before he hailed a cab.